Praise for Karin Gillespie

LOVE LITERARY STYLE

"Witty and smart, entertaining and lyrical, in *Love Literary Style* author Karin Gillespie explores all facets of love and language through her evocative characters and charmingly delicious plot."

— Laura Spinella,
Bestselling Author of *Ghost Gifts*

"An intelligently written novel packed with Southern wit. This is a story book clubs will devour. It's warmly humorous, thought-provoking and shines with emotional depth."

— Amy Avanzino,
Author of *From the Sideline*

"Cheeky and charming, Gillespie's sweet, outlandish fable is as much a sendup of books, authors, and the publishing industry as it is a love letter to it all."

— Phoebe Fox,
Author of *Out of Practice*

GIRL MEETS CLASS

"Funny, empathetic, and wise. Gillespie shines a light into dark corners we need to examine, but somehow manages to entertain us at the same time. A fantastic read."

— Susan M. Boyer,
USA Today Bestselling Author of *Lowcountry Bordello*

"A delectable page-turner with twists and turns at every corner."
— *San Francisco Book Review*

"Filled with humor and a happy ending, I highly recommend this to anyone looking a humorous read with just a dash of romance!"
— *The Southern Bookworm*

"Gillespie knocks it out of the park...[her] humor is as tender as it is sharp. At first, Toni Lee's figures of speech zip by like jerky ducks in a shooting gallery; but as she orients herself her aim improves. By the time you fall in love with her, bells are ringing all over the place...It's got everything: gymnastic sex, moonlight and madness and love and romance."

– The Augusta Chronicle

THE BOTTOM DOLLAR SERIES

"With a flair for timing and a cheeky southern turn of phrase...Brace for a wild ride chock-full of Southern wit and down-home advice from a clutch of quirky characters you will hope to see again soon."

– Booklist

"A winner of a first novel, filled with Southern-style zingers and funny folks."

– Kirkus Reviews (starred review)

"The characters are the kind of steel magnolias who would make Scarlett O'Hara envious."

– The Atlanta Journal-Constitution

"Laugh-out-loud antics as...Gillespie continues her entertaining Bottom Dollar Girls series...Certain to please women's fiction fans of all ages."

– Romantic Times (Top Pick)

"As tart and delectable as lemon meringue pie...a pure delight."

– Jennifer Weiner,
Author of Good in Bed and In Her Shoes

"A fine romp of a book, well-written and thoroughly entertaining."

– The Winston-Salem Journal

Love
Literary
Style

Books by Karin Gillespie

GIRL MEETS CLASS
LOVE LITERARY STYLE

The Bottom Dollar Series

BET YOUR BOTTOM DOLLAR (#1)
A DOLLAR SHORT (#2)
DOLLAR DAZE (#3)

Love Literary Style

Karin Gillespie

HENERY PRESS

LOVE LITERARY STYLE
Part of the Henery Press Chick Lit Collection

First Edition | November 2016

Henery Press
www.henerypress.com

Trade Paperback ISBN-13: 978-1-63511-085-2
Digital epub ISBN-13: 978-1-63511-086-9
Kindle ISBN-13: 978-1-63511-087-6
Hardcover Paperback ISBN-13: 978-1-63511-088-3

Printed in the United States of America

To Converse MFA program

ACKNOWLEDGMENTS

Thanks to the wonderfully supportive and professional team at Henery Press: Erin George, Art Molinares, and Kendel Lynn. Special thanks to Rachel Jackson for her keen editorial eye, good-natured spirit and endless patience.

Thanks also to Midtown Market for hosting my book parties and Tricia Hughes for tirelessly supporting them.

Always ever grateful to my dear friend and supportive beta reader Laura Spinella. Thanks to supportive writing friends: Rhian Swain, Joann Appleton, Kim Romaner, Laurie Merill, Ann Beth Strelec, Margaret Williams, Jim Garvey, Leonard Todd, John Presley, Rick Davis, Tom Turner, Joseph Barry and Wally Evans.

Great thanks and love to my family: David Neches, Brandon Skelton, Magda Newland, Ken Gillespie, Tim Gillespie and Ed Gillespie.

None of this would be possible without my readers. I hope you enjoy the latest.

One

It was too bad that, as a college professor, Aaron Mite was expected to be approachable. Approachability was contrary to his nature. Thus, when a swingy-haired tanned blonde female barreled toward his podium, he steeled himself against the encounter. Students rarely lingered after composition class to say, "What an enthralling lecture." Particularly since the day's presentation covered misplaced and dangling modifiers.

The blonde was one of hundreds who prowled the grounds of Metro Atlanta University, usually in perfumed packs of four or five. Her name was Megan or Chelsea or perhaps Payton. Aaron could tell by the determined set of her jaw that she wanted something from him, and it was probably a grade change. If so, she was wasting her time. Aaron's grades were as permanent as the polar ice caps. Well, as permanent as polar ice caps were before the dawn of global warming.

"So," she began.

This was a new habit of students, starting sentences with the word "so." It wasn't as distressing as misusing the word "literally," as in "I'm literally starving to death." It did, however, grate on Aaron every time he heard it.

"What does this say?" She rattled a paper in front of his nose and pointed her finger at a comment he'd written in red ink. Some of his colleagues had switched to less threatening ink colors—blue, purple, and even hard-to-read orange—but Aaron still preferred the authoritative power of red.

He squinted at the scrawl. He often had trouble reading his own writing, but not in this case. Aaron recognized the phrase as one he frequently wrote in the margins of student composition papers: "This essay is not worth the papyrus it was penned on."

He read the comment aloud and the girl—Leslie, Brittany, or Taylor—wrinkled her nose. "I don't get it."

"It's simply another way of saying, 'this essay isn't worth the paper it's written on,' but that would be cliché. As I've said several times in this class, clichés are the enemies of good writing."

Her previously benign features turned cross. "You think I wasted paper writing my essay?"

"Yes. But, happily for you, paper is plentiful."

She stared at him. Aaron stared back. For a moment they were engaged in a standoff, but the girl looked away first. "Whatever," she said.

She wandered off, eyes fastened to her phone, poor grade seemingly forgotten. Not a surprise. Young people's minds flitted about like gnats.

Another student remained in the classroom, Sabrina, a woman in her early thirties who'd recently gone back to school. She worked part-time as an administrative assistant in the English and Foreign Language department at Metro Atlanta University.

Sabrina's appearance in Aaron's class at the beginning of the semester worried him. What if she was a terrible writer and he had to give her poor marks? Would she ever make photocopies for him again?

But she proved to be a competent writer and would likely receive an A for the semester. In fact, he was so impressed with her narrative essay, he urged her to take a creative writing class as an elective.

Sabrina was still gathering her things. Unlike the younger students, she didn't start packing up her belongings ten minutes before dismissal time in anticipation of a hasty getaway.

She glanced up at him and said, "Professor Mite, I wanted to tell you how much I'm enjoying your class."

Aaron was slightly taken aback. It was unusual for him to receive praise from students. In his teaching evaluations, he usually got comments like: "If Professor Mite ruled the world, a comma splice would be punishable by fifty lashes," or "Dude hates the word 'very.' Use in essays at your own risk."

Sometimes the comments were more personal: "Kind of cute, but needs a major wardrobe rehab. Wears the same jacket every day. Also, what's with the limp?"

"Thank you very much, Sabrina. I've enjoyed having you as well."

"I admire your fervent love for our language and excellent writing. You've inspired me to write a novel of my own."

"That's ambitious, and I wish you the best of luck. Do you have any idea what themes you want to explore? I can recommend some novels as inspiration."

She thought for a moment and said, "Death, I guess."

Her answer surprised Aaron. Sabrina was a chipper soul, continually smiling, always greeting everyone who came into the English department office suite and offering them candy from a seemingly bottomless dish on her desk. (Aaron was partial to the butterscotch disks.) Her desk was also littered with photographs of twin toddlers smashing their chubby faces into birthday cakes or cavorting in a kiddie pool. Death was the last thing he'd guessed she'd want to write about.

"Bravo to you for tackling such a challenging theme. You may want to consider reading *Death of Ivan Ilyich*, *Slaughterhouse Five*, or maybe even *White Noise*."

"Are those mysteries?"

"Excuse me?"

"I want to write a cozy."

Cozy? A cozy, when used as a noun, referred to a padded covering for a teapot.

"I don't follow."

"You've never heard of cozies?" Suddenly Sabrina was very animated. Her curls bounced on her shoulders and her cheeks flushed. "They're a category of mystery novels set in a small village, and the amateur sleuth is usually a female. There's always a murder, but it's never gruesome, and the victim tends to be a mean person who deserves to die."

Aaron was momentarily taken aback. "Are you saying you want to write genre fiction?"

"Yes. I love to read cozies."

"I see." Aaron noisily cleared his throat. "What was the last...*cozy* you read?"

"It was called *Dread and Breakfast*. The sleuth is Abigail Appleworth, the owner of a bed and breakfast called the Pleasant Dreams Inn. One of her guests—a developer who wants to cut down the hundred-year-old oak tree in the town square and put up a parking lot—is bludgeoned to death with an overcooked crumpet."

Aaron took a moment to absorb the highly improbable particulars. Then he said, "I'd like to know how you felt after you read the book. Did it change you?"

"I'm not sure what you mean."

"Were you affected by the themes? Did it prompt you to think critically? Did you spend time considering the underlying issues?"

"Well, no, but—"

"Or did it pass through you like cheap fast food?"

Her expression was quizzical. "I hadn't really thought about it like that."

Aaron smiled, preparing himself for a lengthy discourse on the superiority of literary fiction over genre—a pet subject of his—but an unexpected male visitor interrupted him. The man fixed his steely gaze on Aaron. "Stop by my office when you're finished here. I'd like a word."

"Yes, Father," he said without thinking.

Once he was gone, Sabrina stared at him, her mouth open so wide he could have chipped a golf ball into it.

"Your father's Dr. Horace Flowers?"

Aaron nodded. He rarely mentioned the relationship to anyone, especially to the people who worked in the English department.

"You've had dealings with him, I'm sure," Aaron said.

"Yes, I have. He's so..."

Churlish? Stern? Ill-mannered? Pompous? Demanding? There were dozens of negative adjectives that could describe Dr. Horace Flowers.

"Accomplished," Sabrina said. She was being kind.

Aaron's father *was* extremely accomplished, which allowed him to get away with all of his other less pleasant traits. He was the author of a definitive book on fiction writing called *Craft* as well as seventeen books on literary criticism. His favorite subject was the renowned author Nicholas Windust, and he wrote extensively about him.

"My husband gave me the latest Nicholas Windust novel for my birthday," Sabrina said. "I stayed up all night reading it. Are you as big a Nicholas Windust fan as your father?"

"I think he's a genius at the sentence level. My only quibble with his work is that his endings tend to be too upbeat."

"Are you saying you don't care for happily-ever-afters?"

"I don't believe in them. To me, the most important quality in fiction is authenticity. One only has to watch a few minutes of a twenty-four-hour news channel to know real life is a series of child abductions, school shootings and tsunamis. You'd do well to remember that when you begin writing your own novel."

"I'll keep that in mind. By the way, I never would've guessed you and Dr. Flowers were related. You don't have the same last name."

Aaron heard her comment but he was distracted. He touched his tie as if to remind himself it was still there. His fingers raked through his hair; they came back a shade too oily. When was the last time he had a haircut?

"I'm sorry," Sabrina said. "That was too personal. I didn't mean to—"

"It's fine." He didn't like to discuss his history with Horace Flowers. "Please excuse me. I don't want to keep my father waiting. He can be prickly."

"I know." Sabrina blushed as she caught herself. "I mean...Rather—"

"No worries. I know exactly how my father comes across. Good luck with your writing. I do hope you reconsider your plans to write genre fiction. You're quite talented and perfectly capable of tackling something more challenging. I'd be glad to look at your work even after the semester is over."

"That's so generous of you. I'd be happy to do something in exchange...Do you have any decorating needs? Everyone says I have a flair."

"Not necessary." Aaron rented a one hundred and fifty square-foot room in a boarding house with a hot plate and a communal bathroom. His decorating needs were nonexistent.

He left the classroom. The elevator was being repaired, so he climbed the stairs to Horace Flowers' corner office, his bad leg dragging slightly behind. His loafers were loud against the tile flooring. The closer he got, the more gingerly he walked. By the time he arrived at his destination his stride was nearly soundless. He and his father worked at the same university but it'd been over a month since Aaron saw him last. Usually the only time Horace Flowers summoned him to his office was when he was miffed about something.

Aaron followed the strains of Mendelssohn and paused at a slightly ajar door. He knocked, but the knock was too timid to be heard over the music. He tried again, this time harder. A voice invited him to enter.

Horace Flowers' office was probably six times as large as his own. Framed photographs adorned the wall—images of his father posing with several notable authors, although none of them were Nicholas Windust. Windust was so reclusive he refused to pose for an author photo.

There was a sitting area where tea and tinned butter cookies were sometimes served, but Aaron had never been offered either.

He nodded a greeting and sat across from his father, who was hunched behind his massive dark-wood pedestal desk, holding his head as if he had a severe migraine. People who didn't know Horace Flowers well were always asking him if his head hurt, but Aaron knew it was just a mannerism.

Aaron set his briefcase on his lap as a protective shield and meekly waited for his father to speak. Meetings between them usually had the formality and warmth of a parole hearing.

Horace Flowers had wispy gray hair, long teeth, and a permanently wrinkled forehead. Disappointment had settled so deeply into the muscles of his face that on the rare occasion he tried to smile, it got swallowed in the sagging folds of his skin. His father switched off the music.

"How are you, Aaron? Doing well, I trust?"

"Fine." Aaron was surprised by his father's conviviality. Horace Flowers usually dispensed with social preambles and got straight to the point.

"Would you care for a cup of tea? I had one of the girls in the office make a fresh pot."

His father's uncharacteristic hospitality unnerved Aaron. Why was he being so nice? Had someone died? If so, he couldn't imagine who. He had a great aunt Priscilla in Iowa City whom he'd only met once or twice. She was their only living relative as far as he knew.

"No tea for me, thank you," Aaron said.

"You're probably wondering why I asked you here today."

"I am."

"I had a little extra time this weekend..." His father paused to take a long slurp of tea; all of his motions were deliberate and exacting. Whenever Aaron was in his company, time seemed to sputter to a stop.

"Would you care for a cookie?"

"No." Aaron was feeling more agitated with every second. Please come out with it, he thought.

"As I was saying, I had some spare time this weekend..."

Aaron scooted his chair a bit closer to his father's desk in anticipation.

"And I read your novel."

The tendons in the back of Aaron's neck went taut, and his briefcase slipped from his lap to the floor. Six months ago his father had asked for a copy of his manuscript and promised he'd peruse it when he had time. It was the second novel Aaron had given his father to read. His previous novel, *Klieg*, was written during the first semester of his MFA program five years ago. Aaron had been ridiculously proud of that novel, and his fellow workshop members had praised it, but his father said it was amateurish.

Deeply embarrassed, Aaron immediately deleted the offensive document from his computer. His second novel, *Chiaroscuro*, took him five years to write, and he felt as if he'd made enormous strides in Craft during that time.

In fact, nine months ago, he managed to sign with a literary agent. Aaron had no notion how to find an agent—the skill wasn't taught in school. Thankfully his MFA mentor had recommended Aaron to his own agent. Unfortunately, seven editors had already rejected his novel.

There was a long silence, so long Aaron felt compelled to prod his father along. "And...?"

His father stared beyond Aaron's shoulder as if his next thought was written on the far wall of his office. Then he said "This is exceedingly painful for me."

Aaron's chest hitched. His father wasn't reticent about speaking his mind. What he had to say must be very, very bad. Aaron splayed his palms across the ridges of his corduroy slacks; his hands seemed oversized and cumbersome, like gloves stuffed with gravel. What did he normally do with them? He couldn't recall.

"Your work's competent."

He waited, armpits sweaty with dread, knowing his father had far more to say.

"But it falls far short of greatness on a number of levels. I'm sad to say that I suspect you were offered literary representation because of our relationship."

The tips of Aaron's ears heated up. When he was distressed they looked severely inflamed.

"I didn't mention our relationship to my agent," Aaron said. He was determined not to be published as Horace Flowers' son.

"Someone at the agency obviously found out. It hardly takes any research to discover our relationship."

"My agent's very complimentary about my work." His voice sounded squeaky, much younger than his twenty-nine years.

"Son, I think you should withdraw your submission. It'll never attract the attention of an editor."

"You can't be sure about that." Aaron decided not to mention the seven rejections.

"Here's what I suggest: Apply for the PhD program. I know the deadline's passed, but one word from me and it'll be extended."

His father had been pushing a PhD on Aaron for over two years. He'd have liked to see his son follow his lead and become a literary critic. The best compliment his father ever gave him was that Aaron's sense of literary aesthetics rivaled his own. Growing up, Aaron usually bowed to his father's wishes, but not when it came to writing.

"I want to be a novelist," Aaron said. The sentence came out as a near whisper, which sounded wimpy even to him. He cleared his throat and spoke louder. "I am a novelist."

His father shook his head; his eyes were filled with pity, which was more distressing than the usual arrogance. "Do you honestly want to be an adjunct the rest of your life, making less than the towel boy at my club?"

"It's temporary." Supposedly seven rejections was a modest number in the publishing world. He once read that Nabokov, author of *Lolita*, received numerous rejection letters, one which said, "I recommend that [the manuscript] be buried under a stone for a thousand years." No one had yet to be that scathing about Aaron's work.

"I'm trying to save you years of disappointment."

"Maybe this novel will sell. Maybe it'll—"

"You're not a terrible writer. And with practice and study you may very well improve. I've seen poor writers become mediocre writers, and mediocre writers become serviceable writers. But to elevate a serviceable writer to a brilliant writer, one who deserves a place in the pantheons..." He threw out his hands. "I'm so sorry."

Horace Flowers believed there were only four living American novelists writing worthwhile fiction: Philip Roth, Cormac McCarthy, Thomas Pynchon, and Nicholas Windust.

"Maybe I don't want to be in pantheons. Maybe I could simply be—"

"A genre writer?"

"Of course not! I was thinking of a midlist literary writer."

"Not with this novel, and most likely not with the next one either. I'm sorry. There's something essential lacking in your work."

Aaron wanted to ask his father to clarify, but he was afraid to hear the answer, afraid it was something he couldn't rectify. Being a published novelist was Aaron's one and only ambition. Writing was all he cared about.

"You're absolutely certain about this?"

The skin around his father's eyes was wrinkled and pillowed; his irises were so faded they were almost colorless. Yet, weary as his eyes appeared, Aaron knew they could easily discern excellent fiction after reading a paragraph or even a sentence or two.

"I'm a literary critic," he said gently. "Novels are my reason for existence. If I thought my own flesh and blood had the potential for greatness, don't you think I'd nurture that gift?"

Aaron sat still in his chair. The office seemed unnaturally quiet, as if it was somehow suspended in outer space instead of being on the floor of a bustling university.

Horace Flowers said, "Please check your box before you leave campus today."

Aaron exited the office and headed to the English department suite. A cluster of students chatted in the halls, obstacles on the way to his destination. "Did you see Comedy Central last night? That guy...what's his name? He's hysterical."

Aaron limped ahead, pretending he didn't hear a student misusing the word "hysterical." Normally he'd stop and say, "Hysterical is not a synonym for hilarious." But who cared about proper word usage when his reason for existence was falling apart?

He nearly sideswiped an Asian female custodian emptying a trash bin. She mumbled something in Mandarin, but Aaron forged onward without a second glance. Once in the office suite, the secretary greeted him. Aaron couldn't even manage his usual head nod. He checked his box. Inside was a manila envelope that contained the admission materials for the PhD program. Aaron held the envelope in his hands for several seconds and then tossed it into the garbage can.

Two

Laurie Lee sat on a grassy knoll outside the Central Georgia Library in a suburb outside of Atlanta. A Colonial bread truck rattled by, and the driver honked and yelled, "Hey gorgeous." She didn't bother to look up. Catcalls and whistles were the soundtrack of her life.

She was enjoying the feel of the afternoon sun warming her scalp and the tickle of clover on her bare legs. Laurie was on her lunch break from her temp job as a library assistant, and she was jotting down thoughts about Brock Wilder, the male hero in her romance novel-in-progress.

Her coworker Ramona arrived for her shift in a battered hearse which she purchased from a bankrupt mortuary. She emerged from the vehicle wearing a t-shirt that said, "Banshees Do It Better."

Once Ramona got within hearing range, Laurie said, "Helga's going to give you grief for that shirt." Helga was the head librarian and their mutual boss.

"I have a shirt to cover it in my backpack." Ramona sat beside Laurie and the smell of licorice drifted over. She liked to chew on fennel seeds.

Laurie consulted her notebook. "Tell me which description you like better. Piercing sapphire orbs or orbs the color of a South Carolina sky on a June afternoon."

"Orbs?"

"I'm trying to decide what color orbs I should give my hero, Brock."

"Why are you calling eyeballs orbs?"

"Don't you think it sounds more poetic?"

Ramona pulled a face, but Laurie paid her no mind. Her coworker wasn't a writer and didn't understand the need to vary words now and then. "How's the proofreading going?" Laurie hired Ramona to proofread the novel she'd completed a few weeks ago.

"Almost finished." Ramona popped another fennel seed into her mouth and flicked a section of her shoe-polish black hair over her shoulder.

"That's so quick. Thank you. Now I'll be able to make my deadline."

"I don't understand. Why do you have a deadline when you self-publish your books?"

"You mean indie publish."

Laurie thought "indie publishing" sounded more appealing than self-publishing. Some bold writers were even calling it artisanal publishing, which made their books sound like very fine cheese or chocolate. But maybe that was a little pretentious.

"It's my own deadline," Laurie continued. "But I'm strict about keeping to it."

She waited for Ramona to say something complimentary about her novel, but instead of offering praise, her coworker withdrew a long-sleeved black shirt from her backpack. She flapped it to smooth out the wrinkles, and a musty odor rose from the fabric.

Laurie couldn't stand it a second longer. "What did you think?"

"About what?"

"My novel, silly."

Ramona put on the shirt, pulled up a section of the fabric to her nose, and took a long contemplative sniff.

"Were you disappointed that no one gets bitten in the neck?" Laurie said in a teasing voice.

Ramona was a fan of paranormal romances; the covers were usually either blood-red or a deep moody blue, and the artwork featured pale brooding people with dead, soulless eyes. Laurie got goosebumps every time she encountered one.

Her coworker poked at a scab on her forearm. "I don't read vampire novels anymore. Nobody does."

"Is that so?" It was almost impossible to keep up with all the various trends in romance. There were so many. Recently Laurie discovered Amish romance, or bonnet rippers as they were called.

"But, in answer to your question, I found your characters to be somewhat unrealistic."

Laurie quirked an eyebrow. It seemed odd that someone who liked to read about werewolf sex could accuse her of writing unrealistically.

"Well, I am writing a romantic comedy, so the characters are supposed to be a little broad."

Ramona slapped at a housefly on her arm and missed.

"Think of Reese Witherspoon in *Legally Blonde*."

The fly landed on Ramona's lace-up boot, and this time her palm flattened it.

"Or Sandra Bullock in—"

"I don't watch romantic comedies."

"Oh." Laurie couldn't imagine that. She watched them so frequently she considered herself a rom-com expert.

"And maybe broad characters work better in movies?" Ramona hefted herself off the ground. "I better go in. Don't want Helga on my case."

"Wait. What about the hero, Brock? Surely you liked him?" Brock was Laurie's own personal masterpiece. She got a little woozy just thinking about his crooked grin and superb kissing techniques.

"He was too perfect."

"Isn't that a good thing? If you want imperfect, why bother reading romance? You can simply go to a singles' bar and flirt with a guy who picks his teeth with a knife."

"Brock was so perfect he was unbelievable."

Laurie disagreed. She wanted to defend Brock as if he were her own husband.

"And the conflicts seemed manufactured and a little silly."

"But it's a romantic comedy. A certain amount of silliness is inevitable."

"Maybe. But to be honest, I had the most problems with Lily."

"Lily?" Laurie inhaled sharply. "What was wrong with her?"

"She was too wimpy and eager to please. I like strong female protagonists."

Laurie's cheeks felt hot and not from the sun. She'd based the character of Lily on herself. In fact, all of her main characters were loosely based on herself.

"Maybe she's just very girlish?"

"Maybe," Ramona said, a tad reluctantly. "Anything else you want to know?"

"No. I appreciate the honesty. Truly I do."

Actually, she cringed from the honesty. Mostly because she desperately wanted to be a good writer. It was so magical to create characters and settings, all from her imagination. And Laurie had been working on her writing for six months. That was practically a lifetime for her. Her late grandmother used to say to her, "You have the attention span of a two-year-old who's just gobbled a sugar cookie."

That wasn't completely untrue, but that's because her grandmother had pressed activities on Laurie that she didn't much care for. Calligraphy. So tedious. Needlepoint. No, thank you. Still, if she didn't get some validation for her writing soon she might lose heart.

Break over, Laurie returned to the library and went about her duties smiling at patrons, checking out books, and collecting fines. She tried not to think about what Ramona said, but every now and then, the criticism rose up in her consciousness like dirty water from a backed-up sink.

Six months ago she'd stumbled across an article about a romance writer who made a fine living selling self-published novels over the internet, and, to Laurie, it seemed like a missive from heaven. How many times had she watched a bad rom-com or read a novel and thought, good Lord, I could do better writing with the tip of my nose?

Laurie was perfectly poised to be a romance writer. She devoured at least a dozen romance novels a month (particularly funny ones) and had seen practically every romantic comedy in existence, even the dispiriting ones like *Fool's Gold* (What was Kate Hudson thinking?) and that awful one where Patrick Dempsey dressed up as a bridesmaid.

Did she know how to write novels? Frankly, no. That was the single hitch in her plan. Yet she was determined to learn.

After reading the article, she immediately ordered *Romance Writers' Phrasebook* and had been writing romance novels ever since. She believed she was improving every day and was particularly proud of the one she'd recently finished. That's why it bothered her so much that Ramona didn't like it.

A young black woman with a prominent overbite and springy chocolate-colored hair came up to Laurie's desk. She asked if the library had Toni Morrison's latest.

Laurie consulted her computer and said, "I'm sorry. I don't see any of his books in our system."

"He is a she."

"Oh. Well, I'm sorry but we don't have any of her books either."

The girl flared her nostrils. "What kind of library doesn't have Toni Morrison?"

Actually, it was a small library, and it mostly served a nearby retirement village. The majority of patrons were older women who wore track suits and padded about in spongy-soled shoes. They favored romances and mysteries. Currently there was a fifty-person hold on the latest Mary Higgins Clark.

"Maybe I'm spelling it wrong? It is T-o-n-y?"

"You work in a library, and you don't know who Toni Morrison is?" The girl's tone was accusatory.

Laurie had only picked up the library job a little over a month ago, since she'd moved to Atlanta from Swainsboro, Georgia.

"What kind of books does Toni write? Mysteries, thrillers, sci-fi?"

"Never mind. I'll check myself." The girl disappeared into the stacks, backpack slapping against her shoulder blades.

She was the last patron in line. Laurie decided to use the afternoon lull to pull up her blog on the computer and dash off a post.

The Heart Spot, Official Blog of Romance Author Laurie Lee
Tags: cute, sensitive, warm, muffins

Hello, my darling readers. Don't forget tomorrow is Cute Guy of the Week day here at the Heart Spot. This week's cutie is named Cody, and he's a firefighter. Wait until you see his dimples. Might turn a few of you into arsonists. (Kidding!!!) But Cody's not just cute. He also likes to make homemade blueberry muffins and bring them to you as breakfast in bed.

Romantically yours,
Laurie Lee

Laurie borrowed the concept of Cutie of the Week from another romance writer. The other writer called her feature Hunk of the Week, and always posted photos of men with their shirts off. Laurie didn't care for the naked-chest aspect. All of her cuties were clothed, because wouldn't you want to know a person before you were confronted with his pectoral muscles?

Although, the more she learned about romance writing, the more she realized how naive she was about it. The most popular books were filled with steamy sex scenes and had women sleeping with either billionaires or their stepbrothers. Didn't anyone want to read a romance that featured a man who sent flowers and said heartfelt things like "You're my everything" instead of "Let me tie you to the bed so I can bludgeon you with a riding crop."

But then again, maybe women wanted to be bludgeoned. Laurie wasn't selling a lot of books, and she suspected her blog readership was small. WordPress provided a stat counter, but she never looked at it, afraid it would discourage her. The indie publishing books all said the same thing: It was a long-tail business, and nothing happened overnight. She was trying to practice patience, which was not one of her strengths. She was ashamed to admit she'd actually bought a few of those racy novels in hopes of spicing up her own novel.

After work, Laurie checked her mailbox outside the stucco cottage she'd recently subletted and found an envelope from a writers' colony in the Georgia Mountains, which she eagerly ripped open. She saw the ad for the colony in the back of *Writer's Digest* and applied several weeks ago, hoping to write undistracted in a lovely setting.

Her name on the envelope was misspelled—Laura Leer instead of Laurie Lee—but the letter contained thrilling news. Not only had she been accepted to the colony, she'd been awarded a full scholarship, something she'd never once dreamed of getting. Ironically, the writing sample she'd sent in was a chapter from the novel Ramona didn't like.

"Woo hoo!" She was so loud she spooked a squirrel rooting around in the flowerbed.

Laurie stood in her yard under the shade of a mimosa tree and read the letter two more times, even though the air was still and heavy and sweat pooled in the hollows of her collarbone. She especially adored this sentence: "We were bowled over with your writing sample and would be honored to offer you the Distinguished Scribe scholarship. It's the only one we offer."

Honored. As if she were doing them a favor. Laurie did a little dance of victory every time she read it.

It was one of the first validations she'd gotten as a writer, and it was a relief after her coworker's criticism of her latest novel. Then again, poor Ramona probably didn't recognize good writing when she saw it. The staff at the writing colony were trained to identify promising work and obviously her writing must have leaped out at them and said, "Choose me!"

Three

"How many male novelists does it take to screw in a light bulb?"

It was Saturday morning. Aaron was in a coffee shop, drinking his usual cup of black coffee and sitting with his girlfriend, Emma. She was tight with a dollar and had only two indulgences: gin and coffee. Every Saturday she liked to sample a different coffee shop in Atlanta, and she insisted Aaron accompany her. To Aaron, all the coffee shops seemed similar. They all had too-clever names. (This one was called Brewed Awakening.) They all hung jarring amateur art on the walls and employed scary-looking female baristas whose bare arms bloomed with tattoos or whose ears bristled with piercings. He would much rather pick up a Styrofoam coffee at a convenience store.

Emma was sipping one of her complicated coffee drinks—a nonfat Frappuccino with extra whipped cream and chocolate sauce—and eyeing him over the rim of her cup.

"How many male novelists does it take to screw in a light bulb?" she repeated

Aaron shrugged. He wasn't much for riddles. Puns, on the other hand, could be amusing, especially Shakespearean puns.

"Four thousand words from the narrator about his feelings on his childhood circumcision," Emma said.

"What's that?" The steam from the coffee fogged his glasses, and he wiped them with his sleeve.

"How many male novelists does it take to screw in a light bulb?"

"I have no idea."

"The light bulb is inauthentic."

If that was the punchline of the joke, it wasn't particularly funny. Not that he'd say so to Emma. She didn't take criticism well.

"You don't get it, do you?" Her eyebrows were at half-mast, and she was glaring at him. Obviously she was disgruntled about something and was waiting for him to ask her what's wrong. Aaron refused to bite.

"I read your novel last night," she said.

Emma managed a literary bookstore called The Spine. She'd been angling to read Aaron's novel ever since he finished it, but he'd been reluctant to give it to her. Emma had a cruel streak when it came to evaluating literature. Her sharp mind unmercifully dissected novels, stripping them of their flesh, revealing weaknesses in their bones and innards. If a work didn't possess the intellectual rigor she expected, she'd write a negative Amazon review that read like a death wish.

On the other hand, if she admired a work, she wasn't stingy with her praise. The day after his father said he'd never be an important novelist, Aaron, in a weak moment, asked Emma's opinion, hoping to be reassured. Now he wished he hadn't. Emma didn't look like a woman about to shower accolades on his head. Pebbles, rocks, maybe even anvils, but not accolades.

Emma paused for a long while. (For evil effect, Aaron imagined.) A shaft of sunlight fell on her shoulder-length dark hair, revealing auburn undertones. In the background beans groaned in a grinder; an espresso machine gurgled and whistled. It was a noisy endeavor, making coffee in a café.

Finally, she spoke. "Everything that's wrong with you and our relationship is reflected in the pages of your novel."

Aaron fidgeted in his chair. Lately Emma had been looking for any excuse to turn the most innocent exchange into a "State of the Relationship" discussion.

"I don't see any connection between our relationship and my novel."

"No connection?" Her eyebrows leaped into the upper quadrant of her forehead like acrobatic caterpillars. "You barely disguise any of the characters. Louise is clearly based on me."

"Louise is fiction. You and she have little in common."

"My middle name is Louise."

"Coincidence."

"She works in a bookstore."

"As a clerk, not a manager."

"She's withholding in bed."

"Yes, well...what did you think of Eric?"

"Hmm. Let me see." She stroked her chin in an exaggerated manner. "He's emotionally deadened, pessimistic and lives entirely in his head. He's never seen Louise as a fully developed and complex person. Eric defines her according to the function she fulfills in his life, and that's why Louise is sexually withholding. She doesn't feel cherished by Eric; she feels like she could disappear from his life and he would barely notice."

"Not true. Eric admires Louise's intellect."

"Yes, but Eric also thinks he's so much smarter than Louise."

Aaron took a sip of his coffee. "That's because Eric *is* smarter than Louise."

Emma's eyebrows turned into aerialists, nearly flying off her forehead. A plastic creamer sailed through the air, and Aaron ducked. After five years of dating Emma, he'd become a practiced ducker and rarely got hit anymore.

"It's because of Eric's uppity attitude that Louise is fed up. She doesn't want a relationship that's completely cerebral. She's a woman, not an intellectual sparring partner. Louise has a soft side that longs to be loved. She might not always show it, but it definitely exists."

Aaron swallowed a reply. Emma might like to believe she had a soft side but she was mostly sharp elbows, sharp fingernails and especially sharp tongue.

"Aaron. This has gotten out of hand."

"I agree. It was a mistake to ask you to critique my novel. You're too close to the material."

"This isn't about you, Mr. Self-Involved. It's about our relationship. What you fail to realize is, I need a man who—"

Emma launched into what was sure to be a long diatribe on his various failings. He tried to pay attention but after a moment or two his mind wandered.

Her nose flared and flattened like a chimney bellow.

"Our relationship is a microcosm—"

The soot of her discontent sullied the room.

"I feel disenfranchised and—"

It settled on his shoulders like the ashes of—

"Are you writing in your head again?"

"No. Of course not."

Did a chimney bellow flare and flatten? He couldn't recall seeing one in operation before.

Emma banged her coffee cup against the table; the wire sugar canister jumped, tossing about pink and yellow packets of Sweet N' Low and Splenda. "How many male novelists does it take to screw in a light bulb?"

"I don't know."

She stood and flung her purse over her shoulder. It nearly clipped Aaron in the head. "The woman left the room. The male novelist was too busy navel-gazing to notice the relationship was over."

"Over?" Aaron said. He was suddenly more alert. "Again?"

Emma had broken up with Aaron many times during their five-year relationship. The breakups lasted anywhere from a week to a couple of months, depending on her level of annoyance. When she was ready to have him back, she'd call and invite him over. Then they'd resume their relationship as if nothing had happened.

"I mean it this time. I'm not happy."

He'd also heard that before. Emma always implied that Aaron was responsible for her happiness, which perplexed him, because he had no idea how to make himself happy, much less another person.

"I'll take the MARTA home."

Emma tossed some money on the table. On her way out, she nearly sideswiped a man in a baseball cap holding a tray of coffees. Legs well-muscled from years of prep school field hockey propelled her across the shop. (On more than one occasion, Aaron had found himself caught in the python-like grip of those legs.)

A sense of wistfulness stole over him. He was fond of Emma and would miss her. But he always missed her less when she broke up with him during the summer. Summer was the best time to write, and with Emma absent from his life, he wouldn't have to worry about the everyday *sturm and drang* of a relationship. Recently he'd applied to several writing colonies, and a colony in the Georgia Mountains had accepted him. Emma tended to be proprietary over his time and would probably resent his absence.

He added a couple of dollars to Emma's stingy tip and left the coffee shop. Outside the sky was gray, and the sound of thunder rumbled in the distance, which surprised him. Every morning he diligently checked the forecast and no inclement weather was predicted.

Aaron quickened his pace to his old Buick, hoping to arrive home before the storm. It seemed to be getting closer every second. A block away from his car thunder clapped loudly, and he broke into a gimpy trot. A whimpering sound emerged from behind a dumpster.

"I didn't hear that."

Another whimper followed as if to say, "Oh, yes you did."

He reluctantly paused and peered behind the dumpster. A black puppy with matted fur and no collar gave him a piteous look.

Aaron glanced about his surroundings, hoping to spy an anxious owner, but no one was around. The puppy was cowering up against a dirty piece of burlap for comfort and was so tiny Aaron wondered if he was weaned.

"I'm sorry, but I live in a room that doesn't allow pets. I'm also due to leave for a writers' colony in several days. In case you didn't notice, a storm's brewing and if I don't go immediately to my car—"

More thunder, louder still, which caused the puppy to whimper again and made Aaron even more anxious to flee, but he continued to linger. The animal was shaking, and its eyes were wide and terrified.

"Let me reiterate. I don't have time for this type of inconvenience."

The puppy responded with another whine which sounded eerily like "mama."

Aaron paused for a moment, considering, but after the puppy's last utterance, he knew he had no choice. He scooped up the trembling animal, tucked it under his jacket, and made a dash for his car.

Four

"Vall-der-ri, Vall-der-ra! A knapsack on my back."

Laurie sang while exploring her accommodations at the writers' colony, located deep in the mountains of Georgia. She was staying in one half of a duplex house, and it was utterly charming: Eyelet curtains. Porcelain claw-foot tub. Antique desk with an inkwell.

It made her feel like Jane Austen who, incidentally, was the great-great grandmother of the romantic comedy. She hadn't read any of Austen's work—the books were as thick as doorstops with tiny type—but she'd watched *Clueless*, *Bridget Jones's Diary*, and *Pride and Prejudice*. (The Kiera Knightly version, not the BBC, which was eight hours long. Who had the time?)

There was no phone or TV in the duplex but she had her cell phone. Internet was optional. Laurie decided to request it, because she didn't want to be off the grid for two whole weeks. She spent the morning unpacking and exploring the grounds. At noon someone tippy-toed up to her back porch and left lunch wrapped in a gingham napkin and tucked into a wooden basket.

The good clean air made her ravenous. She gobbled up a turkey sandwich and fruit salad in a few bites. After lunch she sat down at the desk to write a love scene.

Usually her search-and-peck typing couldn't keep up with her imagination, but today the words refused to come. Two hours passed and she'd only written a paragraph, and not a particularly good one.

At least it was almost time for dinner. Dinnertime was the only opportunity for socializing with fellow writers; the rest of the day they were closeted away in their duplexes working. This surprised her. She'd imagined the colony to be more like camp, where writing time was broken up with other activities like hikes, canoeing or games of charades. Maybe even a round or two of "Kumbaya."

Before getting ready for dinner, Laurie called her dearest friend Delilah, who lived in her hometown of Swainsboro, Georgia.

"Aren't you supposed to be writing?" Delilah said. Laurie could hear her friend's two children babbling in the background and the jangly music of cartoons.

"That doesn't sound like PBS to me," Laurie teased. Delilah told people she only allowed her kids to watch educational TV. What a fibber. Those children knew more about Sponge Bob than his own mother did.

"Don't change the subject. Why are you calling me from the writer's cult? Bored already?"

"It's a colony, not a cult."

"Colony, then. Shouldn't you be pounding your keyboard?"

"I'm writing a love scene and having a bit of a block."

"That's what you get for choosing a challenging hobby like writing. You should try adult coloring books. After the kids go to bed, I pour myself a big-girl glass of Yellow Tail, get out my sixty-four Crayola box and I'm as content as a little neck clam. Until I pass out. Those coloring books are better than a Lunesta."

Laurie smiled. No doubt Delilah didn't color within the lines, which was one of things she always liked about her old friend. "I've told you. This isn't a hobby. This is—"

"Annabelle Louise. Don't you dare smear Nutella in your brother's hair."

"It's a calling and so much fun. I really want to stick with it."

"Well, I have a solution to your block, but you will probably resist it."

"I'll keep an open mind."

"You write romance, correct?"

"Yes."

"Then get some into your life, for St. Pete's sake."

Silence.

"Are you there?"

"I am. I'm not sure I'm ready to—"

"I'm not suggesting you run out and get engaged. Just sleep with someone. This is the perfect opportunity. Grab one of your fellow scribes and toss him into your bed."

"You're proposing a fling?"

"Exactly."

Laurie lowered her voice to a near whisper, even though she was alone in the duplex. "I've never done anything like that before."

"No one will know. Except you, your fling mate and hopefully me."

"A fling. Hmmm."

"Sorry. Gotta go. Bart Junior just spilled his orange juice on Snowflake *again*. What was I thinking, having kids and an angora cat in one household?"

Laurie ended the call. If all had gone to plan, she might have a child of her own by now. Instead she was sitting in a room alone, in the backwoods mountains, contemplating sex with a stranger. Which, to be honest, was a bit thrilling.

You're what?

She could practically hear her late grandmother's voice in her head. Come to think of it, Bella Mae Jenkins would skip the question and probably power wash Laurie with holy water. She'd been ninety-three at the time of her death three years ago, and lived in Swainsboro all of her life. Women of her generation never thought about flings. (Or if they did, they probably recited the Lord's Prayer over and over to scrub their brains of lewd thoughts.) They mostly certainly didn't think about flings when they were widows, and their husbands had only been dead for a year.

Widow.

Laurie still couldn't believe the word applied to her. She, who up until her husband's funeral, didn't own a single thread of black clothing. She, who was only twenty-two when she watched dirt being thrown on Jake's grave.

Widows had gnarled fingers and rheumy eyes and were generally ornery. *Don't cut through the Widow Lee's yard. She'll throw pinecones at you.*

They were expected to maintain a certain decorum: Laugh infrequently and not too loudly. Always wear a pained expression when saying your late husband's name. Listen patiently when people talk about his football triumph stories over and over.

Those expectations were ten-fold in a small town like Swainsboro. It was one of the reasons she needed to get away for a while.

Yes, she was a widow, and for the first few months after Jake's death, she behaved like one. She lost ten pounds, rarely smiled and had zero carnal needs. But, in recent months, she'd been plagued by sexy thoughts, and those erotic novels she'd recently been reading caused them to multiply like fruit flies. Jake was buried in the cold soil, but her sexual drive had not been buried with him.

She glanced at her phone. Time for supper, thank goodness. Laurie changed into her most cheerful outfit, a hot-pink top, Capri pants and strappy sandals, and then left her duplex to head to the main house on the colony grounds. The sandals weren't the wisest choice because the dirt path was strewn with sharp stones that stabbed at her feet through her thin soles. She picked the sandals to show off her toes painted in "That's Berry Daring," but now she wished she'd worn more practical shoes. The closer she got to the house, the more her stomach grumbled. A yellow Victorian loomed ahead, and upon entry, she followed the food aroma down a hallway to a large dining room.

Her heels made a terrific clatter on the hardwood floor, and it seemed as if dozens of eyes (mostly bespectacled ones) were checking her out. She was used to being stared at, especially by men, but this staring wasn't lustful. She suspected everyone was looking at because her clothes were so loud they could wake the dead. If the colony director sent out a memo about dressing in gloomy attire only, Laurie didn't get it.

About thirty writers filled the dining room. They looked terribly serious. So different from the romance writers she'd met.

When she first decided she wanted to be a writer, she attended a conference for pre-pubbed romance writers in Savannah called Moonlight and Mink. The attendees wore bright colors like fuchsia and purple, and she remembered thinking, these are my people. On the last night when a Fabio lookalike gave out the coveted Pink Heart Award, the room was filled with more sequins and feathers than in a line of Las Vegas showgirls.

But colony writers were a different breed and probably wrote books as bleak as their attire. A couple of years ago Laurie belonged to a book club, led by her future sister-in-law, Kate, who was a high school English teacher. The women chose boring books and conducted in-depth conversations about motifs and symbolism. She didn't last a month.

Afterward Laurie started her own book club called Well Red, and the women drank Cupcake cabernet and barely discussed the novel, which was always a lighthearted beach read.

She was tempted to leave the dining room—intellectual types intimidated her. In their company she always felt a little too blonde and big-breasted.

But she reminded herself she'd won a scholarship to the colony. They only gave out one, which meant the colony staff thought her work was better than anyone else's. She might be dressed like a flamingo, but she was a writer and belonged at the colony.

Laurie filed through the buffet line and heaped her tray with rib-sticking Southern eats: fried chicken, mac and cheese, cathead biscuits and a mess of turnip greens. Laurie was not one of those Southern women who picked at their grains of food like malnourished chickadees; she had the appetite of a Saint Bernard. Luckily, she was such a fidgety person she usually burned off the calories.

The room contained a collection of large picnic-style tables, and she plunked down on the end, several feet from the nearest person. Laurie doubted she'd be by herself for long. Some bold male was bound to sit next to her and start flirting.

Normally she would already have a prepared reply to discourage would-be suitors, but not tonight. Delilah had a point. Who would know if she decided to coax one of these writers into her bed? As they said in creative circles, she needed to refill the well, literally. (The thought simultaneously embarrassed and titillated her.)

A writers' colony was the perfect place for well-filling. There was little danger of emotional attachments. It'd be a meeting of bodies and sexual appetites, not hearts, souls and emotions. All in the name of research, she thought.

She glanced about and didn't yet see anyone who immediately interested her. Most of the men were a little scruffy-looking. Laurie was attracted to broad-shouldered clean-cut guys who wore button-down shirts and khakis and said, "Yes, ma'am" and "no ma'am." Guys who went to church with their mothers, drove new Chevy pick-up trucks and smelled like Irish Spring and...

Stop it, she thought. There wasn't a guy like that here or anywhere else. That guy was gone forever. She shook the image of Jake from her head. Sad thoughts had a way of smothering sexy thoughts.

Minutes passed and oddly no one, male or female, sat with her. She dined by herself, and eavesdropped on conversations among the writers in the dining hall. None of the topics of discussion made sense to her. The intellectual appropriation of poetry? Pedagogical tools? Maximalism? It was as if they were speaking a different language. When they discussed their favorite authors, none were familiar: Jonathan Franzen, Karen Russell, and David Foster somebody. Occasionally she noticed both the men and women sneaking glances at her as if she were some weird attraction. She ate as quickly as possible, and vowed that, from now on, she'd request meal delivery.

Back in her cottage, she tried to write again but made little progress and was getting discouraged. She heard stirrings outside and looked out the window. Her duplex mate, a shaggy-haired male, was on the patio eating what looked like a peanut butter sandwich. He hadn't bothered to cut the sandwich in half, and the bread looked so cheap even ducks would turn up their beaks.

Drizzle fell but her neighbor didn't move from his spot. His hair flopped into his face as he ate, and he kept touching the bridge of his glasses, which were reinforced with electrical tape. He looked as if he was thinking extremely deep and complicated thoughts, but there was an air of sadness about him. Was he plotting a novel out there? If so, she suspected it was a tragedy.

Laurie's writing was still stalled, and she was as jittery as a June bug from all the solitude and quiet. For amusement she'd been spying on her neighbor. He always ate his dinner on the patio, which made her wonder if the smarty pants in the dining room intimidated him as well.

"He's out there now." Laurie was talking to Delilah on her cell phone. She'd been reporting on her neighbor for a couple of days now. "Eating that sad little dinner of his. He's actually very cute, in sort of a downtrodden way."

"Well, what are you waiting for? Trot on out there and flirt." Laurie could tell that Delilah was enjoying this immensely.

"I've tried that already. He's skittish. As soon as I step out, he flees, but not too fast. He limps."

"What's his name?"

"I don't know. The colony director sent out a flyer with everyone's bio on it, but I misplaced it."

"Have you tried hiding out there before he comes out, and then springing yourself on him?"

"Way ahead of you. Did that last night. Still went scuttling back inside."

"Sounds like he's going to be a challenge."

Good, Laurie thought. She thrilled to a challenge; most men were such pushovers. And her neighbor was perfect for her purposes. He was cute and convenient, both very important factors when contemplating a fling.

"Is it time for damsel-in-distress?" Delilah said.

Laurie gasped. "I love damsel-in-distress! I'll get right on it."

She hung up the phone. Plotting a fling was such fun.

$\mathcal{F}ive$

Aaron should have been working on his next novel—that's what you were supposed to do at a writers' colony—but instead he'd spent the last few minutes writing an Amazon customer review for the latest Francis Zenn novel.

"Misanthropic with a dizzying lack of originality" June 12, 2016
By A Reader of Discernment—(See All My Reviews)
Verified Purchase
Bondage is an 800-page tome that follows the travails of the Dixon family, a bourbon-soaked Southern tribe who trace their roots back to the Civil War. This novel is so flawed it's hard to know where to begin.

Ding!
Aaron eagerly switched screens to check his email. Before he left for the colony, an editor from Wilner, a semi-respectable literary imprint, expressed interest in his novel. He kept hoping to get an update from his agent.

From: Living Social Deals
Subject: Kale Juice Detox Diet
Delete.

He continued his Amazon review: "Characterization is thin and unpalatable."

Ding!

From: Live and Eat Well

Subject: The Number One Food That Causes Belly Fat

Delete.

"Zenn's prose is bloated and overwrought...."

Ding!

From: Male Pills 61

Subject: Make your happy stick bigger. Fast, effective penis enlargement

Delete.

"Turgid in some sections, flaccid in others, *Bondage* is not worth the papyrus it was penned on."

Aaron hit the send button on the Amazon review, satisfied he'd made a contribution in the name of literary honesty. He was envious of Zenn's writing career. His publisher was the prestigious Featherstone, and his first two novels received praise so glowing, it was a wonder Zenn's head wasn't the size of a minor planet.

Zenn's second novel, however, was a failure on almost every level, yet it hadn't received a single negative review. Even the notoriously cranky *Kirkus* dubbed it "Dickensian and galvanic." Aaron suspected it was a case of the "Emperor's New Clothes." Zenn had become such an icon no one dared to admit he'd written a stinker.

"What're your thoughts on the matter, Dusty?"

Aaron was addressing Windust—Dusty for short—the puppy he'd rescued from behind the dumpster. The dog cocked his glossy black head and looked up at him, as if soaking up every syllable. Dusty was so attentive Aaron often found himself talking to the dog, even though he realized the animal was limited in its understanding of the King's English.

Dusty knew the word "hush"—at home, Aaron said it frequently to keep his landlord from discovering the *verboten* pet— and the word "treat." Dusty was a fool for a form of fake bacon called Wavy Treats, even though they tasted more like smoked rubber than bacon. (One day Aaron was curious about their appeal and stole a nibble.) Dusty also knew the phrases, "Come to Da," (Da being Aaron) and "Who wants a tummy scratch?"

Aaron uttered the latter phrase, and Dusty flopped on his back and presented his belly, which was ghostly white in comparison to his black fur.

Shortly after rescuing Dusty from the storm (which quickly petered out into a drizzle), Aaron drove to the Humane Society and discovered they weren't accepting any more animals that week. Then he called the dog pound to see what would happen to the puppy if he left it in their charge.

"Puppies are usually adopted," said the woman who answered the phone. "It's the older dogs that have trouble finding placement."

Aaron decided to increase the puppy's chances of adoption by buying it a handsome collar appliquéd with bones and giving it a bath and a brush. When the dog was dry, its fur was soft and silky to the touch. Its ears, in particular, felt like chamois between his fingertips.

After bath time, the animal got playful with the towel and tried to engage Aaron in a game of tug-of-war. It was acting so feisty and endearing that Aaron cut the game short so as not to get too attached.

When he arrived at the pound and set the puppy on the counter, the young woman in charge scratched it under its chin and said, "Are you sure you want to leave this cute snip here? There's little chance he'll be adopted."

"That's odd. I called earlier and was told that puppies almost always get adopted."

"Not black puppies." She was twirling a pencil in her hair, which was dyed a vivid shade of purple.

"Why not?"

"People have this silly idea that black dogs are more menacing because you can't always read their expressions. We also post pictures of adoptable dogs on our website, and black dogs aren't as photogenic."

"That's absurd. Look at this animal's coat; it shines like obsidian. I can practically see my reflection in it. And his little face is very expressive. Sometimes he's pensive, other times he's eager, and right now he's—"

"Adoring," the girl said. "That's how he's looking at you. Like you hold all the keys to the kibble cupboard." She scratched the animal's head. "Isn't that right, buddy?"

The girl was correct; the animal was gazing at him intently with dark inquisitive eyes as if trying to memorize his every feature. He couldn't remember the last time any living thing looked at him that way.

"I can't have a dog," he said as he picked it up and left the pound. He said it again on the car ride to the pet store where he bought tins of food, a retractable leash, snacks, a harness to keep the animal stationary during car rides, and a collection of squeak toys. When he got home and the dog settled itself beside him on the futon, he opened his mouth to say it once more, but then the puppy rested its muzzle on his thigh and the words died in his throat.

Aaron was scratching Dusty's belly when he heard the scream. He didn't immediately respond, hoping someone else would investigate. A few moments passed, but the screams didn't cease. He came to the unhappy conclusion that he was the only one hearing them, which meant he was obligated to see what was going on. Reluctantly he stepped outside on the patio.

A woman rushed toward him, a blur of hot pink and platinum hair. He recognized her as his neighbor. "Thank God you're here!" She smelled of overripe peaches and baby powder.

"What is it?"

"A spider. It crawled on my foot."

"Did it bite you?"

"Not yet, but I think that's what it's planning."

"Where is it?"

She pointed a trembling finger at a corner of the deck. He expected to see a fearsome-looking variety of arachnid—a wolf spider or similar—but the interloper was a harmless daddy longlegs.

"That's not a spider."

"Is too." She jutted out her bottom lip.

"Daddy longlegs aren't technically spiders; they're opiliones. Note the lack of separation between the abdomen and cephalothorax. If you were to examine it closely—"

"No, thank you."

"You'd discover it only has two eyes; spiders have eight. Also daddy long legs don't build webs."

"But daddy longlegs are extremely poisonous; I remember reading that. And the only reason they don't kill people is because their fangs are too short. I was lucky to escape with my life."

"What's your source?" Aaron was a prolific reader and didn't remember anything about daddy longlegs being venomous.

"What?"

"Where did you get that information?"

"I don't know. Wikipedia, maybe?"

"Not credible." It was a statement he'd repeated many times to students.

Aaron took his first good look at his neighbor. Mink black lashes fringed blue eyes. Short wavy golden hair glinted in the sun. A plump strawberry of a mouth ripened below a nose so delicate it was difficult to believe it had a practical function as a breathing apparatus.

He wondered what she was doing at a writers' colony since she looked more like a pin-up girl than a writer.

Regardless, he had no interest in prolonging the conversation—he was woefully unskilled at making small talk—so he headed back to the duplex.

"Wait! Can't you do something about..." She lowered her voice to a whisper as if the spider could hear. "You-know-who?"

Aaron picked up a twig and gently coaxed the creature off the patio.

"Thank you. Thank you. Thank you."

He waved off her gratitude. His actions hardly deserved that level of effusiveness.

"So are you enjoying the colony?"

"I suppose."

"Me too. Although it feels a little too quiet, you know what I mean?"

"Actually, as a writer, I don't think there's such a thing as a place being 'too quiet.'"

"Really? Because sometimes I'll sit at my desk and think I'm the only person in the world. Sometimes I think the rapture happened or that some deadly plague wiped out humanity."

She certainly had a vivid imagination.

"I'm sorry to hear that, but I'm afraid I need to return to my duplex. I'm trying to get some writing done."

"Of course. Sorry to be a bother."

He felt her eyes on him as he went back inside. He had an odd urge to peer over his shoulder and take one last look at her—she really was quite pretty, in an old-fashioned fifties way—but he resisted the impulse.

"Damsel-in-distress didn't work?" Delilah said. "That's usually a sure thing."

"I know," Laurie said. "But I got a really good look at my neighbor, and he's even cuter close up. Also he was so sweet with the spider. Most men would have squashed it. Suggestions?"

"Did you pack a sheer dress?"

"I did."

"Why don't you forget to put on a slip and then stand in the sunlight?"

"Scandalous!"

"But damn effective, especially with your figure."

*   *   *

Aaron was spying on his neighbor through an opening in the duplex's curtains, and it wasn't the first time. Today she was sitting outside with her face tilted toward the sun, her flawless features arranged in a beatific expression.

In addition to her lovely face, she had a curvaceous and well-proportioned physique. Yesterday she was standing outside in a bright pink dress made of a sheer material, and the sun was shining behind her, distinctly outlining all of her many attributes. Quickly he backed away from the window, feeling like a peeping Tom, but now, here he was again, watching her without her knowledge.

She pulled a book from her satchel, and Aaron was surprised to see that it was *Alphabetical Africa* by Walter Abish. *Alphabetical Africa* was rough sledding for most readers because of its unusual structure. The first chapter only had words that began with the letter A, the second chapter had words that began with only A and B, and so on. Emma, who was exceedingly well-read, became so frustrated with the novel, she threw it across the room, nearly grazing Aaron's temple.

Aaron watched his neighbor read. Her big blue eyes greedily devoured the material. Her tongue occasionally peeked out of her mouth to lick her bee-stung lips. The expression on her face was rapturous; clearly she was savoring every syllable. Aaron wanted to ask her which chapter she was reading, but then she would know he was spying, and besides, he rarely initiated conversations, especially with beautiful women.

Aaron had limited experience with females, attractive or otherwise. Emma has been his only girlfriend, and she was the one who pursued him. They attended the same MFA program, and their first conversation was about the conclusion of Cormac McCarthy's *Blood Meridian*. (He thought it was trenchant; she deemed it stylishly impressive but facile.) Except for a few breaks, they'd been a couple ever since.

He backed away from the curtains. Up until now the neighbor

had merely been a pleasant sensory diversion, but because of the book she was reading, he was curious about her identity. He rifled through his briefcase, looking for the flier that the writers' colony director sent him a week prior to his departure. There was a listing and a short bio for everyone in attendance but Aaron hadn't glanced at it. He wasn't at the colony to socialize.

The flier not only listed the attendees but also said where they were staying on the colony grounds. His duplex was called the Fitzgerald. He occupied the *Great Gatsby* side, and his neighbor resided in *The Beautiful and the Damned*. Her bio said her name was Laura T. Leer, an author whose name seemed vaguely familiar. Perhaps he'd encountered her work on an online journal? Aaron continued to read and was astonished to discover she was the recipient of a MacArthur Genius Grant. Talk about appearances being deceiving. But what really seized his attention was the publisher of her novel.

"Featherstone!" he said. He startled Dusty, who let out a yelp.

Ever since Aaron started writing he had dreamed of being a Featherstone author. They were the most prestigious publisher of literary fiction in the country, and because Featherstone had published her novel, his neighbor completely outclassed him. Literary writers tended to be very status conscious and most likely Laura T. Leer wouldn't want anything to do with an unpublished author like himself.

"He's been spying on me," Laurie said to Delilah. "And he isn't very sneaky about it either. The curtains twitch, his breath makes clouds on the window, and sometimes I can even see his nose. A perfectly decent aquiline nose, just in case you were wondering."

"Ouch!"

"What's wrong with an aquiline nose?"

"Not a thing. I stepped on a Lego," Delilah said. "But never mind that. Tell me everything."

"Well, I was outside reading a fairly racy novel called *Enter*

Me—hoping for inspiration—and getting a little worked up. That's when I sensed his eyes on me. Not that he knew what I was reading. I always cover up my hot novels with a dust jacket from books the library's discarding."

"But he still didn't come out?"

"Sadly, no."

"Time for the big guns then. Operation carnivore. If that doesn't work, I don't know what will."

Aaron no longer spied on his neighbor. It was undignified to gape at a person of her literary caliber. Still, he thought about her frequently, marveling that a single layer of sheet rock separated him from her brilliance. Sometimes he also dreamed about her, and frankly, they were not the type of dreams he should be having about a MacArthur Genius Grant recipient.

She was grilling out a lot lately; his nostrils had picked up the scent of meat. Dusty kept scratching at the door, hoping to beg for a scrap or two. The temptation to peek at her was strong, but he restrained himself. Aaron wasn't her equal, not nearly, and it was best if he forgot all about her. Obviously she wanted to keep to herself. Like him, she never went to dinner in the main house.

"I thought for sure last night's rib eyes would lure my neighbor out of his lair, but *nada*," Laurie said to Delilah.

"Could he be a vegetarian?"

"Maybe. He's a bit on the pasty-faced side, which could be from a lack of iron. What should I cook for a vegetarian?"

"I have no idea. My Bart insists on having some poor charred mammal on the plate every night. He doesn't even like chicken. You know, there's always the direct approach."

"That takes all the fun out of it. And I don't think it's effective. Men like the conquest. There must be a better way."

"Time's running out."

"True, but I already have so much energy invested."

"Good luck and keep me posted."

"I will. Oops. Another call. Talk soon."

Laurie switched over. Marvel, Jake's mother, was on the line. Laurie never knew how to refer to her. Was she her former mother-in-law or did the mother-in-law status remain in perpetuity? Being a widow was complicated.

"How are things in the big city, dear?"

Laurie had not told Marvel about the writing conference; it would generate too many questions. Plus it'd get back to Jake's sister, who would probably think it was laughable that Laurie, with her humble high-school education, was trying to write a book.

"It's noisy and absolutely filthy."

Marvel was very suspicious of big cities, and Laurie knew she didn't want to hear anything positive. Laurie lived in Decatur, which was just outside of the city limits of Atlanta, and it resembled a small town with a tidy square and courthouse. It was very clean and generally peaceful. But unlike most small towns, Decatur was home to all manner of hip and diverse people. Laurie thrilled to walk the streets, never knowing if she might bump into a lesbian couple, a person covered in head-to-toe tattoos or exotic people speaking foreign tongues.

"I know you're counting the days when you come back home to Swainsboro," Marvel said. "It's a shame you had to leave."

Jake wanted several children, and Laurie had planned to be a stay-at-home mom. They'd only been married a month when he was repairing a shingle and fell off the roof, cracking his skull. Suddenly she was a widow with no future plans. For six months she did nothing but grieve, but she also knew she couldn't languish forever. She had to figure out a way to support herself. Eventually she settled on being a nail technician. Something to make money until her writing panned out.

Her grandmother had left her some money, and Laurie used it to sublet a house in Decatur and pay for the tuition at nail school, which would start in the fall. The program lasted a year, and when she finished, she'd been promised a position at a salon in Swainsboro called Just Teasing.

"I do miss Swainsboro," Laurie said. She'd been in Decatur for only a month and she already adored it. But everyone she knew and loved was back in Swainsboro, Delilah especially.

"You be careful. I'm sure there's plenty of predatory men in the city."

Actually, right now, Laurie was the predator. Marvel would be appalled if she knew that Laurie was plotting a fling. She'd taken on a motherly role in Laurie's life since her grandmother died, and, of course, she probably couldn't imagine her daughter-in-law with anyone but Jake. His death had crushed her.

"I will."

"Wear loose clothing."

"Yes, ma'am."

"And study hard. I know Jake is looking down at you from heaven."

Laurie certainly hoped not. If all went to plan, he wouldn't like what he saw.

Aaron had a vividly carnal dream about his neighbor during his afternoon nap. When he woke up, he laid in bed, panting; his body was covered in sweat. A few seconds later, someone knocked at his door and Dusty barked. Aaron shushed him. Who could it be? His neighbor? Did she hear him through the walls? They weren't particularly solid. The sound of running water and her off-key singing often drifted over to his side of the duplex.

Aaron left Dusty in the bedroom and padded to answer the door, still caught up in a fog from his nap. The young man who brought the lunch baskets was standing outside, but lunch was two hours ago.

"I'm sorry to interrupt, but you have a phone call from someone named Andrea. She wants you to call her right away."

"Where's the phone?" Aaron said. His elderly flip phone failed a day before he was due to leave, and thus he'd alerted Bernie, his literary agent's assistant, about his stay at the colony on the off chance his book got an offer.

"In the study. I'll show you."

Aaron wasn't generally a fast mover, but today he hustled as fast as his limp would allow in the direction of the main house. The lunch man trotted beside him. He was pudgy-faced with a hairstyle similar to a Kewpie doll's.

"Say, have you run into your neighbor? Everyone at the conference is talking about Laura T. Leer. They all want to meet her, but they're intimidated by her accomplishments."

"Could we please walk faster?"

"Sure. We've never had someone of her caliber here. Did you know she's won a—"

"Talking is slowing us down."

Aaron barely remembered the trek across the colony grounds; he was too preoccupied with the phone message. The young man delivered him to the study. The dated early American furnishings barely registered; the one thing in the room that Aaron cared about was the phone which sat atop a small spindly desk. He punched in his literary agent's number, but his fingers felt as cumbersome as sausage links. He had to input the numbers three times before he got it right. Bernie, Andrea's assistant, answered.

"Hey there, cowboy. Good to hear from you. How's the writing conference coming? Soaking up a lot of knowledge, I hope."

"It's a colony. Not a conference."

"Not the same thing?"

"Not at all."

"My bad. What's the diff anyway?"

Normally Aaron would be only too happy to explain the difference—he disliked imprecision in words—but he was too anxious.

"Is Andrea available? I was told she called, and it sounded urgent."

"Calm down. Pour yourself a scotch or a gimlet or whatever

poison people drink at writers' colonies. Andrea's here but she's on the horn. I think she's wrapping it up. Hold onto your boxers...Wait a second...Here's our girl."

"Aaron! Glad you could tear yourself away from your work to give me a call. How's the new novel coming?"

His agent was using her happy voice. Aaron couldn't remember the last time he'd heard her happy voice. Maybe when he first signed with her. Since then he'd only heard her curt, can't-be-bothered voice.

"You called? They came and fetched me."

All the suspense and preambles were wearing him down. He simply wanted to hear the news.

"You ready for this? Max Porter at Wilner loves your novel. They're offering a five-thousand-dollar advance, and yes, I know that's a little bit on the malnourished side, but it's a decent advance for a literary novel these days."

"Five thousand dollars?"

"That's right."

"Wilner?"

"You got it. I also contacted Featherstone to let them know we had an offer. They never got back to me, so I assume they aren't interested."

Silence

"Aaron?"

"I am..."

"Yes?"

"I'm overwhelmed."

Overwhelmed was an ineffectual word for what he felt, but it was the only word he was capable of unearthing from the thousands stored in his mind.

"Of course you are. It'll take a while to get the contracts, but Bernie will shoot them your way once they arrive. In the meantime, have a drink. Celebrate. Cozy up to a fellow writer if you haven't already." She laughed. "I've heard what goes on at those conferences."

"You mean colonies."

"Right."

Aaron sensed she was about to wrap up the conversation, but he wanted to keep her on the phone longer. He wished this moment could go on and on, but he couldn't think of anything to say to prolong the exchange. Literary agents were like soap bubbles; they popped in for a few magical seconds and then they were gone.

"I'm overwhelmed."

"So you said." Terseness crept into Andrea's voice. "My other line is ringing. We'll talk again soon."

Aaron hung up the phone. He stared at it for a long time, thinking he should call someone, but who? Not his father, obviously, nor Emma. No colleagues. As an adjunct, he was isolated from his fellow professors. Adjuncts weren't expected to go to meetings or serve on committees. And he didn't have much time for a social life. His free time was spent working on his novels.

He wandered out of the main house, dazed. He wished he'd run into the colony director or even the man who delivered the lunches, just so he could say the words, "Wilner's publishing my novel."

For the first time, he was acutely aware of his outdoorsy surroundings. It rained recently, and the sun was picking up the water droplets on the rhododendron leaves and transforming them into blinding diamonds. The air smelled freshly scrubbed, and water gurgled in a nearby brook. Mist circled the surrounding mountains, visible from the porch of the house.

Aaron headed back to his duplex. He paused before entering. Inside there was only Dusty, and while he was an attentive companion, Aaron's news would zoom over his dear canine head. His neighbor's door loomed large. She was just behind it, most likely laboring over a future Pulitzer Prize-winning novel.

He was not her equal—far from it—but now that he was about to sign a publishing contract with Wilner, he was a tiny bit closer. Wilner wasn't Featherstone, but it was still a somewhat respectable imprint. And an unpublished novel was all about potential. Before its release, the author could be anything: a National Book Award Winner, a Nobel Prize Winner, the next Nick Windust.

His feet moved in the direction of her door, his fist poised over the wood. He was about to break the most important rule in a writers' colony: Do not disturb the writer.

That's why writers came to colonies. So their work wouldn't be interrupted by the mundane: a Jehovah's Witness brandishing tracts, a clothes dryer buzzing at the end of its cycle, an over-eager neighbor barging in with good news.

He knocked several times, and the deed was done. His offense might get him kicked out of the colony, but he didn't care. His book deal news was like a sneeze; it must be released.

Scurrying sounds were heard behind the door and after a moment or two, she appeared. She wore a bright pink romper that revealed a pair of shapely alabaster legs.

It was late afternoon, and the outdoor light lent a golden tint to her complexion. Most women relied on face paint, costumes and hair potions to achieve the illusion of beauty. His neighbor needed only the light of the sun.

"Well, if it isn't my spider rescuer." Her expression was one of mild surprise, and Aaron temporarily forgot why he'd disturbed her.

"Sorry to interrupt, but there's been an occurrence."

"What is it?"

"It's...It's..." He couldn't seem to say the words.

She tugged him inside, and they sat at her kitchen table. Her attention was so rapt it made him feel foolish. No doubt she was expecting a disaster—a relative felled by a stroke or a copperhead in his bathtub—not a book contract. He abruptly stood.

"Sorry. I shouldn't have disturbed you."

"No, I'm glad you're here. You didn't interrupt one tiny thing."

"You're certain?"

"Positive. Talk to me. By the way, what's your name?"

Aaron introduced himself and she said her name was Laurie. (As if he didn't already know. He liked that she was encouraging him to use the more informal Laurie instead of Laura.)

"You were saying?" Laurie said.

"I got a call...From my agent..."

"Insurance? Oh dear. That's never good news. What happened?"

Her response momentarily befuddled him. "Not insurance."

"Real estate then?"

"No. My literary agent."

"You have a literary agent? Wow. That's so impressive."

Was she mocking him?

"I do, and she called to tell me...Wilner wants to buy my novel."

"Wilbur?" She raised an eyebrow. "Well, that's very nice for you. I hope he enjoys it."

Was she being ironic? Or making a joke? Aaron had no idea. Who could keep up with a genius's mind?

"Not Wilbur. Wilner. The publishing imprint?"

"Of course. Silly me. I don't know what I was thinking...Wilner! This calls for champagne. I've got a bottle in the fridge."

Aaron was about to object. It was several hours before five, and he only imbibed on special occasions. Then he remembered this *was* a special occasion, the most special one of his life.

Moments later his neighbor handed him champagne in a juice cup. The vessel was moist to the touch, and the carbonation rose up and tickled his nose. His hostess planted her elbows on the table and held her head in her hands, looking at him with wide-eyed attention.

"Tell me exactly how this came about. Don't skip over a single detail."

He told her the story, and she oohed and ahhed in all the right places, and said encouraging things like "So thrilling!" or "Oh my gosh. Do you think you'll get to see your book in libraries?"

Her behavior was puzzling. It wasn't as if she'd never met anyone who'd published a book before. Being a distinguished writer, she surely had dozens of novelist friends. In her circle, his accomplishment was not out of the ordinary.

But her enthusiasm was so genuine it was hard to imagine her faking it. She honestly seemed excited for him, and, in turn, he allowed himself to get slightly giddy, a distinctly unfamiliar emotion. His default mood was usually one of low-grade misery.

When he'd exhausted all angles of his publication story and felt as if he no longer had an excuse to linger, she asked him what his book was about.

"It's not easy to describe. At least not in a few sentences."

"That's okay." She poured more champagne, and the silvery bubbles danced and popped in his cup. "I have all the time in the world."

He gave a lengthy description of his novel, *Chiaroscuro*, and his neighbor listened with her whole body, gradually leaning in closer.

"It sounds like a romance," she said. "Funny, I wouldn't have pegged you as a romance writer."

"That's what you got from my description?"

"I did."

Obviously she was not referring to supermarket romances. She must be referencing Northrop Frye's *Anatomy of Critics*. Frye was an influence on Aaron's father, and the premise of his book was that all literature could be divided into four genres: novel, romance, anatomy, and confession.

Aaron remembered Frye characterizing McCarthy's *The Road* as a romance, and he recalled something about romances being nihilistic. *Hmmm.* Perhaps *Chiaroscuro* was a romance after all. He'd definitely look into it.

"There's just one thing missing from your novel."

"Yes?"

"You don't have an HEA."

"An HEA. Ah yes, of course."

He had no idea what an HEA was, but didn't want to reveal his ignorance.

"It's the most important characteristic of a romance."

"Very astute. Thank you for the observation." As soon as he returned home he was going to reread *Anatomy of Criticism* and find out what an HEA is.

"And how would you characterize your work?"

She smiled, and it was like sunlight seeping through a seam in the clouds. "I write romance too."

"Is that so?" No wonder she was such an expert.

"Right now I'm struggling with my hero. I can't get a handle on him."

Yes. Aaron remembered reading something about romance characters being stylized archetypes, i.e., heroes in the vein of Don Quixote.

"Maybe you could help me?"

His neighbor was so close to him he could almost rub noses with her. But lovely as her nose was, her lips were more so. They were lush and pink, the most inviting of confections.

But he couldn't help her because he didn't know enough about the topic. *Dammit.* If only he'd read Frye's work more carefully.

"Well?" she said.

Aaron had never been one to take the lead in male-female interactions (that was always Emma's role), but since he didn't want to admit his lack of knowledge, he decided the only thing to do was kiss her.

He leaned in, and when his lips met hers, he completely forgot about her question or *Anatomy of Criticism*. The kiss went on and on like a comet streaking across the sky.

Six

About Last Night.

It was one of Laurie's favorite rom-coms and featured a very young Demi Moore falling in love with Rob Lowe. They hooked up with each other at a Chicago bar called Mother's, and slept with each other that very night. The next morning Debbi (Demi Moore's character) said to her roommate Joan, "I crawled away in shame...I can't believe I slept with him on the first date." Joan, played by a very prickly Elizabeth Perkins, said, "It wasn't even a date, Deb."

That about summed up the situation between her and Aaron, although her time with him didn't seem the least bit tawdry. Maybe the champagne cast a golden sheen on everything, and maybe if she were sober she'd have thought otherwise.

After some frantic kissing—it had been far too long since she'd been with a man—Aaron started to slow things down, which initially made her crazy, because every inch of her wanted to head pell-mell into the main event.

But Aaron persisted and then...oh my God. Her cheeks got warm every time she thought about it, and other parts of her body got warm too. Aaron had taken her places she'd only read about in romance novels. Places she'd never gone with...She loathed to admit it: Places she'd never gone with Jake.

For some reason orgasms always alluded her when she made love to her late husband. However, she'd watched *When Harry Met*

Sally a half dozen times, so she knew the right noises to make and thankfully he never knew.

But with Aaron, all the moans and gasps of pleasure were genuine. After their first time together, she turned into a wild, wanton woman who couldn't get enough. Laurie scarcely recognized herself. She lost count of how many times they did it.

At some point Aaron glanced at his watch and said, "It's late. I need to get back to my side of the duplex."

His abrupt announcement startled her. Was this a slam-bam-thank-you-ma'am? Suddenly she felt a little trashy. Maybe he read her mind because he said, "I'm sorry. I've never done this sort of thing before so I don't know the protocol."

"You haven't?"

Oh dear, she thought. It was the blind leading the blind. *About Last Night* was her only reference point when it came to these things.

"Have you?" Aaron said.

"No!"

"I didn't mean to imply—"

"It's fine. I didn't want you to think—"

"I don't."

Long silence. Laurie longed to fill it, but Aaron had to be the one to make the next move. Especially in this situation. But finally she couldn't stand it anymore. "Maybe..." she said, and he said it at the very same time.

She laughed. "Go ahead."

"No. You."

"No, you, Aaron." Her tone was firm. He was the male and needed to take the lead.

"Maybe we could do this again?" He blushed furiously. "I don't mean *exactly* this—"

"I know what you mean and yes, I'd like that. We could have dinner together."

"Excellent. Dinner would be great. Well, then..." He extended his hand.

"I think we're past handshakes." She gave him a goodbye kiss on the cheek and then it moved over to his lips and before she knew it, their tongues were entangling and she was ready for another go, but one more time and she probably wouldn't be able to walk the next day. Before it went too far, she pulled away.

"We have the rest of the colony."

He smiled. "Yes, we do, don't we?"

She nodded. It was official then. They were having a writer colony fling.

He left and she planned to go to sleep but it was impossible. She kept replaying the shivery highlights of their evening together. That's when she decided to get up and write. The minute she sat down at her computer, the words rained out of her.

"Writer's block over," she texted Delilah, who would know exactly what Laurie meant. Luckily she wouldn't press for details. It was one thing to plot a fling, but another to kiss and tell.

Through the thin walls on Aaron's side of the duplex she could hear a few yips and even a growl. It sounded as if her new fling partner was having a restless night.

Aaron couldn't sleep. Not after that incredible evening. He felt as if he'd been locked in a dark stuffy room for years, and suddenly the door flung open and bright light, bracing sea air and a cloud of monarch butterflies swooped in.

He had no idea that intercourse could be so playful and fun. (Emma was gravely serious about sex; it was as if the two of them were dismantling a bomb. One false move and it could blow up in their faces.) With Laurie, it was all tickles, titillation and teases.

He also admired her sexual inventiveness. In a single evening they'd utilized almost every square foot of the duplex, some to better effect than others. (The kitchen table sadly did not live up to *The Postman Always Rings Twice* expectations.) Aaron's favorite venue was the clawfoot tub.

At first he was skeptical, because in his experience, sex in water presented a number of friction challenges. But Laurie turned it into a delightful experience, and, at one point, they were splashing each other like children.

She brought out a silly side in Aaron that he didn't know he had. Who would have expected a respected literary author to have such a lighthearted spirit? In fact, when he was with her, he almost forgot about her elevated status.

When the evening ended, he was worried that she might not want to see him again. Luckily it all worked out, and they were having dinner together.

The next evening Laurie was heating up supper, a tomato pie she picked up at the local market. Aaron sat at the kitchen table drinking wine. "I thought we might discuss the elephant in the room," he said.

Laurie looked around the duplex. "The elephant?"

"You've not heard that expression?"

"Not that I recall."

"It's derived from a fable entitled 'The Inquisitive Man' which tells of a gentleman who goes to a museum and notices all sorts of tiny things, but fails to notice an elephant."

"Okay." Laurie said. She still didn't get it. Honestly, she really should have paid more attention when she was in high school.

"After that, it became proverbial. Meaning there's something significant to talk about, but the people in the room are avoiding the subject."

"Now I understand."

She felt herself blushing. He wanted to talk about the fling. Laurie was under the impression that you weren't supposed to talk about the fling, you were simply supposed to have it. Otherwise you were acknowledging the fling and that made everything seem a little bit more sordid than it needed to be. But then again, maybe it was wise to have ground rules, like in the movie *Friends With Benefits*. That way people wouldn't get hurt.

"Would you like to go first?" he said.

"You brought it up. Maybe you should."

"Okay." He put down his wine goblet and looked directly into her eyes. "I very much enjoyed last night."

His statement was enough to cause her tummy to feel fluttery again.

"I did too."

"I've never quite experienced...That was..."

Her breath sped up. "I know."

"When we were on the chaise..."

"Oh my gosh. The chaise."

"And then the second time. With the wing chair."

"The wing chair," she said breathlessly.

"And I can't look at that throw rug without thinking about...well...."

"The rug." A small moan involuntarily escaped her lips. "Are you hungry? Because I could reheat this pie."

He pulled his chair out from the table, and she crushed herself into his chest. They started kissing and she was fumbling with his belt when he said, "Wait."

"What's wrong?"

"The elephant. Before we go any further, we should discuss our lives back home, outside this conference."

Why? Then it dawned on Laurie. He wanted to tell her there was somebody else back home. A wife or a girlfriend, and that she shouldn't get too attached. But Laurie didn't want to hear it, especially not this very second, when her motor was all revved up. If he had someone at home, she might, in good conscience, be reluctant to proceed with the fling. And at this moment she definitely wanted more of Aaron.

"Don't worry about any of that," she said quickly. "It's not important. In fact, let's make a pact not to talk about our lives outside these walls. For the rest of our time here why don't we pretend this duplex is our entire world? What do you say?"

"Is that what you want?"

"Yes. I think it's for the best."

"Okay."

A few minutes later, they were entangled naked on the rug. As the largest orgasm of Laurie's life rose up from her deepest recesses, her pronouncement about the duplex being their entire world came true. Everything slowly collapsed, the woods, the entire world outside. It was only his hands and mouth on her bare skin, and she never wanted the moment to end.

Last night Aaron brought up "the elephant in the room" and by elephant, he meant his and Laurie's vastly different statuses in the literary world. Aaron was acutely aware he was at the bottom of the pecking order while she was at the top, and he wondered if that was a concern for her.

Laurie made it clear she didn't want to talk about it. Maybe she was one of those rare modest writers who didn't like being fussed over. Certainly she had yet to lord her genius status over him, and, in fact, seemed to almost dumb herself down a shade so as not to intimidate him. Compared to her, he was certainly as dull as an old butter knife.

Or maybe the reason she didn't want to talk about their different statuses was because she had no intention of continuing contact with him after the colony was over. That was understandable. Long-distance relationships weren't practical. He didn't know where she lived, although her accent suggested the South.

Still, writers came to colonies from all over the country. She could be from anywhere. As beguiling as she was, it was probably wise not to get too attached to Laurie or to have unrealistic expectations. Such a mindset was easy for Aaron. He'd gone through most of his life expecting very little pleasures or happiness, so when they came along they were always pleasant surprises.

*   *   *

Aaron and Laurie were going at it like rabbits on her side of the duplex. After they finished, a wall-shaking thunder clap immediately followed.

"That's what I'm talking about," Laurie said happily.

Aaron was on top of her, but instead of savoring the moment as usual, he scrambled off. *Slap.* His feet hit the floor, and he shimmied into his boxers.

"What's wrong?"

Lightning flashed, along with deafening thunder. The storm sounded as if it had a grudge against them. Heavy rain pummeled the roof.

"Can you smell the air? Feel the stickiness? It's coming."

"What's coming?"

"I have to save Dusty. I'll be right back."

"Who's Dusty?"

Lightning slashed the sky like a knife to an easel; this time it seemed like it was just outside their window. Heavy rain hardened into hail and rattled the roof; it sounded like it might break through the ceiling. Laurie grabbed her nightie and pulled it over her head.

"Where are you going?"

"I can't leave Dusty by himself in this storm." Aaron limped toward the exit.

"Who is—?" The sentence died on her tongue; Aaron was already gone.

Laurie padded across the room and opened the door. Lightning illuminated the sky and the wind tossed the trees. Cool air, pricked with moisture, blasted her skin. Nothing like a lively storm, she thought. Besides turkey shoots, thunderstorms were one of the few sources of entertainment in Swainsboro.

Aaron returned, holding something wrapped up in a baby blanket. His boxers were soaked through, and his hair was plastered to his forehead.

"What are you doing out here?" he said. "Get inside."

He sounded so authoritative, which was actually quite sexy. Laurie pointed to the blanket. "Is that Dusty?"

"Into the bathroom," he said, ignoring her question.

Laurie followed, saying, "Why are we going into the bathroom?"

Did he want another lovemaking session in the tub? Why bring the dog?

"It's the safest place," Aaron said.

He climbed in the tub, and Laurie joined him, although she wasn't sure why they were riding out a thunderstorm in a bathtub. Whimpering sounds came from under the blanket.

"This is Dusty." Aaron pulled away the covering to reveal a trembling black puppy. "More formally known as Windust 'Wavy Treat' Mite."

"He's adorable."

"He's contraband. I'm fairly certain pets aren't allowed. Please don't tell the people in charge."

"I would never—"

Thunder clapped. Both Aaron and the puppy quivered violently.

"Are you okay?"

"I'm fine."

It was obvious Aaron was not, in fact, fine. His face was the color of bone, and he was trembling so much she half expected him to fly apart. One clap of thunder followed another and another. Aaron whispered something under his breath to the puppy. A prayer? Laurie put her arms around him. His skin was damp from perspiration.

"Everything's going to be okay. It's just a summer squall."

His eyes were wide and staring as if he was caught in a trance. Over the next few minutes the thunder went from a wall-shaking crash to a distant grumble, but Aaron's shaking and frantic whispering didn't subside. It seemed even worse.

"I think it's over, Aaron," she said.

"No. They come after thunderstorms. They make a low

rumbling sound that gets louder and louder until it sounds like a locomotive passing through the house."

"What comes after thunderstorms? Except for strolls through puddles, which are always fun."

"Tornados," Aaron said with a fierce whisper.

"Tornados? I'm not even sure they have those in the mountains. What makes you think—?"

"It's coming. Did you hear that?"

"I didn't hear—"

"Now!" Aaron balled up in the tub, his chest protecting the puppy. Laurie heard nothing, just Aaron's ragged whispering and the slow drip in the sink faucet. The porcelain of the tub was cool against her bare legs. Her baby doll nightie kept riding up her back.

Five minutes later she said, "Aaron. I really think it's safe now."

"A little longer."

Laurie didn't move. The smell of her honeysuckle soap competed with her peach body wash. Her legs started to cramp, and her stomach let out a low rumble. Aaron startled.

"That's just my belly," she said.

A few more minutes passed. Laurie said, "I have to stand up. I'm getting a Charley horse." Also she was feeling a little claustrophobic.

He didn't respond. Laurie unfolded herself and stepped out of the tub, flexing her leg. Aaron lifted up his head.

"Look. Dusty's not even shaking anymore, and animals have a sixth sense for these things," Laurie said. "Come on. I'll make us some tea."

Slowly Aaron got out of the tub with Dusty in his arms. They both left the bathroom, and Aaron looked around warily as if he expected a tornado to steal out from under the bed or leap out of a closet.

"It could still happen," he said. His longish hair was sticking up in haphazard tufts. He was bare-chested and his skin gleamed milk-white in the lamp light. "You can't see tornados at night."

"Let me check the weather on the computer."

She pulled up the weather map on her laptop; the storm system had moved away from the Dillard, Georgia area, the site of the colony. Aaron was looking over her shoulder. She felt the heat of him behind her and heard his uneven breathing.

"Looks like we're going to survive." She got up from the desk chair. "Let me get that tea."

She put the water on and joined Aaron at the kitchen table. Dusty was on his lap, and he was staring out the window even though it was too dark to see anything. Without his glasses his eyes looked oversized and vulnerable.

"Are you feeling better?"

He nodded. One ear was poking out from his shaggy mane, and it was bright red.

"Tea should be ready soon. It's Sleepy Time and very calming."

"I'm sorry. I overreacted."

"What's a little overreaction among friends?"

"When I was a child I used to live in Norman, Oklahoma with my mother and stepfather. Norman's in the apex of tornado alley and..." He glanced away. "I'm sorry. I forgot. We agreed not to talk about our lives outside the colony."

"We can break the rule this one time. So you had a lot of tornados in Norman?"

"Dozens every year. I can't tell you how many times we had to go into the basement to ride them out, and it was especially terrifying when the tornado siren went off at night. It was often just my mother and me. My stepfather was always away on business trips."

"That does sound scary."

"You'd think I'd be used to them. But I was young when they happened. It's embarrassing, but I guess I'm still traumatized."

Some adults were almost impossible to imagine as children, but not Aaron with his floppy hair and dreamy gaze; she could easily imagine the scared little boy inside of him, especially with a puppy snuggled on his lap.

She placed a hand over his. "Everyone has something like that. I'm actually claustrophobic. Don't stick me in a tight place."

"You seemed to be fine in the bathroom."

"It was getting to me after a while."

"And I guess you're also afraid of spiders?"

"Spiders? Shoot, no. I grew up in an old house and spiders lurked in every corner and cranny so—"

"But you screamed when you saw the daddy longlegs."

Heat flowed up Laurie's neck. "To be honest, that was a trick to meet you."

"Really?"

Laurie nodded. "Now you know all my wily ways."

The tea kettle sounded

"Saved by the whistle," she said.

She prepared the tea and placed a cup in front of Aaron.

"This might be too personal, but I'm curious. What were you whispering to Dusty in the bathroom?"

Aaron colored, as if embarrassed. "I was reciting from a book called *Words of Comfort*; it included works by Keats, Emerson and some others. Every time we had to take shelter in the basement my mother would read from it. A couple of selections were short enough to commit to memory."

"Which one were you whispering in there?"

"It was a hymn from George Matheson."

"Will you recite it for me?"

"You don't want me to do that."

"I absolutely do. I adore recitations. They're so sweet and old-fashioned."

Aaron closed his eyes and tilted his head to the ceiling. He said, "There is an Eye that never sleeps, beneath the wind of night. There is an Ear that never shuts, when sinks the beams of light. There is an Arm that never tires, when human strength gives way. There is a Love that never fails, when earthly loves decay."

Laurie let the words soak in her brain cells for a moment. Her favorite part was "A love that never fails."

"It's lovely."

"I've been reciting it for so long the words have almost lost their meaning. I'm not sure I believe much of it. I'm a pragmatist."

And I tend to be the opposite, Laurie thought. "Do you still have the book?"

"It was lost a long time ago."

"Maybe your mother has it?"

"No." He swallowed and gazed at his bare feet. "She died."

He looked terribly sad, and Laurie's heart leaped in his direction. "I'm so sorry."

"It's been a number of years, and I'm not particularly close to my father. So I do miss her. "

"I actually lost my parents in a car accident when I just a toddler."

"That's terrible."

"It is, but sadly I don't remember them. My grandmother raised me, and she passed almost three years ago. She's the one I miss." Laurie decided not to mention Jake. Who wanted to have a fling with a widow? It wasn't very sexy.

Aaron put a hand over hers. They were both silent. The mood had gotten unexpectedly serious. He seemed to realize that and said, "I didn't mean to bring up sad topics."

"No. It's fine." But changing the subject would probably be wise, considering the temporary nature of their relationship. "Why don't you tell me how you came across that cute fur face in your arms?" Laurie said brightly.

Aaron told the story, and Laurie watched him as he petted Dusty—he was so gentle and affectionate with the pup—and she felt a twinge of longing that didn't fit in with their fling.

Laurie gave her head a little shake as if to chase away her sentimental thoughts and suggested they celebrate the end of the storm by having another go-around under the covers.

"Lights out so we won't traumatize Dusty."

Aaron eagerly nodded and she shouted, "Last one to bed is a rotten—"

"Egg?" When people used clichés, Aaron had a habit of finishing their sentences for them.

"No! A rotten chicken neck smells much worse. That's why people use them to catch crabs. Last one to bed is a rotten chicken neck."

Laurie ran to the bed and pounced on it, giggling, and Aaron joined her. They started kissing and the heavy mood dissipated.

Seven

Laurie was teaching Aaron how to do the Carolina Shag, a dance that originated in Myrtle Beach, South Carolina. He'd never heard of the shag, but then again, he'd never been worldly about pop culture. Nor had he ever danced with a woman, but he was enjoying it and found he was surprisingly agile, despite his limp.

She asked him about his limp when they first met, and he gave his standard answer: One of his legs was slightly longer than the other. Not true, but that's what he told everyone, and yet the night of the thunderstorm he'd been briefly tempted to tell her more. She'd been so kind that night. Emma always chided him for his fear of thunderstorms. "Buck up, girlie," she'd say.

The front door of Laurie's cottage was open, and a breeze infused with the smell of cut grass cooled their skin. Dusk pushed the sun into the horizon, reducing it to a purple-orange smudge. The diminishing light threw Laurie's face into shadows but a few stray strands of hair around her face were lit as if electric. She was singing "Carolina Girl" in a soft soprano, the chirps of crickets her only accompaniment.

The floorboards creaked as their feet pattered across them; the homey smell of their fried pork chop supper still clung to the air.

"I have a surprise for you later," Laurie said. She was breathless from the exertion of the dance.

"What is it?"

"No hints. You'll have to wait and see."

Aaron had a surprise for her as well. He wanted to see if she might consider getting together some point after their colony time was over. The thought of never seeing her again was unimaginable.

Dusty barked and a voice said, "Where did you come from, sweetie? Dogs aren't allowed on colony grounds."

Aaron stopped dancing. A woman with a choppy blond bob and owlish glasses stood in the doorway. She bent down to give a tail-thumping Dusty a pat on the head. He recognized her as the director of the colony.

He hoped she didn't put him on a colony blacklist or turn them away. There were only two nights left.

"I'm sorry about the dog," Aaron said. "I just got him, and uh, well..."

Laurie scooped up Dusty. "He's an abandoned dog and needs to bond with his new family. Could you leave this dear little face behind?"

"It *is* a dear little face, but...Well, I suppose it'll be okay, so long as you don't let anyone else know—"

"You're such a peach." Laurie flashed her most dazzling smile. "Would you like to join the party? I made margaritas."

Aaron wished Laurie wasn't so welcoming. Tonight he wanted her all to himself. Their time together was running out.

"I don't want to be a crasher," the director said.

Too late, Aaron thought.

"The only reason I'm here is because I ordered a copy of your book, Laura, and I was wondering if you might possibly sign it for me. I'd be very grateful."

"Please call me Laurie," Laurie said. "And you really want my autograph?"

"Yes."

"Wow. I'd be honored!"

Such modesty, Aaron thought. As if she'd never signed a book before. That was one of the qualities Aaron adored about Laurie— her ability to still get excited about the smallest of things. She was the least jaded literary writer he'd ever met.

The director withdrew the book from a bag and handed it to Laurie.

Laurie cocked her head, looking bewildered. "I'm sorry. What's this?"

"Your book."

"No, it's not. There's not a speck of pink on the cover."

"But—"

"And this book looks so serious." Laurie studied the cover. "Plus it's written by Laura T. Leer."

"That's not you?"

"No. I'm Laurie Lee. And my middle initial is K for Kay."

"And you're sure this isn't your novel?"

She laughed. "I think I'd recognize my own book."

"I'm confused..." The director blinked behind smudged glasses. She wasn't the only confused person in the room. What was going on? Aaron thought.

"When I got the acceptance letter from the colony I noticed my name was spelled wrong," Laurie said. "Do you suppose there was a mix-up with the letters?"

"I don't know," the director said. "I have a secretary who sends them out." The brusque way she said "secretary" made Aaron believe the employee was going to pay dearly for her mistake.

"Maybe whoever wrote the colony acceptance letter sent it to me instead of this Laura Leer."

The director glanced back at the book, which was titled *Torpor in the Suburbs*. She took a moment to digest the news. "Oh my."

"I guess that means the scholarship and the acceptance to the colony was supposed to go to Laura Leer. Not me."

"What an inexcusable error," she said. "I'm so sorry."

"No need to apologize. I feel bad for Laura T. Leer. She's the one who missed out."

"Still I...can't believe this happened..." The director remained in place, as if uncertain about her next move. Moths pummeled their soft bodies against the porch light outside. The sound of cicadas rose and fell.

"Well, I'll leave you to your evening," she said, backing out of the duplex.

"You're sure you don't want a margarita?" Laurie said. "They're strawberry."

"No, thank you. Good night."

The director departed. Laurie dropped into the sofa and flung her long legs over one of the arms.

"Crazy. Can you believe that?"

Aaron didn't reply. He was still trying to process what just occurred.

"It was fun being a scholarship-winning writer while it lasted." She jiggled her foot and her flimsy gold sandal dropped to the ground. "But you know what?"

"What?"

"I'm not going to think about it. No sense in ruining our evening together. We were having too much fun." She gave him a seductive look and crooked her finger. "Why are you so far away? Come here."

Aaron gingerly approached. The woman he'd grown to know as Laura T. Leer nuzzled up against him, and he felt the soft down of her cheek.

But now it felt like a stranger's cheek.

"You seem tense," she said. "What's wrong?"

"To be frank I'm...discombobulated."

"Why?"

"I too thought you were Laura T. Leer."

Her pale eyebrows knitted together, creating a pink spot in the middle of her forehead. "You did?"

"Hers was the name on the colony flier."

"I never saw that flier; it's probably in my bag somewhere. I'm forever losing stuff. So who is this Laura T. Leer person anyway? The colony director acted like she was the new Danielle Steel."

Aaron had no idea who Danielle Steel was. He listed Laura T. Leer's accomplishments, and a twinge of loss accompanied each one.

"A genius?" Laurie laughed so hard her face turned red. "They give out awards for that?"

"They do."

She let out a low whistle. "And you thought I was her? I'm flattered, but honestly if you're that gullible I've got a state park I can sell you."

"Well, I—"

"This is hysterical!"

"Actually hysterical is not a synonym for humorous," he said quietly.

"What?"

"Never mind."

Laurie smiled. "You know what this is?"

Aaron shook his head.

"It's the imposter story line. Like in *Maid in Manhattan* or *While You Were Sleeping*. It's my favorite complication in a rom-com. To be honest, it's tricky to extend it for the length of a movie or a book. Talk about your suspension of disbelief."

Aaron felt like she was speaking a foreign language. *What was a rom-com?*

"If you're not Laura T. Leer—" he said.

"Ha! Not even close."

"Then who are you?"

"No genius, I can tell you that. I can barely solve the Jumble in the newspaper, although I'm pretty decent at the *People* crossword puzzle. I'm plain old Laurie Lee who works as a temp and is planning to go to school in the fall."

At least she was furthering her education. "What are you studying?"

"Nails."

"Nails?" Aaron was thinking of nails that were hammered into walls.

"Nails." Laurie wagged her ten red fingernails.

Aaron had no idea such schools existed. "And what do you write?"

"I already told you. Romance."

"Ahem...When you say romance...Are you to referring to parlor fiction?"

"*What* fiction?"

"Books with heaving bosoms and tumescent breeches?"

She ran a hand down his chest. "You keep talking like that, mister, and you're going to lose your breeches."

Aaron captured her hand. "Can we be serious for a moment?"

"If you insist." She pouted. "What was your question again? Oh yes, breeches. No breeches in my books, only blue jeans that are constantly shimmying down my hero's hips. I write contemporary romances. Like you."

"You're mistaken. I don't write romance."

"But you told me your novel is about the relationship between a man and a woman."

"There's a relationship in my novel, but it's not a romance."

"Are you sure? Because sometimes when men write romances publishers like to call them 'love stories.' Like with R.K. Harris's books."

"Who?"

"I told you about him. He's the gold standard of male-authored love stories. Although his first one, *Love's Prophet*, is definitely the best."

"For once and for all, I don't—"

"How does Wilbur categorize your work?"

"It's not Wilbur, it's Wilner, which is an imprint of W&W."

"W&W? Woo hoo! That humongous publisher?"

"Yes."

"Cherry St. James, my favorite romance writer, is published by W&W...You're sure you're not writing romance?"

"I keep telling you. I don't write—"

She wound a strand of Aaron's hair around her index finger. "Are you balking at the romance label because you're a guy? You'd be surprised at how many guys—"

"I don't write romance!"

Laurie untangled her fingers from his hair; she sat up straight. "Good gravy. You don't have to yell."

"I apologize, but you weren't listening to me."

"And I don't particularly like your tone. You said 'romance' like you'd say 'hog entrails' or 'raw sewage.'"

"I didn't."

"You did."

Maybe his tone was a little negative. Aaron always maintained that genre writers were formulaic, predictable and had no respect for Craft. And romance was the least appealing of all the genres. Why bother reading a book when you knew what the outcome would be?

"I didn't mean to use a tone. Who's the publisher of your romance novels?"

"Breathless Press."

"I've never heard of it."

"That's because it's my publishing company."

"You own a small press?"

"I suppose you could say that. But I'm the only author."

"You're self-published?"

"Indie-published, but yes. That's me. I know it's not Wilbur but—"

"Wilner. What are your aspirations? Are you hoping one day to be traditionally published?"

"Maybe. But honestly, right now all I want is a few more readers. And I would love to win the Pink Heart." She got a faraway look in her eyes. "I can just imagine that beautiful trophy on my mantel."

"I'm not familiar with—"

"The Pink Heart is a romance award for pre-pubbed authors. If I won it, I'd feel like the Cinderella of the romance world."

How did they determine a winner? Aaron wondered. Did they pick out the least banal?

"What about you? If you don't write romance, what do you write?"

"Literary fiction."

"You mean book club fiction?"

"Definitely not." Aaron had strong objections to book club fiction, because it was commercial fiction masquerading as important fiction.

"Give me an example."

"*Blood Meridian.*"

She feigned a shiver. "Sounds like horror."

"*The Body Artist.*"

She smiled. "Kinky."

"*The Human Stain.*"

"Eww. Get out the Comet."

"I take it you haven't read any of these novels?" He was trying to keep the disappointment out of his voice.

"I stick with romantic comedies mostly. It's what I like to write too. Are you upset I'm not Laura T. Leer?"

She waited for his answer, and for the first time he saw how affected her mannerisms were. Cocked head, pursed lips, almost as if she was posing for a cheesecake shot. A parody of a coquette. There was nothing quite real about her.

Under any other circumstances he'd have never coupled with her; they had nothing in common, and yes, to be honest, he was a little let down. All this time her impressive resume had colored his view of her.

When she made a seemingly silly comment, it surely had a double meaning that escaped him. When she cracked a joke, he judged it to be more clever than it might have been. When she did something unexpected, he deemed it to be fresh instead of silly or impulsive.

Being with her these past few day was like watching a film with an unexpected plot twist at the end. Aaron felt as if he has to rewind his entire colony experience to pick up on clues he'd missed.

But did he need to say this to her? Not particularly. Their time together was almost done. She had yet to express a desire to see him when they returned home, which, considering the recent development, was probably for the best. The heightened atmosphere of the writers' colony, along with frequent and energetic sex, had obviously disguised their numerous differences.

"I'm not upset. I'm pleased that you are...uh..."

"Laurie Lee."

"Right."

"Great." She jumped up from the couch. "Let me get your surprise."

He'd forgotten all about that. She returned, hands behind her back.

"Pick a hand."

"Right hand?"

She extended an empty hand. "Nope."

"Left hand then?"

"Wrong again!"

Would he have enjoyed this game if she was still a MacArthur Genius recipient? Now that she was a self-published romance author it seemed a little childish. "It appears we've run out of hands."

She glanced down at her bosom and winked. While she went to retrieve the surprise, she'd donned a light summer sweater over her dress, and she now looked boxy in the chest area.

Aaron decided to play along. He unbuttoned her sweater and fished out a small square package that was nestled in her cleavage.

"That tickles."

He unwrapped the package and turned it over in his hands. She'd given him *Words of Comfort*, the book his mother used to read to him during tornados.

Aaron couldn't speak for a moment. Finally he said, "I would have assumed this was out of print."

"It was. A used bookstore had it, and they sent it via overnight mail."

He hadn't seen the book in years and the familiar cover awakened the smell of peppermint on his mother's breath and his small trembling form pressed against the warmth of her chest. It also brought to light a very specific day, parts of which continued to haunt him.

"Do you like it?"

Aaron nodded.

"I'm glad."

He looked up from the book and when he did, his gaze met hers. Aaron no longer saw Laura T. Leer, revered Featherstone author. Nor did he see the cartoonish romance author he'd reduced her to only moments ago. Instead a new version of Laurie assembled itself before him, someone he couldn't easily categorize, but felt a visceral urge to know.

It was obvious Aaron was disappointed she wasn't Ms. Genius Girl. His jaw was dragging so much she was surprised he didn't get carpet burn. His reaction wounded Laurie, even though she tried not to show it. All this time and Aaron hadn't been smitten with her at all, but with some smarty pants writer who was so different from Laurie she might as well have been from another planet called Brainiac.

Fine, she thought. I'll just give him his stupid gift—which she shouldn't have bought because people in flings didn't buy each other presents—and then I'll leave the colony early and never see him again. But then she gave him *Words of Comfort*, and when she saw the naked expression on his face, it was as if someone had reached into her rib cage and gave her heart a twist.

"I apologize," Aaron said. "I was just startled...All this time, I thought..."

"I understand."

He glanced down at the book. "This is a wonderful gift. One of the best I've ever received."

"I debated whether or not I should order it...I didn't want you to think...You made it pretty clear from the onset that you had this whole other life back home."

"What are you talking about?"

"The hippo in the room?"

Aaron laughed. "Do you mean the elephant? And I was referring to the fact that back home you were a renowned author and I'm just a man with a book contract."

"You couldn't have been more wrong about that. So you're not involved with someone else?"

"My girlfriend broke up with me before I came here. You?"

"No one. But...."

"What?"

"I was married. For only a month. But then my husband died."

"I'm so sorry. How long ago?"

"Over a year. It was really hard at first, but...I'm trying to move on from my grief."

Silence and then they both spoke at the same time.

"I don't imagine—"

"I was thinking that maybe—"

Aaron laughed. "Ladies first."

"We haven't talked about where we're from, but I'm from Atlanta...Well, Decatur—"

"I live in Atlanta too. Virginia Highlands."

"That's so close to me."

"We're practically neighbors."

But in some ways we're really far apart, Laurie thought. Their roles had been reversed. She was the lowly self-published author, and he was the man with a book contract from a big publisher. That didn't bother her, but she couldn't speak for Aaron.

Aaron glanced down at the book and back at her. "I'd like to see you after our colony time is over."

Laurie flung her arms around him. "I thought you'd never ask."

Eight

Being in love was an utterly unfamiliar state to Aaron. With Emma it had always been more about companionship. There was no euphoria, sleeplessness, loss of appetite or excessive attention to insignificant details about a lover's appearance. (Laurie had a tiny birthmark on her right thigh that looked exactly like a map of Italy, and Aaron stumbled into a state of wonderment over this tiny imperfection every time he saw it.)

The only state he could compare it to was when he first started MFA school and became obsessed with the craft of writing. For an entire magical year he could think of nothing else, and it made him giddy. That state ended when his father read his first novel and found it lacking. Now Aaron approached Craft in a more intellectually appropriate manner.

But his feelings for Laurie seemed to resist intellectual examination, common sense or restraint. Any well-read person knew that happy endings belonged in the realm of children's fairy tales, and that most romantic relationships were doomed, particularly when they involved a couple of opposites. There was *Romeo and Juliet*, *The Hunchback of Notre Dame*, *The Great Gatsby*, *Anna Karenina* and *Tristan and Isolde*. He could go on.

Opposites attracting worked in novels because it kept the conflict level high. Without conflict, fiction was dead on the page. But in real life, too much conflict could kill a relationship.

On the other hand, over time, Aaron might influence Laurie to broaden her reading horizons. One of the reasons she was immature in her literary tastes was because she'd had little exposure to excellent writing.

A week after they got back from the colony, Aaron ordered two copies of Laura T. Leer's novel, *Torpor in the Suburbs*, and suggested to Laurie they both read it and discuss it.

Aaron was pleased to discover that while the novel had sophisticated themes and was deeply layered, it was also extremely accessible. (In no way was he implying Laurie couldn't handle a denser book.)

Still, he hadn't wanted to hit her with something too challenging like *Alphabetical Africa*. During one of their conversations he discovered she hadn't read the work, and was only using the dust jacket to cover up a romance novel.

Their discussion of *Torpor in the Suburbs* went fairly well. She agreed with him that the novel was lyrical and meditative. There was some awkwardness when he called it a fabulist tale and she said, "Yes. It was fabulous."

Aaron let it go. If she kept reading good books she would eventually pick up on literary terms. Most importantly, they both loved the ending.

Laurie hated *Torpor in the Suburbs*. It was depressing, and never once was the reader introduced to anyone named Torpor. But that was a small complaint.

The most aggravating aspect of the book was the author's tendency to take off on long detours. While Laurie was reading, she'd think, Hey, lyrical lady, let's get back to the action, but then she remembered...there was no action to get back to.

And the ending? Worst ever...The main character turned into a sofa. Literally. Maybe that would have made sense if other characters had been turning into furniture throughout the entire novel, but no. The ending was the first and last instance of such a drastic transformation. Talk about being farfetched. It was as if the author got tired and said, "I don't know how to end this catastrophe, so I guess I'll do something completely bizarre and let the readers sort out what it means."

And Aaron fell for it. For days he went on and on about how apt the ending was because the main character was withdrawn and glum. So, of course, it made perfect sense that she would turn into the most useless piece of furniture in the house. (The sofa was butt sprung, covered in cat hair and hulked in a corner of the basement; no one ever sat on it.)

But it was okay that they had such different opinions. Some of Laurie's favorite rom-coms were about opposites attracting: *Pretty Woman, The Way We Were, Notting Hill, Knocked Up.* She could go on and on. All those films had happy endings so she had high hopes for her and Aaron.

In fact, her hopes were so high she asked him to move in with her. One afternoon she visited the grim little cell Aaron and Dusty were living in. It was a basement room with one tiny window and it smelled like wet wool and all the clothes in his closet were speckled with mildew. Laurie wouldn't keep a guinea pig in that room.

Aaron told her his landlady was kicking him out because of Dusty, and he was looking for another place. That's when she issued the invitation. Normally Laurie wouldn't be so bold, but he was at her house almost every night anyway. It seemed to make sense, and she could also use help with expenses.

He didn't hesitate. That very day Laurie helped him pack his meager possessions, and just like that, she had herself a new roomie.

Growing up she never imagined she'd "shack up" with a man. She was definitely a girl enamored with marriage. Her Barbie doll had an extensive collection of wedding gowns, all white, of course. But with Aaron, shacking up seemed sweet instead of seedy.

"Please don't tell anyone in town about my living in sin," Laurie said to Delilah when she gave her the news over the phone. "In fact, no need to mention I have a boyfriend at all."

"My lips are sealed with Crazy glue. You couldn't pry them apart with a pair of pliers."

"Not even Bart." Bart was Delilah's husband.

"I promise, but you shouldn't have to keep Aaron a secret. It's been over a year since Jake's death. It's only natural to move on."

"Some people might think it's too soon." By "some people" she was thinking of Jake's family, all his friends and probably most of Swainsboro.

Everybody loved him.

"Does that mean you're not going to come back to Swainsboro after nail school is over?"

Laurie hadn't even thought about that. She knew everyone was expecting her return. "I'm just taking this one day at a time."

Another symptom of being in love was impulsivity. That's why Aaron immediately said yes to Laurie's cohabitation invitation. Anything to be close to her.

She lived in a yellow ranch the color of sunny-side-up eggs, surrounded by a rose-vine-covered white picket fence. One of the rooms she called her flamingo room. (Everything in the room—drapes, sofa, rug—was patterned with pink flamingos and the shelves were filled with flamingo figurines.) It was a ridiculous room, but it lifted Aaron's spirits every time he walked into it. Possibly because it was also Laurie's favorite place to engage in sexual romps.

She'd offered him her Florida room as a workplace, but it was far too cheerful, with tree-lizard green walls and a trio of windows. Aaron preferred to work in garret-like quarters, so her walk-in closet was near perfect. (It smelled of lavender potpourri, but he'd learned to live with that.)

At five p.m. when Laurie came home from her temp job, she'd go into the kitchen and prepare elaborate girly cocktails complete with plastic umbrellas. Aaron had developed a taste for them. Currently his favorite was a Pink Lady.

One afternoon she came home to find him eating his typical snack of bread and peanut butter.

"Why didn't you put jelly on it?" she said.

Aaron shrugged. "When I was a child there was never jelly in my father's house. I always went without."

"You can't have a peanut butter sandwich without jelly. Not in this house, mister."

She showed him where the jelly was stored in her pantry. She had a jar of apricot; not a favorite of his. Displeasure must have registered on his face, because Laurie left to run an errand. When she returned, it was with ten flavors of jelly. She said, "As long as I'm around, you'll never eat a peanut butter sandwich without jelly again."

Aaron had eaten sandwiches with only peanut butter for such a long time, he preferred them that way. (Also jelly had an off-putting viscous quality, like a chemical masquerading as a food.) Still, Laurie was so proud to have brought jelly into his jelly-less world that Aaron now prepared all of his sandwiches with it.

At night they snuggled in her four-poster rice bed with her soft sheets, a perfect end to a perfect day. He held her in his arms and gazed into her eyes, feeling as if he might fall into them and never emerge.

One night, after Aaron had been living with Laurie a month, he woke up and she was gently shaking his shoulder. Dusty was licking his foot.

"What is it? What's wrong?" Aaron said. He sat up in bed.

"You were having a nightmare."

Aaron was glad it was dark so she couldn't sense his embarrassment. "I'm sorry. I didn't mean to wake you."

"It's okay. You were reciting that hymn again."

Aaron swung a leg out of bed. "I should probably sleep on the couch. I don't want to keep you up." When he had nightmares with Emma she always made him leave the room.

"I don't mind." She slipped an arm around him. "Do you want to talk about it?"

Aaron was silent. Then he said, "It's a recurring nightmare."

"About what?"

"My mother's death."

"Oh." Her voice dropped slightly.

"It's pretty grim. I shouldn't—"

"No. Please tell me."

The concern on her face was so genuine it loosened something in Aaron. Suddenly he wanted to share this very important part of his history with her.

"My mother died in a tornado. That's why I'm nervous around bad weather. I was seven at the time, and I was with her."

"What happened?" Laurie asked gently.

Aaron raised his hand to push up his glasses, but they weren't on his nose. "There was a tornado warning, and like usual, my mother and I went down to the basement. She turned on the radio, but it wasn't working because the batteries were dead and the extra batteries had gone missing. We stayed in the basement until seven p.m. when the warning was supposed to be over. Seven o'clock arrived and we climbed the stairs. It was quiet. Calm. My mother turned on the electric radio in the kitchen. No music. Instead there was this terrible metallic voice. It said, 'Take cover now.'"

He paused and Laurie said softly, "Go on."

"It was too late to take cover. I heard the roar. Glass broke, a deafening *crack* followed. It sounded like the whole world was splitting in two. My mother screamed, and she lunged for me but didn't make it. There was a thud so deafening it drowned out the screaming wind."

"Oh my God," Laurie whispered.

"That was the last time I ever saw my mother." Aaron nearly choked on his words. "Afterward it was dark, like being in the belly of a large beast, and the smell of sap was overwhelming. I was buried in leaves and branches, and one of the branches trapped my leg. I couldn't see or hear my mother, although I called out for her several times. The silence seemed to stretch on for a long while, but at some point I heard a sound. It was faint at first, and I had to stay absolutely still to hear it. It was my mother; she was reciting poems from *Words of Comfort*. She must have been in agony. The tree fell directly on her torso, and she was surely bleeding internally, but she kept reciting poems from *Words of Comfort*."

"Oh, Aaron."

"She didn't stop until help arrived. As soon as she knew I was safe she..." Aaron swallowed hard. "She let go."

Laurie touched Aaron's leg. "And that's how you got your limp."

Aaron nodded.

Laurie embraced Aaron, and he could feel wetness on her cheeks. "It's going to be all right," she said. "No matter what happens. That's something I've always known."

He wished he could adopt her attitude. He was always waiting for the worst to happen. But when he was in Laurie's arms he could almost believe everything would turn out well.

Laurie laid back down and fell asleep, but Aaron stayed awake for a long while. The moonlight seeped in from the window and bathed her beautiful face.

"I love you," he said.

She stirred a little, which caught him by surprise. He hadn't meant to wake her. Groggily she said, "I love you too."

Aaron's heart soared; Laurie Lee loved him! She'd said so even though she was half asleep. He couldn't have been more elated.

"Night, night, Jake," she said. Then she rolled away from him. It took him at least another hour before he could go back to sleep.

Laurie started taking night classes at the International Institute of Nail Technology. Aaron thought that sounded like a pretentious name for a school that trained people to care for fingernails. She was taking classes like Fabric and Sculpting 101, Bacteriology and Other Nail Disorders and History of Nail Care. (Was the latter strictly necessary? Aaron wondered. Was it relevant, for instance, what Cleopatra did to her nails, or was the school padding the curriculum?)

In preparation for her first test, Laurie went around whispering the nail parts under her breath: "Distal free, distal nail fold, lunula, proximal."

After she left for her class, Aaron grew restless. He was used to having her around in the evenings. He wandered the house like a lost man and caught his hip on a narrow table in her sun room, disturbing her display of photos.

Aaron hadn't paid much attention to them before, but as he was righting them, he found it odd there were no pictures of her husband Jake.

Several photos featured Laurie and a pretty brunette with teased hair and heavy makeup whom Aaron assumed was Delilah. (Aaron heard Laurie talking to her on the phone all the time.) There were also photos of an unsmiling elderly woman with a stiff posture, whom he assumed was Laurie's late grandmother, and photos of small children who probably belonged to Delilah. But not one photo of a man. Laurie surely had photos of her late husband, but for some reason she wasn't displaying them. Were the memories still too painful?

The table had a drawer, a perfect place to store photos you'd rather not display, but if he opened it, he'd definitely be snooping. But the drawer was open just a little. So technically...

Impulsively he yanked it open all the way and just as he suspected, photos were stored there. All were upside down. He uprighted one and came face to face with a brawny Nordic-looking fellow with piercing blue eyes. His muscular arm was around Laurie's tiny waist and she was looking up at him adoringly. If Aaron was prone to using clichés, he'd say they looked like "a match made in Heaven."

The contrast between himself and Jake was so distressing Aaron slammed the drawer. It got stuck halfway, and he couldn't make it budge. He struggled with it for several minutes while Jake's image stared up at him. Aaron could imagine him saying to Laurie, "This is who you ended up with? Some weakling who can't even shut a drawer?"

Bang. It finally shut, but the impact knocked over the pictures again. Aaron righted them, hopefully in their former positions. He tried not to think about the photograph he'd seen, but Jake's image and Laurie's worshipful look kept popping up in his mind. Finally he decided to do a Google search to see if he could learn more about the man Laurie was obviously still mourning.

He found the obituary for Jake "Smiley" Parker, and his all-American looks matched his biography. Jake was a football star in high school, but a knee injury kept him from going further with the sport. Instead, he took a job as a salesman at John Deere and was swiftly promoted to district manager. He was an alderman at his church, a Kiwanis Club member and a board member of Habitat for Humanity. During his spare time he enjoyed participating in triathlons.

Laurie's pink VW bug purred up the driveway. Aaron quickly closed the webpage with the obituary and deleted it from the history.

When she came inside, instead of greeting him with her usual squeal of delight, she limply waved and gave him a dry peck on the cheek.

"What's wrong?" he said.

"I flunked nail anatomy and hygiene."

"But you studied so hard."

"I know, but I choked on the test. That used to happen to me all the time in school. It was a wonder I made it through. I almost got kicked off the cheerleading squad for poor grades."

"You were a cheerleader?" Not a surprise. She was exceedingly agile.

"You bet I was. Captain of the squad."

Yes. That's the way high school worked. The football players went out with the cheerleaders. Aaron was president of the English club and never had a single date in high school.

"Do you mind if go in and write for a while? That always cheers me up."

"It does?" Aaron didn't look at writing that way. Not since his first year in the MFA program. He often repeated a popular writing quote to his students, "Writing is easy. You just open a vein and bleed."

"Yes! I adore it. Writing's so much fun."

He was tempted to snort. It might be fun to write light, mindless romances but writing literary fiction was very serious business. She kissed him and frolicked off. Aaron was a little disappointed. He'd like her to spend time with him now that she was home.

Later she made enthusiastic love to him for over an hour. Aaron couldn't help but wonder while her eyes were closed and she was screaming, "Yes, yes," who was she thinking of? Him or Jake? Sometimes Aaron wondered what she could possibly see in him.

Nine

On Saturday Aaron suggested a visit to his favorite bookstore, The Spine, which was located in a mostly empty strip mall in Decatur. He hadn't gone to The Spine since he and Emma broke up. Today it was safe to stop by because Emma always took Saturday off. That was the day of her coffee shop excursions.

They arrived at The Spine, and Aaron inhaled the rarified smell of books and wooden flooring. The store was dimly lit and had no cutesy bookstore feline, no knick-knacks at the cash register and no tables or end caps to display the latest slick-covered offerings. All the volumes were located in the forest of dark wood stacks that soared to the ceiling. Laurie said she was craving something sweet and wanted to know where the café was located.

"There's no café."

"I've never been in a bookstore without a café before...Oh well. My sweet tooth will have to wait. Where do they keep the cards? I need to pick out one for Ramona's birthday."

"No cards either. The Spine just sells books."

"Just books?"

"Yes." That was one thing he and Emma had always agreed on. Neither cared for bookstores that tried to be part toy store, part restaurant or part novelty store.

"I don't think I've ever been in a bookstore that sells only books," Laurie said.

"Then you've been to the wrong bookstores," said a voice.

Emma slunk out from one of the narrow aisles, soundless as a cat burglar. Obviously she'd overheard the entire conversation.

"Hello, Aaron." She didn't bother to disguise the contempt in her voice.

"I thought you didn't work on Saturday."

"I'm filling in for my assistant manager who broke his leg."

Emma cast a critical glance at Laurie, who was dressed in a red and white polka-dot dress with matching red pumps. Her dress emphasized her considerable curves.

His ex-girlfriend wore a black shirt, denim skirt and a clunky pair of clogs, chosen not for style—they made her ankles look thick as stumps—but for comfort. Her dark brown hair hung limply on her shoulders. (Aaron knew she washed it with Dial soap, thinking shampoo was a waste of money.) For a few awkward seconds nobody said a word, and then Laurie extended her hand to Emma.

"Hi. I'm Laurie Lee." She seemed to have turned down her wattage, as if it not to overwhelm Emma.

Emma ignored the hand with five gleaming pink nails. She glared at Aaron, and her eyes were dark and menacing, like holes in a double-barreled shotgun.

Laurie read people well and by now, she had surely figured out this was Emma. "I think I'll browse," she said. "Point me in the direction of the romance section."

It was the worst thing she could have said.

"We don't have a romance section at The Spine," Emma said in a haughty voice. "This is a literary bookstore. We only carry literature of merit." She said the word "literature" with an affected British accent even though she'd lived in Atlanta all her life.

"Well then, I'll browse among the books of merit."

Laurie left, and Emma continued to glare.

"This is who you replaced me with? A romance-reading sex kitten."

"I didn't replace you. As you surely recall, you ended our relationship. And Laurie isn't a sex kitten."

Laurie *was* a bit of a sex kitten, but Aaron was compelled to defend her against Emma, who was definitely not. Although she did have claws.

"How long have you been seeing this little piece of cotton candy?"

"We met at the writers' colony."

"That bottle blonde is a writer?"

"She isn't a bottle blonde. Her hair color's natural and yes, she is a writer." Aaron used the term "writer" loosely.

Emma's brows were low as thunderclouds, and Aaron feared an outburst. Something flickered in her eyes. "Wait. Are you trying to make me jealous?"

"No."

"You're lying. I can tell. I know you like the back of my hand."

Aaron had always thought that expression was imprecise. The back of his hand was generic-looking, and he was fairly certain he wouldn't be able to identify it in a police lineup.

"But your scheme's not going to work," Emma said. "If I come back to you, and I'm not saying I will, I won't be prodded into it. So you can take your fake chippy and—"

"She's not a fake chippy. She's my girlfriend."

"Yeah, right. And I'm Margaret Atwood."

"And we now live together."

"What?"

Emma was extremely competitive. He probably should have kept quiet about his new living arrangements.

"Never mind."

"Don't you 'never mind' me. I heard you. And how dare you live with someone else just after we've broken up. Is this about sex? It has to be. I can't imagine you have anything to talk about with this girl."

Aaron didn't care for the conversation's turn. Time to change the subject. "I have news. I sold my novel. To Wilner. It's not Featherstone, but I suppose it'll have to do."

Emma didn't speak for a minute but darkness brewed in her eyes. Was it a mistake to tell her? He assumed she'd want to know.

"I suppose congratulations are in order," she said. Her tone was not the least bit congratulatory, and her upper lip beaded with sweat, a very bad sign indeed.

"Thank you," he said nervously.

"You were working on that novel for what? Five years?"

"Yes."

"And we were together that whole time?"

"Yes."

"That means five years of watching you write in your head while I'm trying to talk to you. Five years of curtailed social activities because of your novel. Five years of having to put up with your moping when the work wasn't going well or even when it was."

"Yes, but—"

"Five years when your overly precious novel dominated every damn aspect of our lives..."

Emma was using her pre-projectile tone. Time to make an exit. He glanced about for Laurie.

"And when you finally get a publishing contract...Who benefits? Not me. Oh, no. Instead you take up with this marshmallow fluff..."

Emma's face turned red, and her breath was labored; she shot him a lethal look and stormed into the back room.

Aaron scanned the store, searching for Laurie. She was an aisle away pretending to read a Nicholas Windust novel. He knew she was pretending because the book was upside down. He wondered how much she'd overheard.

"We should probably go."

"But I was—"

"Now."

He took her by the arm and steered her out of the store. Emma emerged from the back room, a cup of coffee in her hand. She smiled at the two of them.

"Run," Aaron whispered.

Laurie obeyed, and Aaron followed. He heard a splat behind him; it was hot coffee hitting the floor.

*   *   *

When they were safely back in the car, Laurie said, "What a wildcat."

Aaron nodded. "Yes. I'm sorry. I didn't think Emma would be there."

"She seemed really smart."

"Too smart for her own good." He kissed her cheek and turned the key in the ignition.

"I should have bought that book, maybe. That Nick Windex."

Windust, Aaron thought.

"Maybe I should read more stuff like that."

"That's an excellent novel. I'll be glad to buy it for you. Just not here, obviously."

Laurie laughed. "I agree. Too dangerous...Umm...Aaron?"

"Yes."

"I didn't embarrass you, did I?"

"Of course not."

Well, maybe a little. He could have done without her question about where to find the romance section. At least it didn't come up that she wrote them or that she was a nail scholar, or rather, a failed nail scholar. He'd hate to think what Emma would have said about that.

"How long did you and Emma date?"

"Over five years."

"I suppose she's met your father?"

"She has." Emma and Horace actually got along well. He admired her extensive literary knowledge.

"What does he do again?"

Aaron didn't ever remember mentioning his father's profession. Not that his prominence in the literary world would register with Laurie.

"My father's an academic," he said.

"A smarty-pants then. Like his son." She smiled. "When am I going to get to meet him?"

Not anytime soon, Aaron thought. He simply couldn't imagine Horace Flowers and Laurie conversing. His father had little patience for people who weren't intellectuals. Their meeting would be a disaster.

"Right now we're barely speaking. Someday, I suppose."

"I'll look forward to it," Laurie said. She seemed satisfied with his answer.

Ten

From: Ellen Sideman, Events coordinator of Yards of Books
To: Laurie Lee
Subject: Book Signing

Dear Ms. Lee,
I'm sorry but we can't host a book signing for your novel *Don't Mess With Tex*. It's our policy to only host authors who have been traditionally published. Yards of Books has built a reputation on stocking and recommending quality titles, and we don't have the time to evaluate every self-published title. Should you ever sign a book deal with a traditional publisher, please consider contacting us again.

Sincerely,
Ellen Sideman

"Phooey!" Laurie said. She was looking at her recent Amazon sales on the computer. Despite her near constant Facebooking, blogging and tweeting, her novel sales were flat. Had she gotten into the indie publishing boom too late?

The writing, however, was going well. In fact, a cute idea for a novel recently popped into her head, and she was already thirty thousand words in. She intended to participate in an upcoming Pitch Frenzy conference.

Laurie decided she wanted to be a hybrid author, meaning she'd like to publish some of her books with a traditional publisher and also continue to indie publish. Getting a traditional publishing contract would help her get name recognition.

She was envious of Aaron's career. In a week he'd be flying to New York City to meet his publisher, and, of course, once his novel came out, he wouldn't have to beg the local bookstore to carry it.

Laurie intended to push herself to get as much writing done as possible before Pitch Frenzy. She was able to sneak in some work during slow periods at her various jobs. Sometimes she woke up in the middle of night inspired and wrote a few pages. She found it much easier to write romance when she was in the throes of one.

Things were going so well between her and Aaron. Of course, they had a few tiny speed bumps. Aaron, for instance, never asked how her writing was going, and that hurt her feelings. She was always quizzing him about his work.

Also, the other day she caught him paging through *The Romance Writer's Phrase Book*, which she'd accidentally left out. He was reading it with open-mouthed horror, almost as if he'd run across a magazine featuring chained naked men with ball gags in their mouths.

"Anything wrong?" she said.

He dropped the book. "Not at all."

She tried not to worry too much about his reaction to the phrase book. Most men weren't into mushy romance stuff. Also she only borrowed some of the phrases when she was in a real pinch.

"His eyes smoldered with fire."

"She was wrapped in a silken cocoon of euphoria."

"An ache was sparked by that one indelible kiss."

The Romance Writer's Phrase Book confirmed Aaron's worst prejudices against the genre. It contained over three thousand descriptive phrases organized by categories which included physical characteristics ("his legs, brown and firm as tree trunks"), emotions ("icy fear twisted her heart"), and sexual phrases ("gusts of desire shook through her").

Did writers actually lift these tired phrases and insert them into their manuscripts? If so, it was the antithesis of Craft.

Laurie caught him with the book. He immediately put it down and acted like nothing had happened. But it bothered him enough to prompt him to ask her about it that evening at happy hour.

"I'm curious," he said, trying to affect a casual tone. "What's the purpose of that book you have? The phrase book?"

"It's just a tool. Like a dictionary or a thesaurus."

"You don't actually use those phrases in your writing, do you? Word for word?"

"No. Never. Ever."

Did she protest too much?

"Because that would be cheating," Aaron said.

"Absolutely."

"Very good to hear," Aaron said. He decided not to pursue the issue any further. After all, Laurie's true vocation was to be a nail technician, not a writer. The other day he'd even let her give him a pedicure. It was quite enjoyable, particularly the pre-pedicure foot massage.

It was time for Aaron to leave for New York, and Laurie insisted on taking him to the airport. He tried to discourage her, citing traffic snarls, her busy schedule and the readily available long-term parking, but she said, "I love airports. All that emotion zipping around. My favorite terminal is the international terminal because people are usually going away for a long time so the goodbyes are so lovely to watch. Sometimes I go there for inspiration. Also, so many rom-coms have airport scenes."

"Rom-coms?" Laurie had used the term before but Aaron didn't remember what it meant.

"The movies I love to watch. *The Wedding Singer, She's Out of My League, Sleepless in Seattle, Garden State* and *Love Actually.* All have memorable airport scenes."

"Shall we make our own memorable scene at the airport?" Aaron said.

"Oh yes. Let's do."

When they arrived at the terminal, she jumped out of the car with him and stood on tiptoe and gave him a long drawn-out kiss. She smelled faintly of the sex they had that morning, and Aaron sensed fellow travelers watching them.

"Was that memorable enough?" he asked.

"Very," she said.

Slowly Laurie let him go. A hair-tousled Aaron headed into the terminal. People smiled. The sky caps gave him knowing looks. They could probably guess what he'd been up to all morning. Aaron had to leave behind the sublime and face harsh reality: security guards in too-tight trousers and the obligatory stocking footed walk through the x-ray machine.

But then Laurie was at Aaron's side again; she stole one quick yet passionate kiss and whispered, "When you love someone, you always take them to the airport." Then she ran back to her idling car, white-gold hair flying behind her. It happened so fast Aaron was stunned. People around him were clapping. He couldn't ever remember being this happy. New girlfriend, new novel and New York. He never imagined he'd be deserving of living a life like this. But how was he going to survive three days without Laurie?

Aaron had never been to New York before, but when the cab driver dropped him off at his hotel he didn't feel like a tourist. He felt like someone who belonged. New York was the publishing capital of the country, and soon he'd be a published novelist. He wondered if people could sense his new status in the world, if it somehow showed in the way he walked or how he held his head.

He was staying at a hotel in Midtown. There was barely room

for a luggage rack and the queen-sized bed took up almost all the space. The publishing company wasn't picking up the tab for his trip, but his agent told him it was important for authors to have a face-to-face meeting with their editors, that publishing was all about establishing relationships.

Aaron meandered around Midtown for an hour. It was late October and the air had a nip, and he wished he'd worn a heavier jacket. Because of his limp he didn't walk fast enough at crosswalks and imagined the swarming yellow cabs were gunning for him. On the sidewalk he was out of rhythm with the oncoming surge of pedestrians and was continually sidestepping to avoid being mowed down.

He sought refuge in the public library, which was close to his hotel. The atmosphere inside was hushed and calm. One day *Chiaroscuro* would be in this very building. Why not visit the shelf where it would be displayed? He ventured into the appropriate aisle and approved of his eventual close proximity to Norman Mailer. But who was this Fern Michaels with her flowery covers?

He decided to visit the W&W building where the Wilner imprint was located. He wouldn't be meeting his editor until tomorrow, but it was wise to do a dry run from the hotel to time his walk for the next day.

He made it to the W&W building in under twelve minutes. It was an unexceptional-looking high-rise, not very different from those that house prosaic types of businesses like banks or insurance companies. How much nicer it would be to return to the days when publishers weren't such big conglomerates and were located in quaint older buildings like the old Scribner headquarters on Fifth Avenue. (He read that the bottom floor was now a discount women's clothing store. *Tragic.*) Not all publishers had gone the bigger-is-better route. Featherstone was located in a brownstone in the West Village.

"Aaron? Aaron Mite?"

Aaron squinted at the man addressing him. He was tall with a lantern jaw and vivid blue eyes that competed with the crisp autumn sky behind him. Sunlight glinted from his silver-gold watch, and his suit threw off a moneyed sheen.

"Ross Harris. We attended the same MFA program?"

"Of course. Good to see you."

"You haven't changed." He laughed. "In fact, the last time I saw you, I think you were wearing that same jacket."

Aaron fingered the lapels of his corduroy jacket. It was true he'd owned it since grad school, but it was still serviceable so he saw no reason to discard it.

"What are you doing in the city?" Ross said.

It took him a beat before he answered. His identity as a soon-to-be-published author was still new, and he had a hard time owning it. "I'm visiting with my editor at Wilner. My novel will be published next fall. "

"You're kidding me."

"I'm not."

Ross's incredulity pleased him. Thousands of students graduated from Creative Writing programs each year, but how many published with a major press? Aaron imagined the number was small.

"What have you been doing since graduation?" Aaron asked. Ross's attire suggested a lucrative profession. Investment banker? Or maybe a hedge fund manager?

"I'm a novelist too. I've just now finished a meeting with my editor at W&W."

It'd been five years since the MFA program ended, and Aaron had a hard time recalling Ross's work, which meant it was probably mediocre, but perhaps he'd made strides since then.

"My condo isn't far from here," Ross said. "Would you like to grab a drink and catch up? I have a car waiting for me."

Aaron accepted Ross's invitation; he had nothing to do until morning, and he was curious about Ross's work.

The interior of the black Lincoln Town Car smelled of new leather and Ross's cedar cologne. The thick glass windows and comfortable seats muffled the impact of the city. During the trip,

Ross was occupied with a phone call. He sounded chummy with whoever was on the line, someone named Quip.

He ended the call and said, "Sorry about that. My agent wanted to tell me about some recent film negotiations, but then she went on about her blind date last night. Didn't go well, apparently."

Aaron couldn't imagine talking to his own literary agent for such a long time and in such a familiar manner.

The car deposited the pair in front of a large impressive building on the Upper East Side. "Is Quip your agent's first name or last?" Aaron said.

Ross laughed. "Neither. I call her Quip because she always has a witty comeback. Her name is Andrea Durban."

"Andrea?"

"You know her?"

"She's also my agent."

"How about that? I guess you're familiar with her quick wit. Did she tell you that story about her toy poodle, Kippy, and his run-in with a pigeon? What a scrappy pooch."

"She didn't." Aaron didn't know his agent owned a poodle, scrappy or otherwise.

The entrance to Ross's building was arched and bordered with intricate scrollwork. Ross nodded at the doorman and related the Kippy story. Aaron was barely listening. The opulent surroundings distracted him. The lobby was vast and cathedral-like, reminiscent of a four-star hotel.

Light streamed in through a domed ceiling and fell majestically on marble floors. Touches of affluence were everywhere, from the gleaming wood paneling to the antique leather furnishings. Aaron couldn't imagine a writer being able to afford such a place. Maybe Ross had family money.

They rode the elevator to Ross's apartment. The inside was spacious, and sunlight flooded through the floor-to-ceiling windows. His furnishings were stark and modern with sharp edges or odd shapes. Aaron was about to sit on a chair when Ross stopped him.

"Sorry. That's a sculpture."

He pointed to something that looked like a miniature trampoline. "That's a chair."

The so-called chair didn't seem designed to accommodate the human posterior, but when Aaron sat on it, it cleverly transformed from trampoline to chair. A manservant attired in a white linen tunic top and matching trousers appeared and asked what they'd care to drink.

"I don't suppose you have the makings for...Never mind," Aaron said.

"Anything you want; Sam can mix it for you," Ross said.

Ross sat on a white leather sofa, his arm was draped over the back, legs spread, taking up a considerable amount of square footage.

"Can you make a Pink Lady?" Aaron said.

"My pleasure," Sam said. Ross requested a gin and tonic.

"A Pink Lady, huh?" Ross laughed, but not unkindly. Aaron explained that a Pink Lady was his girlfriend's favorite drink, and he was already missing her a great deal.

"Is this Emma?"

"No. I have a new girlfriend now."

Ross asked several questions about Laurie as if he was genuinely interested, and Aaron was happy to provide answers. Laurie was his favorite topic, and he went on about her much more than he intended, even talking about her fervor for flamingos and romantic comedies. He showed Ross a photograph of her that he kept tucked in his wallet.

"Wow," Ross said. "Quite a departure from Emma."

"True."

"What is she? A model? Actress? She's pretty enough."

"She's still in school."

"What field?"

"Medicine." Nails were *somewhat* medical. Laurie was presently taking a course called Safety, Sterilization and Sanitation, although according to her she was failing it.

Ross winked. "With a face and body like that, who cares what she does? I've underestimated you, Aaron Mite."

Aaron was uncomfortable with a conversation that suggested he chose Laurie for her good looks. He didn't want to share the real story with Ross.

"Do you have a girlfriend?"

"Not at the moment."

"I'm surprised. As I recall, you were always popular with the gentler sex."

Ross's good looks caused a stir among the female members of the MFA program, especially the poets, who dedicated more than one ode to him.

Ross smiled. "Those grad school days were heady. But now it's a matter of not having enough time to go out and find someone. My work keeps me hopping."

Aaron nodded. "Writing can be extremely time-consuming."

"True, but there's also everything that goes along with it. You'll find out soon enough now that you're going to be a published author."

"What do you mean, 'everything that goes along with it'?"

"Do you have a few hundred hours? I'll let your editor clue you in. Lord knows they didn't teach of any of the nuts and bolts of publishing in MFA school. So much of the program was a waste."

Aaron vehemently disagreed. His MFA days were some of the most edifying of his life but he didn't feel like arguing with Ross. "Do you have a copy of your novel here?"

"You mean novels, and I thought you'd never ask." Ross strode to a large cabinet and opened it. Dozens of volumes were displayed within, all bearing the name R.K. Harris on the spine.

"The name R.K. Harris is familiar to me," Aaron said.

"Not to brag, but I've become pretty well-known over the years."

Aaron disapproved of the prefacing phrase "not to brag." It was like saying, "Not to stab," and then going ahead and stabbing someone while assuming the action would be negated.

Numerous titles lined the shelf. It had only been five years since grad school.

"There's so many...How did you...?"

"I've written fifteen since grad school. The reason it looks like so many books is because some of these are foreign editions."

Suddenly he remembered it was Laurie who'd mentioned Ross's books, and he may have even seen one lying about the house. "Do you write romance?"

"Not romance. Love stories, and not to brag..."

Aaron winced.

"But they've all been *New York Times* bestsellers. Four have hit the number one spot."

"My girlfriend's a fan."

"Really?" Ross seemed pleased. "But I'm not surprised. I'm big with the ladies."

"And these books...They paid for this apartment?"

"And a whole lot more. Not too shabby, huh? I bet you wouldn't have expected that from me. You didn't always care for my work, especially during our second year. What was that phrase you always used? Something about cuneiform? It wasn't worth the cuneiform it was chiseled on?"

"I think you mean papyrus."

"That's it. It wasn't worth the papyrus it was penned on."

"Correct." Aaron had to admit he also liked the cuneiform phrase. Maybe he'd try it out for a little variation.

"No hard feelings, by the way. Difficult for me to be mad, considering all the success I've enjoyed. My newest novel came out last week, and the publisher staged a flash mob."

"A flash mob?"

"Everyone in the publishing company—from secretaries to literary assistants to executive editors—showed up on the steps of the New York Public Library and read my book."

The techniques for publicizing commercial fiction were certainly curious. Perhaps hoopla was necessary to distract readers from the pedestrian quality of the writing.

A solicitous Sam delivered their drinks, and Aaron was slightly disappointed that his Pink Lady came without an umbrella. It was, however, tasty.

"You caught me on a good day, Aaron. I'm feeling generous. Publishing's a tough business, and since we went to grad school together I'd like to give you a leg—"

"Up?" Aaron said. "That's very kind of you. What did you have in mind?"

"I hardly ever do this anymore, but I'm going to blurb your book."

"Blurb?" The word sounded undignified, an unholy union between a burp and slurp.

"Endorse it."

"But you haven't read it."

"I will. Or more likely I'll get one of my people to do it. If Quip took it on, it's gotta be good. And you were one of the better writers in our program. Especially during the first year. Whatever happened to that novel of yours, *Klieg*?"

"Discarded. It was amateurish."

"That's funny. I remember it being very accomplished but then again, it's been a while. Anyway, about that endorsement—"

"Thank you. Your offer's generous."

"Yeah, well, I know it's hard to get attention for quiet literary novels. I thought—"

"I'm extremely grateful."

Ross put his hands behind his head and spread out even more on the couch. "Makes me feel good to help out someone who's just jumped on this crazy publishing carousel. I was one of the lucky ones who never had to pay my dues, but—"

"I fear I must decline your kind offer."

"What?"

"We don't have the same readership. You write romance."

"Love stories." He carefully enunciated each syllable. "And incidentally they've been called love stories for thinking people."

"But still genre fiction."

"Upmarket fiction, which marries literary fiction with genre fiction."

What a dreadful union, Aaron thought.

"And speaking of genre fiction, too many people judge it by its worst examples. There's predictable and cliché-riddled genre fiction, and then there's genre fiction where every sentence shines. When's the last time you've picked up a genre novel? I think you'd be surprised—"

Aaron held up a finger. He withdrew a book from Ross's cabinet and began to read.

Ross leaped from the couch to stand behind him. "That actually isn't one of my best."

Aaron ignored him and continued to peruse the book. After a few minutes he looked up from the page. He hoped his expression conveyed his dismay, but if not, he was prepared to offer a detailed verbal critique.

Ross snatched the book away. "I was on deadline. The book you should read is my debut. I wrote it during the MFA program. That one—"

"I've read enough, thank you, to know that we are very different. And may I ask you a personal question?"

"What?"

"You earned your MFA. You studied the Craft. With practice and time you could likely produce fiction that approaches a level of artistry. Why did you make the decision to write genre fiction?"

Ross looked uncomfortable, guilty even, as he should. It was one thing for Laurie to choose to write genre. Unlike Ross, she lacked the advantages of a university education.

"It's not nearly as easy as it looks, doing what I do. I bet you couldn't do it."

"No. I could not."

"So you're admitting there's a skill level involved?"

"That's not what I said. The reason I can't write genre fiction is because it's contrary to everything I believe. I couldn't sell myself out that way."

"You should be thanking genre writers."

"Whatever for?"

"Because the sales of commercial novels make the publication of literary novels possible. What was your advance? Fifteen grand or some other embarrassingly paltry figure? Whatever it was, I promise you it's my sales that are subsidizing your novel."

An uncomfortable truth, since Wilner was an imprint of W&W. Another reason Aaron wished he was with Featherstone. They only published quality literary fiction.

"And while my writing might not be inspiring on the sentence level, it takes artistry to create an engaging plot that sweeps a reader away for hours."

Aaron sighed. He'd had this argument a number of times with students who insisted on inserting pixies and dragons into their narratives.

"Ross, you can talk to me about the future of genre fiction until the dawning of the post-post-post-modernist age, but you yourself just described its purpose: to temporarily sweep readers away from their lives. Once they come back from the trip, they are unchanged. Literary fiction, on the other hand, challenges readers to confront their lives; as the essayist Arthur Krystal says, it melts the 'frozen sea inside of us.'"

Ross stroked his chin, as if considering his point. (As he should. Aaron felt he'd gotten to the marrow of the issue.)

"I assume you read a lot of literary fiction."

"Of course. It's all I read."

"Well then, if literary fiction is so transforming, why the hell are you the same uptight snob you were in grad school?"

Aaron bristled. He was not a snob; he simply appreciated and defended great literature. Normally he was not particularly combative but he felt a retort was in order.

"Better to be a snob than a sellout," he said softly.

"I'm going to pretend I didn't hear that."

"I should probably go."

"You weren't always such a snob. I remember your first

semester in grad school. Your enthusiasm for writing was infectious, but the next semester you came back completely different, all guarded and critical. I always wondered what happened to you."

"My tastes simply grew more sophisticated. It's a perfectly natural evolution in a grad student."

"A shame," Ross said. "Because that first semester you inspired me, and I know I wasn't the only one."

"That was simply youthful exuberance that resulted in some hideously bad writing."

"It wasn't bad writing. Not at all."

Aaron was doubtful that Ross could tell the difference.

"I'm not the only who changed," Aaron said. "Our program was competitive. Obviously the faculty saw merit in your work but now—"

"Enough. I refuse to listen to any more insults about my writing in my own home."

Aaron nodded his assent and headed for the door. It was clear he and Ross would never agree, which was a shame. He'd have enjoyed a lively conversation about literature with an old classmate. Laurie was excellent company in most ways, but she wouldn't know Thomas Pynchon if he pinched her on her lovely posterior. Aaron had bought her a Pynchon novel as well as the Nicholas Windust book she'd looked at during their visit to The Spine. He thought she was reading them but then discovered she'd just used the dust jackets to cover up her romance novels.

"Please have another cheese straw, Laurie. If you don't eat them, my husband will, and the doctor's been after him to watch his sodium."

Laurie smiled at Jake's mother and said, "Yes, ma'am. Don't mind if I do." She wasn't the least bit hungry and there was far too much cayenne pepper in the cheese straws. But she was always eager to please Marvel. Poor thing had been wasting away since

Jake's death. She'd always been thin, but it looked like she'd lost about twenty pounds. She'd also stopped touching up her gray. No traces of her former honey-colored hair remained on her head.

They were sitting in the living room which was now a shrine for Jake. Photos were displayed on every surface, and his athletic trophies glinted from shelves. Laurie happened to know that Marvel spent hours lovingly polishing each and every one. There wasn't a speck of dust on any of them.

"And there she is! The prettiest girl in Emanuel County."

Marvel's husband, Brick, charged into the room in his usual high-energy fashion. He looked mostly the same, still barrel chested and ruddy faced, but in recent visits, the ruddiness had spread and his cheeks were a map of broken blood vessels. Laurie suspected he'd upped his scotch drinking in recent months. On his heels was Jake's older sister, Kate.

Laurie stood and gave both Brick and Kate a hug. Brick's embrace was enthusiastic, Kate's much less so. She lived next door and was always in and out of Brick and Marvel's house.

Brick settled into his easy chair. "How is Hot-lanta treating you?"

"Daddy," Kate said. "No one calls it that anymore."

"Sorry. I guess I'm out of touch. How's the Big Peach?"

"It's fine, sir," Laurie said. "Thanks for asking."

Marvel clutched at her pearls. "I don't know how you stand all those traffic snarls. The way people drive? Like demons out of hell."

"I'll never get used to it." Laurie matched Marvel's dramatic tone. She didn't mind the traffic so much. It meant she lived in a place that was fast-paced and vibrant, and if she got stuck in a long jam, she simply pulled out one of her romance novels.

"Who's this furry thing?" Brick said. He pointed to Dusty.

"My new dog, Dusty." Laurie had called ahead to make sure it was okay to bring him. She didn't want to leave him alone for a full day.

"Very wise of you to have a dog in the city. All that crime," Marvel said.

"How's nail school going?" Kate said. "Mastered cuticles yet?"

Cuticles were more complicated than most people might imagine, but Laurie knew Kate wasn't asking a real question. She and Jake's sister had never been bosom buddies, but after Jake died she was almost hostile with Laurie.

She also treated Laurie as if she were frivolous and dumb. She even told blonde jokes in her presence. (Kate's hair was unruly and brown.) Two weeks after Jake's death, Laurie overheard her saying, "Mama and Daddy are probably going to have to help Laurie out financially. That girl has zero skills." Laurie had no idea why Kate had gotten so testy with her.

"Nail school's going well," Laurie said. That was a lie. She was very close to flunking out. For some reason nothing the textbook or teachers said stuck in her brain.

"We surely do miss seeing you," Marvel said.

"And I miss y'all."

Silence. Their visits were always marked with awkwardness. Nobody seemed to know what to talk about, and Jake's absence always hung over the proceedings. Yet Marvel insisted on them. Likely Laurie's presence was akin to having a little piece of her son in the room. Laurie counted the minutes until she could politely leave. Brick and Marvel's house always made her feel hemmed in.

"I hear you're keeping busy up there in Atlanta," Kate said. "Making new friends?"

Laurie bit her bottom lip. She recognized that smug tone. Delilah must have said something to somebody about Aaron. Laurie was surprised. Her friend was generally good at keeping secrets.

"One very special friend, I hear?" Kate said, her voice a challenge.

"What's Kate talking about, Laurie?" Marvel said, blinking innocently.

Both Brick and Marvel's eyes were on Laurie, waiting for her answer.

"Kate's right. In fact, I've been meaning to tell you...But I just..."

"Laurie has a new beau," Kate said.

"I have a new *friend*."

"And they're living together," Kate said triumphantly. "Have been now for several months."

More silence. This time it was a stunned silence.

"Is that true?" Marvel's voice was pinched with alarm.

"Well, it's expensive living in Atlanta, and Aaron and I thought—"

"Several months? And you didn't tell us?"

"Well..."

Marvel shot up from her chair.

"Marvel, listen. I meant to tell you. But I—"

She was talking to empty air; Marvel had fled the room.

Laurie turned to Brick. "I'm so sorry. I honestly didn't mean to upset her."

Brick wore a weary expression. "It's okay, sugar. You're a young woman, and you aren't expected to wear widow weeds for the rest of your life. Marvel knows that. I think it just came as a shock." He stood. "I best go after her."

Brick left the room, and Laurie was alone with Kate.

"Don't give me that injured look," Kate said. "You deserved that. Why didn't you tell them?"

"I was waiting for the right time," Laurie said. Not that there was such a thing. She should have mentioned it, but she knew the news would be upsetting so she kept putting it off.

"You never did love Jake, did you?"

Laurie widened her eyes at the absurd question. "How can you say that? His death devastated me."

Kate shook her head in disbelief.

"Just because I'm seeing someone new doesn't mean I didn't love your brother," Laurie said. "He was the love of my life. No one can replace him."

Kate shot Laurie a look of such coldness, it made her shiver.

"Why don't I believe that?"

She left the room. Laurie couldn't move for a moment. The

exchange had shaken her. She gazed directly at a photo of Jake in his football uniform, kissed her fingers and touched the photo. "I don't care what Kate said," Laurie said vehemently. "You know I loved you." Then she picked up Dusty, grateful to leave.

Eleven

The elevator opened up into the W&W reception area, and Aaron waited for his editor to come and greet him. Instead, the receptionist told him that Max was on a phone conference and Aaron would first be meeting Rebecca, head of publicity.

Rebecca was a mannish-looking woman in a boxy suit; the only hint of femininity in her appearance was her high heels. Aaron had noted that the women of New York City had a fondness for towering footwear. That seemed counterintuitive considering the amount of walking required to get around the city. You'd think they'd choose sturdy heavy-soled footwear, instead of the flimsy and teetering contraptions he'd seen so far.

Rebecca mentioned they had a fountain-style Diet Coke machine and inquired if he wanted a drink. Aaron declined.

"Let's dive in then, shall we?" She sat behind her desk and swiveled in her chair. "I'd like to talk about platforms. We'll need to start working on yours."

A platform was a flat surface that was raised from the ground, often used by speakers or performers. In middle French it literally meant flat form. Why did Rebecca want him to have one? For author appearances? At five foot nine inches, Aaron wasn't a giant, but he was no midget either.

"I don't have the carpentry skills or tools necessary to construct a platform. Can Wilner provide one for me?"

Rebecca's baritone laugh rang through the small office. "A

platform is what the author brings to the table to publicize the book."

"Does Webster's accept that particular usage?"

"It's mainly a publishing term."

"I see. Well then, I bring the novel to the table. That's my platform."

In fact, Aaron could actually stand on his novel, and it would serve as a platform in the traditional sense of the word. It was a large volume and could easily support his weight.

"Of course you do. And your novel is definitely a vital component to the equation, but there are other matters to consider. You'd be surprised how much influence you already have. First there's your family and friends. They'll certainly buy copies of your novel."

"My father has already read the novel and didn't care for it. I have a girlfriend, but she prefers romance novels over literary novels."

Rebecca playfully wagged her finger. "Come on, Aaron. You surely have more family and friends than that."

"I almost forgot. I also have an ex-girlfriend who owns a bookstore."

"That's great." She jotted notes on a legal pad in front of her. "Are you on good terms with her?"

"The last time I saw her she tried to scald me with a hot cup of coffee."

One corner of Rebecca's lips jutted down. "I see. What about work colleagues?"

"I'm an adjunct, which means I scarcely interact with anyone on campus."

She rubbed her hands together. "Sounds like we have some work ahead of us. Have you thought about a website?"

"No."

"We at Wilner strongly encourage authors to maintain a website. I can give you the names of some companies that specialize in author websites as well as book trailers."

"Trailers?"

"It's like a movie trailer only with a book."

"Forgive me, but don't readers prefer to imagine the characters and situations in their minds? Isn't that the whole point of reading a book?"

Rebecca tapped her pencil against the surface of her desk. "You don't *have* to have a book trailer. It's just another publicity tool. Let's move on. What is your social media involvement?"

"Nil. I spend all my free time writing."

"Wilner encourages authors to have, at the very least, a Facebook and Twitter presence. I'll send you a PDF with tips on using social media."

"I have to confess, I'm not comfortable with social media."

She raised an eyebrow so expertly plucked it seemed slightly unnatural. "We've found that authors who have a social media presence tend to sell more books."

"Wouldn't it be simpler to take out an advertisement in the *New York Times Book Review*?"

She laughed again, although Aaron didn't get the joke. "That's a marketing issue, and I'm afraid a *Times* ad is not included in your current plan."

"Is it possible to contact the marketing people to suggest one?"

"It's not that simple. You may want to discuss marketing concerns with your editor; my bailiwick is publicity. Have you thought about doing some writing that's off the book page? Perhaps you could write an essay on what it was like to grow up as the son of such a famous critic."

Aaron stiffened. Surely he'd misheard. "What was that?"

"Your father's Horace Flowers, correct?"

"How did you know?"

"It was in the materials Max gave me."

"I never mentioned it to Max."

"Your agent must have—"

"I deliberately never told Andrea. I want my work to speak for itself."

"I understand, but from a publicity standpoint it doesn't hurt to—"

"Please don't mention Horace Flowers in any press materials."

Rebecca's pencil tapping grew more rapid. "Aaron, correct me if I'm wrong, but it sounds like you aren't particularly interested in publicizing your novel."

"Frankly I'm a little confused. Isn't that your function?"

"Well, it is, but we like to think of ourselves as partners with the author."

"Haven't I've already done my part? It took me five years to write that novel. Will you be spending five years publicizing it?"

Rebecca tossed the pencil across her desk and picked up the phone.

"Maybe it's time you talked to Max. I'll have his assistant take you to his office."

Max's assistant was pale and thin and wore a black dress with several zippers in illogical places. Her pace was slow and tentative because she, too, was hobbled by a pair of extremely high heels. She paused at an office door and opened it.

"Your author is here, Max," she sang out.

Aaron had imagined his editor to be an older man in a bowler hat, three-piece suit and a gold timepiece on a chain. Thus it was jarring to see a middle-aged man wearing a white suit and a canary-colored shirt talking on the phone at a Lucite desk. Max was small-boned with brown hair that was blonde at the tips. He hung up the phone and shot up from his desk to greet Aaron, breathless and arms aflutter.

"Welcome to the Wilner family." Max's gestures were theatrical and broad, and his voice was unexpectedly high-pitched. Everyone at Wilner seemed slightly manic; perhaps it was the easy access to Diet Coke. He clapped his hands together. "We are so excited about your novel."

"Thrilled," the assistant chimed in.

"I just got off the phone with Rebecca, and she said the two of you had a productive meeting. One teensy bump though."

Aaron frowned. Teensy wasn't a word. He thought an editor would be more precise in his language.

"Rebecca tells me you're reluctant to mention your relationship with your father. Why is that?"

"It's not relevant to my work."

"She also mentioned your father didn't like your book. We can't imagine why. It's stunning."

"Luminous," added the assistant.

"My father disagrees."

"And I'm sure that was devastating to you, but honestly, it's not that uncommon. Not long ago I was reading Steven Martin's autobiography. Do you know that it took his father forever to acknowledge his runaway success?"

The name Steve Martin rang familiar; Aaron wasn't a fan of pop culture but sometimes pop culture was so pervasive it bullied itself into his world. For instance, Aaron had heard of the Kardashians, although he had no idea why they were famous or why people wanted to keep up with them. Perhaps they were a family of long-distance runners.

"Was Steve Martin's father a famous book critic?" Aaron said.

"No."

"Then I don't understand the connection."

"Touché. But my point is this: Even though your father said he didn't like your novel—"

"Correct."

Aaron didn't see the need of getting into specifics.

"But, you see, from a publicity standpoint, that makes the connection even more delicious."

"I'd prefer my novel to stand on its own merit. Even if my father loved *Chiaroscuro*, I wouldn't want people to know about our family relationship."

Max and his assistant exchanged a look. The energy in the room seemed to fizzle.

"It's difficult to get attention for a debut literary novel," Max said.

"Almost impossible," the assistant echoed.

"There are thousands of novels out there. We try to find ways to makes ours stand out in the marketplace," Max said.

"Didn't you just say my novel was stunning?" Aaron said.

"Yes, indeedy," Max said.

"Is it possible the quality of the writing will attract readers?"

Max and his assistant didn't immediately respond. It was as if Aaron had proposed a radical new idea, and they needed time to process it.

The sound of screams in the hallway broke the silence. Aaron startled, but Max and his assistant didn't seem the least bit concerned. They exchanged a smile.

"Someone must have gotten some excellent news about an author," Max said.

"Wasn't Oprah going to announce her pick today?" the assistant said.

"No. That's tomorrow," Max said. "Must be something else."

A tiny brunette woman rushed into the office. Her face was flushed, and she nearly stumbled over her shoes. "Another number one spot on the *Times* list for R.K. Harris!"

Max clutched at his throat as if choking on his surprise. "Oh dear God, that's fabulous news. I'm so thrilled for you and your author. That's four in a row, correct?"

"Five."

The woman rushed out of the office. Max smirked. "Show-off," he said. "Now where were we?"

"What a coincidence. I had drinks with Ross, or rather, R.K., yesterday. We went to grad school together."

Max and his assistant swapped a rapturous look.

"Do you think he might be willing to blurb your novel?"

"Uh...yes. He offered to endorse it," Aaron said quietly.

"Wonderful!" Max and his assistant said in unison.

Aaron cleared his throat. "I turned him down."

Both faces fell simultaneously as if yanked by invisible puppet strings.

"Why, for God's sakes?" Max said.

"He's a genre writer. We have a completely different readership."

Max's smile was brittle. "Actually, you don't yet have a readership. Ross, on the other hand, has—"

"Millions of readers," the assistant said.

"He's considered a cut above the usual genre novelist, and he rarely gives blurbs, so that makes his endorsement all the more valuable," Max said. "A nod from him could move thousands of units."

"Units?" Aaron said.

"He means novels," the assistant whispered.

"Of course I did," Max said.

"You make it sound like it's all about commerce," Aaron said.

"Crass as it may seem, Wilner is in the business of making money," Max said. "Yes, we have more literary sensibilities than most imprints, but we still have to pay salaries. The only imprint I know that can publish whatever it wants, regardless of profitability, is Featherstone, but they're partially supported by private donors."

Again, Aaron was regretful he didn't receive an offer from Featherstone. He wished his agent had been more aggressive with them. Then he wouldn't have an editor who thought a novel needed all sorts of extras beyond its literary worth to sell copies, as if it were a box of breakfast cereal.

"Why not call R.K. right now?" Max said. "Tell him you've reconsidered."

"I can't."

"Why?"

"Before I left he called me an uptight snob..."

"Oh," Max said.

"And, in retaliation, I called him a sellout."

"I see," Max said.

"I'm sorry," Aaron said, but he wasn't. No matter what his

editor said, he knew an endorsement from Ross would completely mislead readers about his novel.

"I don't suppose you know Nick Windust?" Max said.

"Sadly, no."

"Just a joke," Max said. "I don't recall him ever blurbing a book. Anyway, we're going to get some galleys together soon and hopefully we'll be able to find someone worthwhile to endorse your novel."

"Fine. Are we done with the publicity part of this conversation?" Aaron asked.

Max exchanged a glance with his assistant. "I think we are."

"Good." Aaron looked around the office; it was spacious but there was only one desk inside. "Where will we be working?"

"Working?"

"I assumed you wanted to put some final touches on the book while I'm here."

Max laughed. "No, Aaron. We're done with the editing. In fact, your novel has been sent to copyediting. I'm afraid the days of an editor editing in the office are long gone. I do almost all my editing at home or on the subway."

"Then what do you do during the working day?"

"Acquire manuscripts, act as an advocate for the books on my list, and, of course, have lunch meetings with literary agents. Speaking of which, I have another appointment. It's been such a great pleasure to meet you, Aaron Mite."

Aaron had nothing else to do for the rest of the day. Tomorrow he was scheduled to have lunch with his agent and then, thankfully, it was time to return home to Laurie and Dusty.

He spent the next few hours in the New York Public Library reading. Laurie would be appalled by the way he was squandering his time in the city. When she heard about his trip she bubbled over with activity suggestions: strolling on the Brooklyn Bridge, eating cupcakes at the Magnolia Bakery, singing "Strawberry Fields" while visiting Strawberry Fields in Central Park. (She'd never been to Manhattan but got most of her knowledge of the borough from the romantic comedies she favored.) Those pastimes would only be enjoyable if Laurie was with him. Aaron had never been one to engage in a lot of leisure pursuits. Writing took too much time.

He could only imagine what she'd think of his dinner that night: a turkey Subway sandwich, which he took back to his room to eat. No doubt she'd be sampling the street food or wandering into whatever restaurant caught her fancy.

Aaron waited for his agent in the foyer of a restaurant called Buds. The space was airy with towering ceilings and heavy molding, and he suspected it may have been a bank in a previous incarnation. The hostess wore a black cocktail dress as if it were nine p.m. instead of noon.

Someone tapped his shoulder. Behind him was a man with unruly salt-and-pepper hair and a bushy mustache. He wore a short-sleeve dress shirt and his tie appeared to be a clip-on.

"Aaron, right?"

"Yes?"

He pumped Aaron's arm. "Great to meet you, cowboy. It's Bernie. Andrea's assistant."

"Where's Andrea?"

"Sorry. She's not going to make it today. I'm here in her place."

"Is she ill?"

"No. She's taking R.K. Harris out to a celebration lunch for hitting the number one spot on the *Times* list. She's sorry but she and R.K. are like this." Bernie crossed his fingers.

"Should we cancel then?"

"And miss out on a free meal? Are you nuts? I've got the agency credit card in my wallet, and I plan to put it through its paces. And there's a couple of things Andrea asked me to pass along to you."

"Fine, then. I'm hungry."

The hostess showed them to a table near the kitchen. They examined menus which were oversized and cumbersome but listed only a few entrées in flowery hard-to-read script.

"Do you have any recommendations?" Aaron said.

Bernie shrugged.

"I've never been here before. I usually pick up a liverwurst sandwich at the bodega. You want a cocktail?"

"I'm flying later. Alcohol and high altitudes are a poor combination."

"Well, I'm having one. A Manhattan. Maybe I'll even have two. Blame it on you. You know what they say about writers hitting the sauce...Hey, quit looking at me like that. I'm kidding."

Bernie's speech was littered with clichés, but Aaron admired his casual ease. They ordered their food. Bernie opted for prime rib, and Aaron echoed his order because it was the only thing on the menu that didn't have a lot of extra embellishments.

"By the way, I'm a huge fan of your novel." Bernie flapped a cloth napkin onto his lap. "Couldn't put it down. A work of genius. Reminds me of Karl Ove Knausgård's *My Struggle*."

"Thank you," Aaron said. Personally he found *My Struggle* to be overly long and self-indulgent, but no need to mention that.

"When your MFA mentor sent it over, I marched it to Andrea's desk and said, 'You need to read this tonight.' She told me to jump in the lake but to fetch her a cup of coffee first. I was a newbie and she didn't trust my judgment yet. But I kept nagging her, and she finally read it and admired it, although she did think the main character was bleak as all get-out. Thought it would be a hard sell, and damned if it didn't get rejected a lot. But I believed in your work, so I did some digging to see if I could find a sales angle. Boy, did I hit pay dirt when I discovered you were Horace Flowers' son."

The drinks were delivered and Bernie stirred his with his pinkie finger and took a big gulp. Aaron ignored his ginger ale. He swallowed hard. "You were the one who told Andrea about my father?"

"That's right. And that's why Wilner bought it. Don't get me wrong; they liked the writing, but they couldn't resist the publicity opportunities."

His father had been right all along; he was the reason Wilner had made an offer on *Chiaroscuro*. Aaron no longer had an appetite.

"I don't want to exploit my connection to Horace Flowers," he said quietly.

"You made that clear to Max, but I gotta level with you here, cowboy. The people at Wilner are getting annoyed with you, and that's not a good thing. You need to throw them a bone or two."

"Such as?"

"A website, definitely. And a social media presence: Facebook and Twitter should be enough to appease them."

"But I have no knowledge of either of those things. I wouldn't even know where to begin."

"It's not rocket science. Rebecca, your publicist, said she was emailing you a social media guide. Opening a Facebook and Twitter account is easy as—"

"Pie?"

"You're reading my mind, cowboy. As for your website, get some college kid to throw one up for you."

"I don't want to spend time on the internet. I want to spend time writing books. Authors are supposed to write, not post what they had for breakfast that morning."

In Aaron's case it was bran flakes to maintain bowel health. Posting that every day could get monotonous. Although now that he was with Laurie he occasionally added berries to his routine.

"The days when an author could cool his heels and let his publisher do all the promotion work are long gone. Authors who sit on their backsides don't sell as many books, simple as that."

"Genre writers I can understand, but literary writers?"

Bernie popped the cherry from his drink into his mouth. "They're all doing it now. Even the Pen Prize and Pushcart nominees."

"Well, you might expect that from Pushcart nominees...It's

hardly a prestigious honor. Do you know how many writers are nominated for a Pushcart each year?"

"Er...I think we're getting off track here."

"Three thousand."

"Damn. That *is* a lot. Guess I won't be impressed anymore when I see that mentioned in a query letter."

"Regardless, someone needs to take a stand against publishers forcing social media on authors."

Bernie dabbed at his moustache with a napkin. "Even if means you might not get published?"

"I have a contract."

"So? Publishers back out of book contracts all the time."

Aaron's mouth was dry. He took a sip of ginger ale. It was flat. "I didn't realize that."

"I've seen it happen more than once."

"Andrea couldn't stop them?"

"Not likely. And even if she could, she's not going to go out on a limb."

"Why wouldn't she? She's my advocate."

"In theory, but don't forget that, for Andrea, Max represents dozens of future book deals. You're just another author to her, and a pain-in-the-butt author to boot. You're already on her bad list. I can tell by this restaurant she picked."

Aaron glanced about. It was nicer than any restaurant he'd ever been to. Not that he went to many restaurants back home. He preferred simple food: a baked potato, a plain chop, tomato soup. Restaurants tended to fuss with food too much.

"What's wrong with this restaurant?"

"It's strictly D-List. The *New York Times* restaurant reviewer's dog wouldn't eat here. It's for clients who need a spanking. The valued clients, like R.K. Harris, are living it up at Michael's with muckety mucks like Barbara Walters and Anna Wintour. This place, on the other hand, is so far off the radar, soap opera extras don't even bother with it." Bernie picked up his glass and rattled the ice. "It does, however, serve a decent Manhattan."

The food arrived, but Aaron barely touched his prime rib. Bernie ended up eating part of Aaron's. He asked for the rest to be boxed up.

After the check was paid, and they were both outside the restaurant, Bernie said, "Sorry to be the bearer of bad news...For what it's worth, I'm on your side. I probably read a hundred or more novels a year. You're the real—"

"McCoy?" Aaron said wearily.

"That's right. A true talent. Fifty years ago you'd get the treatment you deserve, but the world has changed since the days of Hemingway and Fitzgerald."

"Yes," Aaron said in a stricken voice. "It certainly has."

Bernie left, and Aaron walked back to the hotel to collect his carry-on bag before he departed for the airport. For years he'd dreamed of getting his book published. Never once in his fantasies did he imagine that he would have to peddle it himself.

Twelve

Marvel sent a nice little note to Laurie, apologizing for her behavior and saying that of course Laurie needed to move on with her life. She wrote:

I hope this boy treats you well, although it's hard to imagine anyone loving you as much as my Jake did. I remember how he always used to say, "Laurie's the perfect wife. I wouldn't change a thing about her."

I don't know what your plans are with this new beau, but remember a man doesn't buy a cow when he can get the milk for free.

Love,
Marvel

Laurie read the note to Delilah over the phone. Apparently her husband Bart overheard one of their phone conversations and that's how the news about Aaron got out. You couldn't keep a secret in Swainsboro.

"That cow saying is older than spit," Delilah said. "Eve's mother probably said it when her daughter was romping around buck naked with Adam in the Garden of Eden."

"Eve didn't have a mother. Didn't you learn that in Sunday School?"

"I must have cut that day. So what are your plans? Do you want Aaron to buy the cow?"

"Honestly, it's a little soon to be thinking about that. We've only been together for three months. But I can tell you this. I surely did miss him when he was gone."

"Have you told him your good news?"

"Not yet."

A few days after Aaron got home from his New York trip, Laurie attended Pitch Frenzy, which was held in the ballroom of a nearby hotel. She had only one minute to pitch her novel idea to a panel of judges. She pitched *Canine Cupid*, which was about a woman named Lucy who owned a loveable mutt that knocked up a purebred show dog. The uppity owner, Art, was initially irritated but eventually they fell in love.

A film scout was on the panel and he asked Laurie to send her the chapters she'd written and an outline.

"Why haven't you told him?" Delilah said.

"It's a long shot, and Aaron's been in a funk since he got back from New York. His editor's having trouble getting a decent blurb for the novel. If they don't get at least one good blurb, Barnes and Noble might not order any copies."

Silence.

"Delilah? You there?"

"Watch yourself, Laurie."

"What?"

"You used to do the same thing with Jake. It was all about his accomplishments and his glory. In Jake's case, of course, you literally cheered for him. Aren't you tired of being the woman behind the man? It's time for you to shine. Or is Aaron's ego too fragile to handle your success?"

"My *potential* success, and Aaron has a fine, strong ego. Yes, he does get down in the dumps occasionally, but I'm usually able to snap him out of it."

"He's a grown man. Aaron should be able to cheer himself up. Most importantly, does he recognize your dreams? Is he a cheerleader for your writing?"

Cheerleader was not the word Laurie would use.

"He doesn't discourage me."

"Suppose your book does become successful, how will he take it? Some men can't handle a woman's success, and Southern men can be especially touchy about it."

"Aaron's not like most men. If my book sells to the movies, and that's a big if, he'll be the best boyfriend in the history of the world. I'm certain of it."

"I'm glad to hear it. You do seem very happy with him."

"I'm ecstatic."

Laurie wasn't worried in the least. Their relationship was not a competition. After all, Aaron was a successful writer in his own right. Everything would be just dandy.

Facebook status update: (No picture) (Zero friends)

My name is Aaron Mite, and my novel *Chiaroscuro* will be published in the fall. I'd be grateful if you'd purchase it when it's released and perhaps also buy copies for your friends and family. It's vital that my publisher recoup its investment in me. Thank you very much.

First Tweet: (0 followers)

Please purchase Aaron Mite's novel *Chiaroscuro* when it comes out in the fall. I thank you in advance.

Website:

Welcome to the Official Site of Aaron Mite, Novelist and author of *Chiaroscuro*.

My novel will be available in the fall. I urge you to pre-order it. My website designer has provided several links to online retailers to expedite your purchase.

From: Bernie Fields
To: Aaron Mite
Subject: Try again

Cowboy, you're not getting this. First, you need to reach out to people. Second, you gotta be personable. Why not talk about your process? People love to hear how writers write. Be friendly! Don't be so damn formal.

Bernie

Facebook: (1 Friend, Bernie Fields)

Greetings, social media friends. How are you today? What did you have for breakfast? Feel free to share this information on my wallpaper. It's been suggested to me that you might be interested in my writing process. I write longhand, and then I type the entire document into the computer. I hope that satisfies your curiosity and you'll consider purchasing my novel.

Tweet: (1 follower, Bernie)

Fellow tweeters. See my Facebook page. Space constraints prevent me from sharing my writing process here.

From: Bernie Fields

To: Aaron Mite

Subject: None

You know, maybe you're not cut out for this social media stuff after all. Things aren't looking great around here. Andrea had a phone call yesterday with Max, and I overheard her talking about some sad pre-order numbers for *Chiaroscuro*. I think they're close to wiggling out of the contract. You need a miracle, cowboy.

Bernie

Aaron decided to write an essay for his favorite online journal, the *Literary Lion*, in hopes of attracting attention to his novel. Essays appeared weekly, and the timetable in between acceptance and publication was short.

He began the essay talking about his usual pet peeves like the anti-intellectualism of American literature and how genre fiction was dominating the national conversation. Halfway through the essay, he'd gone off subject and began ranting about the increasing expectations publishers were putting on serious authors. He wrote:

"Not only do we write the novel, we're also expected to hawk it with the persistence of a carnival barker."

When he finished, he realized he'd written a completely different essay than he'd intended. Instead of pleasing his editor, it could alienate him even more. Yet he was reluctant to change a word. He suspected he had said what many other authors were thinking but were afraid to express for fear of upsetting their publishers.

For several minutes, his finger hovered over the send button. Finally, he went through with it. The deed was done, and he felt no regrets. As a literary writer he had the duty to uphold the truth. After all, if he wasn't going to be candid, he was no better than a hack. Two days later he received an acceptance email; his essay was going live on Monday.

Monday came, and Aaron visited *Literary Lion* and checked out his essay. There were dozens of comments and most agreed with him. It was comforting to know some sanity still existed.

An email from his editor arrived two days after his essay was published. Max had cc'd Andrea and the subject line read: "Your piece in *Literary Lion*." Aaron didn't immediately open it. Even though it was only two p.m. he decided to pour himself a brandy. He downed the drink and stared at the email, trying to get the courage to open it. Meanwhile, he reread his essay, hoping it was less critical then he remembered. Unfortunately, it was worse.

A moment later another email came in.

From: Bernie Fields, assistant to Andrea Durban

To: Aaron Mite

Subject: Congratulations on your reprieve

A reprieve? That didn't make sense. What happened? He opened Bernie's email:

Hey, cowboy. I'm sure by now you've already heard the news from Max. It looks like you're back in the game. You're a lucky guy. I read the *Literary Lion* piece, and it definitely could have backfired on you.

Bernie

Aaron decided to open the email from Max.

To: Aaron Mite
From: Max Porter
Cc: Andrea Durban
Subject: Your piece in *Literary Lion*
You're a ROCK STAR!! Guess who read your essay in *Literary Lion* and loved it? Frank Zenn himself. He loved it so much he had his editor call me, asking for a galley of your novel. He plans to read it ASAP. If we get a blurb from him, we don't need anyone else.

I'm proud of you for shaking the bushes and getting yourself out there. I haven't read the essay, but I'm sure it's AMAZING!! Next time keep us informed, Mr. Modest. We want to hear about all your publicity triumphs no matter how miniscule. Not that I'm implying *Literary Lion* is miniscule. After all, look what your publication there reaped.

All best,

Max

Liberal use of exclamation marks aside, Aaron was pleased with the editor's email. He hoped Max never got around to reading his piece, but even if he did, he suspected the Frank Zenn endorsement would lessen any insult. After all, Frank Zenn's last novel *Bondage* won the Pulitzer. Aaron wasn't a fan of *Bondage*. However, he respected Zenn's first two novels and thus would be happy to accept his endorsement.

From: Frank Zenn
To: Max Porter
FWD: Aaron Mite
Subject: Endorsement
See the FANTASTIC blurb below. Everyone at Wilner is excited, and there's talk of rethinking your marketing plan. BRAVO to you, Aaron!

Max

Dear Max:

I finished Aaron Mite's excellent novel last night and have spent the morning crafting an endorsement that will hopefully do the work justice:

"A masterpiece of American fiction. *Chiaroscuro* is an intricately ordered narrative that eschews post-modernism and authentically probes the despair clouding one man's mind."

P.S. I would like to have a discussion with Aaron about his novel and other issues. Will you pass along my phone number to him? I write from eight a.m. to six p.m. daily, but would be amenable to a conversation any time after that.

Warm regards,

Frank Zenn

Aaron called Frank at six thirty that evening to thank him for the endorsement, and they spent an enjoyable hour in conversation. At one point Zenn said, "I can't remember the last time I've had such a stimulating conversation. Ever since I read your essay, I had a feeling we'd be simpatico."

"Likewise," Aaron said.

"By the way, have you read Carson Hyatt's latest? Some are calling him the new wunderkind of literary novels."

Aaron sighed. "Finished it last night, in fact."

"And?"

"Pompous and dreadful."

"My thoughts exactly."

"As far as I'm concerned, it wasn't worth the papyrus it was penned on."

Silence.

"Hello? Are you there? Did we lose the connection?"

"That phrase. That damn phrase."

"What phrase?"

"'Not worth the papyrus it was penned on.' I recognize it. You wrote an anonymous Amazon review about *Bondage*, didn't you?"

"Uh, well...I'm not sure if I recall..."

"That's a distinctive phrase. It had to be you. And I remember that review well because it was the most sanctimonious, self-important—"

"Perhaps *Bondage* wasn't my favorite novel of yours, but I was impressed by..." The beep of a dial tone. Frank Zenn had hung up.

From: Max Porter
Subject: WTF?
What did you do? Zenn has withdrawn his blurb from your book. Not happy. Not at all.
Max

From: Andrea Durban
To: Aaron Mite
Subject: Wilner contract
I'm sorry to inform you that Wilner has decided not to publish your novel after all.
Regards,
Andrea Durban

From: Aaron Mite
To: Andrea Durban
Subject: For the best
Dear Andrea,
Initially I was distressed to hear of Wilner's decision not to publish *Chiaroscuro*. However, upon reflection, I've decided that perhaps they weren't the right publishing company. Would you consider making another attempt at contacting the editor at Featherstone? Eager to hear your thoughts on this matter.
Respectfully,
Aaron Mite

From: Andrea Durban
To: Aaron Mite
Subject: No Subject

Dear Mr. Mite,

I regret to inform you that I will no longer be able to serve as your literary representative. My client list has gotten too crowded. Best of luck finding a new agent. You'll need it.

Andrea Durban

To: Aaron Mite
From: Bernie Fields, assistant to Andrea Durban
Subject: You were robbed.

Sorry about the heave-ho. Keep in touch, cowboy, and don't give up the ghost.

Your fan,
The Bernster

"Eeeek!"

Laurie was reading an email from the film scout she met at Pitch Frenzy, and it turned out a big star was interested in her *Canine Cupid* proposal. The film scout refused to give any hints about the star's identity, but Laurie imagined everyone from Katherine Heigl to Emma Stone. After she got the email, she rushed into the bedroom, deciding it was finally time to tell Aaron her news.

Aaron was propped up in bed, fast asleep, his glasses perched on his nose. On the bed was a copy of a book called *The Idiot's Guide to Finding a Literary Agent.*

His poor dear face looked tense and anxious even in sleep. Over the last few days the fates had used him as their personal punching bag, and yet every day he still sequestered himself in the closet and bravely spent his hours writing.

If she were in his shoes (a battered pair of loafers she dearly wished he would replace), she would be tempted to take to bed with a box of sprinkled doughnuts and knock off writing for a few weeks. But Aaron was extremely disciplined, a quality she admired. A few times she'd taken a peek at his writing. Aaron could spend several paragraphs describing the way sunlight fell on the floor of a room, whereas in the same space, Laurie's main character would have endured three major life upheavals. In fact, Aaron's writing was paced the way he made love, slow and methodical.

She took the glasses from his nose, removed the book and kissed his cheek. "Sleep well," she said. She turned out the light and prepared for sweet dreams with her handsome scribe beside her. The news about *Canine Cupid* could wait.

Thirteen

Aaron's briefcase was so stuffed with composition papers it looked like it swallowed a watermelon. A week ago he began a new semester at Metro Atlanta University, which would severely eat into his writing time. He planned to spend the next couple of hours grading, his least favorite pastime.

Yet Aaron was whistling Stravinsky's "Rite of Spring" and feeling upbeat. The reason for his cheery mood was that Laurie surprised him with morning love-making. Nothing kicked off his day better.

Aaron sat at the kitchen table and pulled out the first paper. He gave it an initial cursory read and said to Dusty, "Don't even think about eating this one. It would give you severe indigestion." He slipped Dusty a bite of jelly toast and seized his red pen, preparing to do battle with syntax so mangled it jangled his brain.

Five papers in, the phone rang and Aaron ignored it. The landline seemed to exist for a single purpose: to allow telemarketers and shysters to harass people. The phone had an audio function that announced callers in a mechanical voice and often it botched the pronunciation.

Today it was saying, "Rite Er Plant. Rite Er Plant."

Wait. Was he hearing correctly? Not Rite Er Plant, but Writer Plant. Was it possible his literary agent had changed her mind about him?

Aaron jolted from his chair to answer it.

"Aaron Mite here."

"Aaron?" Andrea said. "That's odd. I guess I misdialed somehow. I was looking for Laurie Lee."

"You have the correct number. Laurie's my girlfriend. We live together."

"I had no idea. Is she available?"

"She's at work. May I take a message?"

"Tell her to call me ASAP. I'm certain she'll be getting other calls from agents, but urge her to call me first."

Ha! As if Andrea was in any position to ask him for a favor.

"Maybe," Aaron said. "If you tell me what this is all about."

"She hasn't told you? Three film studios are fighting over the rights to her novel, *Canine Cupid*. Jennifer Lawrence is attached to the project."

"There must be a mistake...How would a film agent discover Laurie's novel?"

"Just have her call me, will you?"

The phone rang steadily the entire afternoon. The calls were for Laurie, and all were either editors or agents. The film agent also called and said a deal had been negotiated with Weinstein Company.

When Laurie got home, Aaron told her the news. She was so startled she swayed in her sandals and had to sit down on a living room chair. "I honestly didn't think it would go through. That's why I didn't tell you—"

"How did this happen?" Aaron said.

Laurie could barely get the story out. Something about frenzy and pitch. It all sounded foreign to Aaron. Never had he heard of a novel being sold this way. (Not that he was an expert at such things.) But, according to Laurie, *Canine Cupid* wasn't even finished. And talk about your silly titles.

The next day Laurie was composed enough to speak to the editors and agents that left messages, but the decision of how to proceed overwhelmed her. Aaron found himself in the position of adviser to his girlfriend, a traditional male role he enjoyed. She wanted to pick the editor who gave her the best terms and not bother with an agent. Might as well eliminate the middleman, she said.

Aaron was a newbie to the business of publishing in many ways, but he knew this much: A literary agent was likely to broker a much more lucrative deal. Despite the fact that Andrea had dropped him, he knew she was well-connected and known for her superb negotiation tactics.

Laurie heeded Aaron's counsel and hired Andrea. To Aaron's astonishment, Andrea almost immediately sold Laurie's partially finished book at auction for a staggering figure. Aaron was under the impression that the publishing business moved at the pace of the Earth's tectonic plates. That obviously was not true when dealing with a desirable property. Ironically, the publishing house who won the auction was W&W. As a condition of the deal, the company asked Laurie to cease selling novels herself.

The book contract was quickly inked, and W&W arranged for Laurie to fly to New York City to meet with all the key people in the publishing company. Laurie asked Aaron to come with her. When he agreed, she expressed her gratitude by making his favorite dish of chicken and dumplings and serving herself as dessert. (Whip cream and maraschino cherries were involved.) Afterward they showered and fell into bed. Aaron was moments from falling asleep when Laurie said, "Does my book deal bother you?"

Dinner and sex had been extremely satiating, thus nothing was bothering Aaron. He told her so.

"You're sure?"

"Very," he said. He was trying to keep conversation to a minimum because he was exhausted.

She scooted closer to him and wrapped her arms around his back. Her breath was hot on his neck. "You're incredible. Because some guys might feel threatened by my success."

Moments later he heard the soft whistle of her breathing and knew she was asleep. Aaron was suddenly restless. He felt her last statement suggested a misunderstanding about their respective statuses.

It was one thing to find success writing genre fiction, but it was much more difficult to achieve recognition in the world of literary fiction. And he objected to her use of the word "threatened." Did the success of McDonald's McRib threaten a Michelin four-star restaurant? Not that there was anything wrong with a McRib; it could be tasty in a pinch, but it was certainly not memorable.

Then again, he remembered Ross saying that certain genre fiction writers were making great strides in the elevation of their prose. At the time he'd questioned his statement, but maybe there was some truth to it. Perhaps Laurie was one of those rare genre writers, and that's why her work was commanding large amounts of money and attention. And who knew? Maybe, one day, Aaron could motivate her to transcend her genre. She was, after all, a true original.

Fourteen

From: Brandi Barrett
   To: Aaron Mite
   Subject: US Magazine
   Hi Professor Mite,
   So I'm in your eng. comp. class. 3rd period? Anyway I was
reading *US Magazine* and guess who I saw? I literally had a heart
attack when I spied my fav teacher's face. ☺ Your girlfriend's very
pretty. Do you want me to save my copy for you?
   Brandi

Laurie was stretched out on the mattress wearing a pink nightgown
trimmed in marabou. She favored theatrical nightwear and had
even bought Aaron a piped pair of pajamas and a paisley robe with
lapels. The ensemble looked like it belonged in the costume room of
a Noël Coward production. (Aaron had always slept in a t-shirt and
boxers but he frequently wore the pajamas to please Laurie,
marveling that they had a breast pocket.)
   She was so engrossed in a rom-com she didn't notice Aaron
until he climbed into bed. He could tell it was a rom-com, because
there was a falling-in-love montage of characters walking in the
rain, feeding each other brownies, and knocking over furniture
while passionately kissing.

She turned the TV off. "Sorry. Wouldn't want you to catch chick-flick cooties."

"Have you heard of a periodical called *U.S. Magazine?*" he said.

"U.S. as in United States?"

"Maybe. Supposedly you and I were in it."

"Oh. *Us Magazine.*"

"Is it true? Do we appear in this publication?"

Laurie bit her bottom lip. "How did you know about *Us?*"

"A student, who should have been reading something loftier, saw it. Were we in it or not?"

"Remember when that photographer caught us coming out of the Strand?"

On their recent trip to New York the only time Aaron and Laurie were able to spend together was a quick trip to the iconic bookstore the Strand, and, yes, Aaron did remember the flash of a photographer's camera as they left the bookstore.

"May I see a copy, please?" Aaron said.

"I'm not sure if I have that one."

Aaron knew W&W had been sending her packages every week with all the publicity she had received. A thick envelope arrived yesterday.

"Please let me see it or I'll get it myself."

"Okay," Laurie said reluctantly. She slipped out of bed and returned a moment later with a glossy magazine in hand. "It's a lot of nonsense."

The magazine was a supermarket tabloid, and a Post-it stuck out of the page. Aaron turned the slick pages until he came across a photograph of Laurie in a white dress, her teeth and hair almost as bright as the garment. Aaron was at her side.

Celebrities: They're Just Like Us

Laurie Lee, white-hot W&W romance scribe, slipped out of the Strand Bookstore with an unidentified male.

Laurie nuzzled him, her lips scraping over his five-o'clock shadow. "You're so much more to me than an unidentified male."

Aaron had taken off his glasses to retire for the night, but he put them back on. They helped him think.

"This isn't good news."

"I know. I'm sorry. You probably don't like seeing yourself in this type of magazine."

"That's not what I'm concerned about."

"By the way, you're much more handsome in person." She walked her fingers across his chest.

He placed his hand over hers. "You're not listening. This isn't about me; it's about you. They're calling you a celebrity."

"I know. Isn't that the craziest thing? Of course, my publicist loves it. And they're going crazy back home. Delilah said I made the front page of the *Swainsboro Forest-Blade*."

"Is that what you want? To be a celebrity? I thought you were a writer."

"Well, I am a writer. It says so right here in the caption. 'Romance scribe.'" She tapped a tangerine-colored fingernail against the page.

"But the press isn't promoting you as a writer. They're promoting you as an object of desire. Before you know it, men's magazines will be courting you."

"Don't be ridiculous. I'm an author, not a centerfold model. And even if they did ask me, which they won't, I'd never agree. My grandmother would surely come back from the dead if I did that."

"I worry that your identity as an author is being drowned out by your..." Her nightgown was diaphanous, and he could discern her nipples, pink and erect, through the flimsy fabric.

"Aaron?"

"Sorry. I temporarily forgot what I was going to say. I worry that your identity as an author is being drowned out by your white-hotness."

Laurie pounded her pillow and several feathers drifted into the air. She had an entire pre-slumber routine of sheet smoothing and pillow molding before she went to sleep. "I don't think that's true. I think they're just trying to get people familiar with me."

"I've seen this before with literary authors. A writer's good looks outshine his or her work."

"Well, it's different with romance writers; they're supposed to be glamorous. Barbara Cartland never got in front of the camera unless she looked like a queen, and Danielle Steel is always perfectly coiffed and Sophia Nash...Of course you're not familiar with these authors, but trust me, I know what I'm talking about."

Aaron thought this had nothing to do with glamour and everything to do with sex appeal. Laurie was an extremely good-looking woman, and if the press continued in this vein, her writing would always be secondary, until people might forget what came first.

"I think you should talk to your editor about how you want to be portrayed in the media." He didn't know how effective that conversation might be. It seemed as if publishers would do almost anything to sell books.

"You're sweet to worry about me, but honestly, I think everything's going to be fine. You seem wound up. Would you like a massage before bed?"

He knew this was Laurie's way of changing the subject, and even though he was still agitated, her offer was hard to resist. Her massages usually started out therapeutic and gradually evolved into something considerably more erotic. But that didn't mean the discussion was forgotten, just temporarily tabled.

Fifteen

From: Bernie, assistant to Andrea Durban
    To: Aaron Mite
    Subject: Checking in
    Hi, cowboy. You still writing? Can't stop thinking about your novel. Your characters are haunting me. Things are going downhill at the Writers' Plant. Andrea just took on some self-published twinkie with big tits who can't write her way out of a paper bag.
    Bernie

From: Aaron Mite
    To: Bernie
    Subject: Re: Checking in
    Regarding the twinkie. She's my girlfriend.
    Respectfully,
    Aaron

A few minutes after, Aaron's phone rang and it was Bernie.

"You're serious? Laurie Lee is your girlfriend?"

"Correct."

"Congratulations. That's one pretty lady and hey, I'm sorry about the twinkie comment."

"You also said she didn't write well. True?"

Bernie paused for a moment. "You haven't read her work?"

"No, I've not. Have you?"

"Hell no. But that's because romance isn't my thing. I like the heavy-hitting literary guys and gals. Like you."

"Then how do you know she can't write well? Are you making assumptions because she's a genre writer?" It occurred to him that, in his defense of Laurie, he was beginning to sound like Ross.

"Uh, not exactly...Some people around the office have mentioned that her writing chops might be a little...You know what? I shouldn't be talking about this. Privileged information and so forth, especially since you're her boyfriend. And she's hardly the only author who can't...You know, sometimes there are other factors that sell books, and in this case, the film sale absolutely sealed the deal. In movies it's more about the idea than the execution."

"I see. Do you have access to what she's written?"

"No. Sorry. Why?"

"I want to read some of her work and judge its quality for myself. She used to sell self-published novels but W&W asked her to stop."

"Give her a Google and you'll probably run across some bootleg copies."

Aaron kissed Laurie goodbye before she left for her very last temp job. She'd decided to become a full-time writer, and had also recently dropped out of nail school. (Or flunked out. Aaron wasn't quite sure which was the true story.)

After she left, Aaron downloaded a copy of Laurie's latest novel written before the W&W contract. It was called *Don't Mess With Tex*. (Where did she get her titles?) It took him only an hour to read, mostly because he did a fair amount of skimming.

He had never seen so many clichés: eyes twinkled, bosoms heaved, lips pursed. Men's chins were chiseled, women's waists were cinched and in the opening scene, the heroine looked in the mirror and admired her upturned nose and mischievous grin. (Despite Laurie's claims to the contrary, he was almost certain she'd cribbed from the *Romance Writers' Phrase Book*.)

Furthermore, none of her characters simply said anything; they growled, they roared, they purred. They also dutifully plodded through a series of improbable plot turns, and their problems were finally resolved courtesy of deus ex machina.

And yet, through all of the dreck, Aaron could discern some positive aspects. Laurie had an appealing and sympathetic voice, but it faded in and out like a weak radio signal and was sometimes lost completely in the wreckage of the work. The novel also showcased her sweet sense of humor, and her skill at crafting sex scenes. (This talent didn't come as a surprise to Aaron.) But overall, the novel was a colossal mess.

He spent the rest of the day deciding what to do. It was clear to him the people at W&W saw Laurie as a commodity to exploit and had absolutely no interest in her as a writer. He couldn't imagine that she'd improved much with *Canine Cupid*.

At five o'clock Laurie returned from her last day as a temp. This was usually Aaron's favorite time of the day. If it was a writing day instead of a teaching day, the house had been quiet as a mortuary for hours, and Aaron was shut away in the walk-in closet like a pair of brittle bedroom slippers. But as soon as Laurie came home it was like a brisk aromatic breeze blowing in through the kitchen window. She brimmed over with chatter ("There was the most gorgeous sunset on the drive home"), opened and closed kitchen cabinets, kicked off her shoes, turned on the radio to a country station ("A new Dwight Yoakum song!"). But this afternoon he was dreading her arrival instead of anticipating it.

Typically, Laurie mixed them both a drink and prepared a happy hour snack, but today Aaron took the initiative and had a Pink Lady waiting for her. (Sadly the color was more grayish than pink; he must have made a misstep in the mixing.)

He also attempted a snack, saltines topped with Nutella and a green olive garnish. He sampled one, and it wasn't as tasty as the snacks Laurie prepared.

"Would you look at this spread?" Laurie said when he put the tray on the coffee table. "You did this? All by yourself? Martha Stewart couldn't have done a better job."

Aaron was embarrassed about the fuss she was making over such a small gesture, particularly since their conversation was about to get dicey. Laurie sat beside him on the couch, shifting her backside to get comfortable. She sampled a snack and made yum-yum noises. He noticed she ignored her drink. He didn't blame her. It looked like a glass of whale spit.

"What's the occasion?" she said.

"No occasion at all. Did you have a pleasant day?"

"I did, thank you. I'll miss the library the most of all my temping jobs, but at least Ramona has agreed to be my assistant. She can help with proofreading, fan mail, and social media."

Aaron had met Ramona twice and each time she glowered at him as if she were plotting his murder. It was odd that a person as lighthearted as Laurie would choose such a sinister-looking friend.

"My editor said it would be a good idea to hire some help, and with my advance I can afford it." Her voice lilted when she said "my editor," just as it did when she said "my agent." It was still a novelty for her to say those words. Aaron knew how excited Laurie was about the new developments in her life, and that made his task all the more onerous.

"Speaking of which..."

"Yes?"

Aaron cracked his knuckles on both hands as a stalling technique. "I read your book *Don't Mess With Tex*. I finished it a couple of hours ago."

"Really?" Laurie jostled her cracker and olives scattered across her lap. "How did you get it?"

"A bootleg site."

"Oh no! I've been emailing those people trying to make them to take my books down...But I can't believe you read it! That's so very sweet. What did you think?" Laurie's cheeks flushed an appealing shade of pink. "I know you aren't wild about romance but—"

Aaron was tempted to say, "It wasn't worth the papyrus it was penned on," but that phrase got him in trouble too often, and he loved Laurie and didn't want to be unduly harsh with her. He remembered once reading an article about using the sandwich method for critiques: First you said something nice and then you pointed out the flaws, and lastly, you ended with another positive comment.

"I laughed several times," he began.

"Really? Which scenes? I want to know." She grabbed his wrist in a dramatic gesture. "Was it the time she locked herself in the pantry and—"

Aaron held up a finger. "In writing workshops it's customary to remain silent while one's work is being evaluated."

"Sorry. I'll hush." She mimed zipping her lips and tossing a key over her shoulder.

Aaron mentioned the things he liked, and he could see Laurie was struggling to remain silent; she fidgeted in her seat.

Then he discussed the problem areas, of which there were many. The longer he went on, the more she drooped. It was like witnessing a stop-gap film of a daisy wilting. Was it possible she'd never been critiqued before?

It was time to end with something positive, and he realized he couldn't think of anything else good to say so he finished up with the following remarks: "You double spaced your document, and the formatting looks very professional."

Laurie took in a big noisy gulp of air as if she'd been holding her breath during the entire critique. "Okay...I guess there are a few problems, and luckily I have an editor who can help me with my new book. But overall, you thought it was funny and sexy...right?"

Obviously she'd only taken in the bread of the sandwich and had completely ignored the meat.

"Overall I thought it was..."

Laurie cocked her head. Her eyes were large and pleading, like Dusty when he'd gone wee-wee in the house. For a brief moment he considered telling her what she wanted to hear instead of the truth, but no...sugarcoating her flaws would not help her to become a better writer.

"It was..." He lowered his voice a decibel. "Dreadful. In almost every respect."

Laurie flinched as if he'd slapped her.

"I hoped it was going to be an accomplished genre novel, but it wasn't. It's clearly the work of an unschooled writer, albeit a writer with potential for growth. I suspect W&W is not paying you for your abilities as a wordsmith. They're paying you because film rights were sold to your manuscript. I also think the publisher's counting on your obvious physical appeal to move books. I know this is difficult to hear but—"

Laurie violently waved her hands in front of her face as if she were caught in a cloud of gnats. "Stop it. Just stop right now."

"I apologize. I know it's sometimes upsetting to be critiqued and I—"

"This isn't a critique! This is a baby seal clubbing! It's a kitten drowning. It's a—"

"Now, Laurie," he said gently. "If you're ever going to be taken seriously as a writer, you need to develop a thicker skin."

"My skin is as thick as a Hermes bag." She tossed the cracker on the plate and it cracked into several pieces. "And by the way, your snack tastes like mud."

"Laurie, please—"

"I know what this is all about. Oh yes, sir, I do."

"What?"

Her lacquered fingernail was inches from his face; it was like a tiny hot pink bayonet. "Delilah warned me about this. You, Aaron Mite, are jealous of my success. You can't handle it."

"Excuse me?"

"My star's rising just as yours is falling and it's eating away at you. Instead of feeling happy for me, you've decided to undermine me."

Aaron sighed. How could she misread him so completely? Did she have no idea of how agonizing this was for him?

"You're wrong. I'm not envious of you. I'm telling you these things because I think you're being exploited and because I care about you."

"Nice try, buddy. But be honest. You've always considered yourself the real writer in this relationship, haven't you?" She wagged her fingers to indicate air quotes around the word "real."

"Well, I—"

"And you're embarrassed I write romance novels. You think they're beneath you."

"Not beneath me exactly. They're certainly not my favorite—"

"And I'd bet my last dollar that if you didn't initially mistake me for your precious Laura T. Leer, you wouldn't have had anything to do with a lowly genre writer like me."

"Laurie, please."

"But now that I'm outshining you, it's killing you."

Her last statement was more than he could take.

"You are not outshining me."

"Oh really?"

He couldn't stop himself. "I have an MFA. I've studied the Craft. I spent five years working on my novel, and it's my second effort. You've only recently entered into the profession. There's no comparison between us. If this novel is anything like the one you're writing, it will be awful. It's simply not very good."

"So now I'm not good enough for you!"

"Not *you*. Your writing."

"My writing is an extension of me. If you think it's no good, you must also think I'm no good."

"It's very common for amateur writers to mix up their work with their identities. In fact—"

Laurie gasped. "I am *not* an amateur. I'm being paid a whole lot of money by a huge publisher to write a novel, and you're eaten up with envy...You need to leave before I say something I'll regret."

"That might be a good idea. I'll give you some space to process—"

"No. I mean for good."

"What? Move out?"

"Yes. Big changes are happening in my life, and I want a man who will lift me up, not tear me down."

"I'm not—"

"A mistake brought us together. Clearly we were never meant to be together forever. Think about it. You've never even introduced me to your father. And now I understand why. You're ashamed of me."

"I rarely see my father myself. And yes, he's a bit of an elitist and wouldn't understand our relationship, but I'm not like him."

"I think you are," she said softly.

"Laurie. This has gotten out of hand."

She stood and gave him a resigned look. "I'm going on a drive. When I come back, I'd like you to be gone, please."

"Can't we talk about this?"

She ignored him to give Dusty a kiss on the top of his head. "Bye, sweetie." Then she fled the room in tears. A few moments later he heard her VW bug pull out of the drive.

Aaron sat silently on the couch, staring at his sad little snack tray and the untouched Pink or rather Gray Lady. The smell of peaches still lingered in the air. Aaron took one last deep inhale of her fragrance, and then he headed to the bedroom to gather his belongings.

Aaron checked into the Motel 6, smuggling Dusty in with him. He spent the entire night on top of the cheap polyester bedspread, staring listlessly at a dagger-shaped water stain on the ceiling. The next day he rented a room that allowed dogs in an old house near the Metro Atlanta University campus.

It was more of an alcove than a room, and it was infested with fleas. Luckily Dusty was protected with his flea medicine, but Aaron was bitten several times while moving his things in. He stopped by the grocery store and called in sick for his teaching duties and didn't leave for the next five days, except to take Dusty out. The only reason he finally did leave was because Dusty exhausted his jumbo bag of Wavy Treats.

Two days later

From: Bernie
To: Aaron Mite
Subject: Good news
Andrea's promoted me to the foreign rights department. She also said I could take on a client or two. Interested?
Bernie

From: Aaron Mite
To: Bernie
Subject: Okay
Thanks for thinking of me.
Respectfully,
Aaron
P.S. Laurie and I are no longer a couple.

From: Bernie
To: Aaron Mite
Sorry to hear it. Hopefully we can find a home for your book and you can forget about what's-her-name.
Bernie

Bernie called Aaron and said he planned on submitting Aaron's novel to Featherstone. Aaron said, "I can't imagine you'll get a response. As you know, they never got back to Andrea, and you don't have her clout."

"Maybe not," Bernie said. "But I am one of the most persistent guys you'll ever meet. Rachel Fogelstein, the prettiest girl at Hoboken High School, got twenty-two invitations for the senior prom. Guess who took her?"

"You?"

"No. But I was the first runner-up. Anyway, I'm going to work on a pitch letter to Featherstone tonight. I think I got a line on a connection there. Apparently their UPS delivery guy is the same guy who eats every Saturday night at my Uncle Buzz's pizza shop. It's not much, but you never know."

Sixteen

Delilah left the kids with Bart back in Swainsboro and came to Laurie's house bearing five boxes of Girl Scout cookies and five bottles of wine. "Specially paired," she said. "There's an app that does it. Your favorite, Do-si-dos, goes best with a California Zin."

"Let's pop open a bottle now," Laurie said, ushering her inside the house. "I've cried so much I'm dehydrated."

Over the next couple of hours, Delilah, being the awesome bosom buddy that she was, let her friend tell the story of the breakup at least ten times and readily agreed that Laurie was blameless and Aaron behaved like an uncivilized ape.

"You don't suppose he could be right, do you?" Laurie said. They were on their third bottle of wine. "That I'm a terrible writer?"

Delilah's lips were a lurid purple and Thin Mint crumbs dotted her white sundress. "Of course he's not right. Since when do publishers throw money at untalented authors just for kicks?"

"Exactly. And you tried to warn me about this, but I didn't want to listen. Did I tell you what Aaron said about my writing?"

"A dozen times, but I'm happy to hear it again."

"He said it was dreadful! If that isn't the most hateful word."

"A shame. I was hoping I was wrong about Aaron because you seemed so happy with him."

"I was," Laurie said plaintively.

"In a different way than you were with Jake."

"What do you mean?" Laurie said quickly. "I was very happy with Jake."

Delilah opened her mouth and closed it again.

"I adored Jake. For months after his death I could barely function." Her eyes started welling up. "You sound like Kate. Why would anyone think that I didn't love my husband? What kind of person would that make me?"

"I'm not suggesting you didn't love him...I just thought...That you and Aaron... Never mind."

"It's true. I cared about Aaron. But Jake was the love of my life. I assumed you knew that."

"I don't know what I was thinking. Must be the wine." Delilah stood, swaying a bit. "And on that note, I think we need some more."

Delilah left in the morning, and a hungover Laurie went into her office to work on the novel. She was having a hard time of it. She kept thinking about her distressing conversation with Delilah. Also, she couldn't stop hearing Aaron's voice in her head. Every choice she made she second guessed. But write she must. She'd receive a huge portion of her advance once she delivered the full manuscript. That meant she wouldn't have to worry about money for a long while.

She bought an extra desk and computer for Ramona, and now they both worked in the study. Ramona was designing a new website for Laurie and a social media strategy. It was pleasant to have someone around, even if it was a morose someone who was wearing too much of a perfume called Death's Bride. According to Ramona it was made from myrrh, wormwood, and crypt dust with a dribble of blood red musk.

One afternoon, two weeks after the breakup, Laurie and Ramona were working in the study when the phone rang.

"Laurie Lee's cell phone," Ramona said. It was her job to answer the phone. "One moment." She handed Laurie the phone. "It's your editor."

"Hi, Bridget," Laurie said breathlessly. She loved when her editor called. She was the connection to the glamorous world of book publishing, and every call from Bridget validated Laurie's identity as a real-life writer.

"I have great news."

"Another foreign sale?" Laurie couldn't get over the idea that people in other countries would be reading her work. Like the Japanese, who didn't even have the same alphabet, for goodness sakes.

"This isn't related to your novel. I'm sure you're familiar with R.K. Harris. He's one of my authors."

"Of course. I thought *Love's Prophet* was one of the most touching romances I've ever read." Laurie wasn't as wild about R.K. Harris's follow-up books. Still, she usually bought his new releases.

"Ross saw your photo in *Us Magazine,* and guess what? He emailed me saying he'd like to meet you. They're making a movie based on his third book and it's being filmed in Atlanta. He'll be on set for a few weeks as a script consultant."

"He wants to go out with me?" Laurie still remembered certain lines from *Love's Prophet*. She'd read it three or four times, and during each instance she wondered what kind of man could write such a tender love story.

"Yes. Can he call you?"

"Normally I would say yes, but I'm actually so busy these days." She didn't want to share her messy personal life with her editor.

"Are you saying you don't have time for one little phone call?"

Laurie pulled a R.K. Harris novel from the shelf in her study and turned it over to examine the author photo. R.K.'s hair was artfully messy, and his teeth were white and uniform. He resembled a lifeguard, broad-shouldered and sun-kissed.

"He's extremely charming," Bridget said.

"Yes, but—"

"And even better-looking in person. If he ever asked me out—and he never has—I'd be the happiest editor in New York City. And you never know, he might just blurb your book. I can't tell you how helpful that would be."

That clinched it. After what happened with Aaron, she half expected her editor to tell her she'd made a mistake and W&W wouldn't be publishing her book after all. So in effort to keep herself in Bridget's good graces, she agreed, but didn't anticipate anything more than a chat with R.K.

A few minutes later, the phone rang and it was R.K. Harris. For privacy's sake, Laurie left the study and took the call in her bedroom, sitting on her ruffled bedspread. They made small talk for a few moments, and he was easygoing and casual. He even managed to make her laugh, but when he mentioned coming into town, she found herself wanting to get off the phone.

"As I told Bridget, I'm so busy..."

"You're sure I can't coax you?" R.K. said.

He was very nice, but she was far too tender-hearted right now.

"I'm sorry. Maybe the next time you come into town."

"I understand. It's just that I thought you might want to meet China New. I was going to take you to a little party she's having. "

Laurie gasped. "*The* China New?"

"You're familiar with her? I wasn't sure because she's primarily a rom-com actress, and I know that some people think rom-coms are cheesy but—"

"I love rom-coms. I live for them."

"You're not just saying that to be nice?"

"Not at all. I would love to go to the party. But, R.K., there's something you should know."

"Call me Ross," he says. "R.K. is just for book covers."

"Ross then. It would have to be a friendly excursion. I'm not on the dating market right now."

"Point taken. I'll behave myself."

They made some arrangements and then ended the call. Laurie opened *Love's Prophet* and read the first line: "I thought I knew the meaning of love, and then I met Jessica." Ross's entire novel came flooding back to her. If the man was anything like his novel, he had a keen understanding of what women wanted.

Seventeen

Aaron spent too much time watching television, a regrettable habit he'd picked up at Laurie's house. Friday evening he noticed that one of the channels was having a Rom-Com Weekend Watch-A-Thon. Wistful for Laurie, he decided to watch his very first romantic comedy, *When Harry Met Sally*. He was expecting the worst, but instead the strong acting, clever dialogue and situations pleasantly surprised him.

For the whole weekend, Aaron sat in his dark alcove watching rom-coms. Some were full of clichés and insipid, but many were entertaining. Quickly he learned the tropes of the genre: a goofy best friend sidekick, opposites attracting and a romantic false lead. The trope that interested him most was the romantic gesture. Near the end of every movie, things looked grim for the film couple, but then one of them, almost always the male, pulled off a romantic gesture and got the girl back.

Aaron hadn't thought about the possibility of winning Laurie back—he'd never been particularly proactive in relationships—but he was intrigued by the idea. If it worked in the movies that Laurie loved, maybe it would work in real life.

All rom-coms also had declarations of love and his favorite was the one in *Jerry Maguire*. Jerry said to his girlfriend, in front of a gaggle of her female cohorts: "You complete me."

Ever since he moved out of Laurie's cheerful little house, Aaron felt like he'd lost part of himself, perhaps the most important part. He'd like to say, "You complete me" to Laurie, but likely she had already seen *Jerry Maguire*, and stealing the line would be plagiarism.

Perhaps if he paraphrased with proper attribution, of course. He sat on his futon and used his laptop to type some thoughts.

"Without you, I'm Ted Hughes without Sylvia Plath..."

No. She probably wouldn't understand the reference, and even if she did, it was a tad morbid.

He tried again: "Without you, I'm a bookstore without a copy of a Nick Windust novel."

No. Not particularly romantic and not personal enough. He needed something she'd immediately understand, some sort of shared moment between them.

And then an idea came to him. He remembered the time she went out and purchased numerous jars of jelly so he wouldn't have to eat bread with only peanut butter.

"Without you," he wrote, "I am peanut butter without jelly."

Not quite right.

"Without you, I am Jif without jelly."

Better because of the alliteration. And it was also apt because, without Laurie, he was not nearly as palatable. He needed her sweetness as a balance. Furthermore, when he made his love declaration to her, he planned to hold a jar of Jif. He noticed a number of romantic heroes employed props—John Cusak and his boom box in *Say Anything* for example. Who knew? If he was lucky she might even respond to his declaration of love by saying, "You had me at Jif."

Aaron glanced at his watch. It was five p.m., and Laurie was likely drinking her girly cocktail. Wouldn't it be nice if he could spend happy hour with her? He'd sorely missed their nightly ritual.

He stopped by the grocery store to buy a jar of Jif. He only had no-brand almost-gone peanut butter in his room, and it was probably not very romantic to give someone a near empty jar of peanut butter. After making the purchase, he drove to Laurie's house, and on the way he rehearsed his speech. He knocked on her door, jumpy with expectation. In movies romantic gestures always worked beautifully, but it was hard to say what might happen in real life.

Laurie opened the door. Aaron had conjured her up in his mind many times over the last few weeks, but his memories of her couldn't touch the reality. It was the difference between seeing a black-and-white photograph of a peach and biting into the juiciest, most succulent peach of your life. She looked so lovely, he momentarily forgot his lines.

"Aaron? What are you doing here?"

He thrust the jar of peanut butter in her direction and said, "Without you I am jelly without Jif."

Wait. That wasn't right.

"I don't understand...Are you saying you want to borrow some jelly?"

"No. I don't want jelly...You're the jelly, and I'm the peanut butter, or rather the Jif and I—This Jif is for you and I'm the—"

A male voice said, "Who's at the door, Laurie?"

Aaron's stomach dropped. Had she already replaced him?

A familiar face loomed into view. It was Ross Harris, looking aggressively handsome. His skin was bathed in a patina of gold light as if he traveled with his own cinematographer.

"What is he doing here?" Aaron asked. He pointed at Ross. "I went to school with him."

"I heard all about that," Laurie said. She wrinkled her nose, implying that Ross had told her something unpleasant. "Why are you here, Aaron?"

"Is Ross Harris your new male companion?" Aaron said.

"I'd rather not discuss that."

"You can't be with him."

The vehemence in his delivery surprised even him.

Laurie raised an eyebrow. "And why is that may I ask?"

"He's the romantic false lead."

"Excuse me?"

"Like Hugh Grant in *Bridget Jones's Diary* or Warner in *Legally Blonde*."

Laurie widened her eyes. "What do you know about those movies?"

"I viewed a Rom-Com Watch-a-Thon this weekend."

"And how does the peanut butter fit in?" she said.

"It's the, uh... romantic gesture."

Laurie still looked confused. His romantic gesture was turning out to be a flop. "But I don't like Jif," she said. "I eat Planters."

"Planters isn't alliterative."

She was blinking as if agitated. "Aaron, I'm sorry. I don't know why you're here. But a jar of peanut butter isn't going to fix things between us. It's a little naive of you to think that."

"Then what will fix things? I miss you, Laurie."

She stared at him, her eyes wide and shiny. "You do?"

He nodded.

"Maybe you could take back what you said about my novel."

Aaron paused a moment, tempted. But he'd be lying to her, and as much as he wanted Laurie back, dishonesty was not the right way to go about it. What kind of relationship would they have if he only said what she wanted to hear?

"I'm sorry. I can't do that," Aaron said.

"What?"

"I may have been too hard on you. My choice of words might have been—"

"Enough. We're not having this conversation anymore. Goodbye, Aaron. And by the way, Ross loves my writing."

She slammed the door shut. Ross remained on the steps, shaking his head. His eyes were a mesmerizing sapphire color, like a character in Laurie's novel. So different from Aaron's eyes, which were such a light gray they were almost colorless and possessed no mesmerizing qualities whatsoever. Suddenly Aaron wanted to punch Ross square in his oversized jaw. But it would be like a gnat taking on a windshield.

Ross pointed at the jar of peanut butter and laughed. "That's lame, Aaron. Even for you."

"What do you mean?"

"Peanut butter is nobody's idea of a romantic gesture. Romantic gestures have to be grand. You also tried to win Laurie back using tropes from a genre you supposedly despise. How tragic you missed that irony."

Aaron glanced down at the peanut butter jar, not knowing what to say. "I was...I thought that—"

"Save it. Just like you can't learn to write literary fiction overnight, you can't learn how to please a woman like Laurie by watching a few rom-coms. When you showed me her photograph in New York, I knew she was out of your league, and it was only a matter of time before she broke it off. She'll be much happier with me. I specialize in pleasing women."

"Does being a woman pleaser also mean you don't mind lying to Laurie? Because I'm certain even *you* recognized the flaws in her fiction writing."

"Your trouble is you don't understand publishing, Aaron. Good writing simply isn't that important. Laurie has a savvy editor. It'll all work out for her."

"How can you say that? Good writing is the most important thing."

"You're such a dinosaur." He winked. "Better get back to Laurie. You don't keep a woman like that waiting."

He slipped back inside, and Aaron was tempted to lob the peanut butter jar at Ross's head, but he had a lousy throwing arm. He also hated to waste a perfectly good jar of peanut butter, especially since he was almost out at home.

"I gave Aaron a chance to redeem himself," Laurie said to Delilah over the phone. She wore headphones, freeing up her hands so she could tidy up the house. "And he refused to take it. So I say, 'Good riddance.'"

"Exactly. Who needs him?"

"Aaron brought me peanut butter. He thought that was romantic."

"Ha! For our last anniversary Bart gave me Spanx. I wanted to Spanx him. Bart said, 'I overheard you saying you wanted some.' I said, 'Not from you! It'd be like me giving you Rogaine for a gift.' And he said, 'I wouldn't mind you giving me Rogaine.'"

Laurie gathered up a stack of fashion magazines and dropped them in an overflowing recycle bin. "Men truly are from a different planet. Except for Ross. He's always says and does the right thing."

"Funny, but you don't sound too excited about him."

Laurie mashed down the magazines with her foot. "We're still just friends. I haven't even kissed him yet, but I wanted to when he told me how much he loved my writing. Did I tell you Aaron watched a bunch of rom-coms?"

"You may have mentioned it, three or four times."

Laurie moved on to the hamper. She dumped her clothes on the laundry room floor and started separating them into colors and whites. "As if that could win me back. It's clear he doesn't respect me."

"Exactly," Delilah said. "And yet..."

"What?"

"You kind of have to admire the guy for sticking with his opinion."

"Even though it's wrong?"

"In his mind, it wasn't."

"That's because he's a terrible snob. Ross confirmed that. He said that when Aaron was in New York, he criticized Ross's work. And of course, Ross is a bestselling author. If it's not literary writing, Aaron thinks it's garbage...By the way, Ross gave me a wonderful blurb, even though the book isn't finished yet. He said the cutest thing: 'I don't have to eat the whole cake to know it's delicious.' My editor was so pleased."

"It seems like you and Ross have so much more in common than you and Aaron. You know what they say: Birds of a feather."

Laurie sighed. "It's true. Aaron and I would have never gotten together if we didn't have that misunderstanding. It's amazing we stayed together as long as we did."

She picked up a white button-down shirt. It was Aaron's. It must have been at the bottom of the hamper.

"I guess it's for the best then," Delilah said.

"Yes. For the best."

She took a long sniff of Aaron's shirt. It still smelled like him. Maybe she'd wait a bit before washing it.

The next day Aaron woke up and instead of wanting to pull the covers over his head like usual, a crazed kind of energy possessed him.

For a solid week he was caught in a writing frenzy, and whenever he completed a chapter he emailed it to Bernie. He'd been subsisting on Red Bull and No-Doze and hadn't bathed since he began. After he completed the tenth chapter, he called Bernie to see what his agent thought of his new novel thus far.

"Bernie Fields, literary agent extraordinaire, maker of bestsellers."

"You may be the only literary agent who answers his own phone."

"That's because I can't find a secretary who will work for Skittles and sexual favors."

Bernie was kidding. Aaron's literary agent was happily married.

"Did you have a chance to read what I've sent you?"

"I have."

"I can't seem to stop writing. I've never written so fast in my life."

"So I see."

"What do you think?"

"It's definitely a departure from your usual work."

"That's because this one is coming from my gut."

"I'm a little taken aback by all the graphic violence...It's disturbing."

"Excellent. That's what I was going for."

"I'm also wondering if it might be too episodic. You have a serial killer who keeps killing the same type of guy."

"It's his profile. I did the research. Serial killers always have profiles."

"Yeah, well, it might be improbable that the killer would kill only male bestselling novelists who write love stories. How many guys like that could there be?"

"So you don't like the novel?"

"I think it might be less novel and more catharsis. Did something happen? Do you want to talk about it?"

"Are you saying you don't like it? Because if you don't, I can always shop it with someone else."

"You sure you're okay? You sound...peculiar."

"I'm fine. I haven't slept in three days, but I don't seem to miss it. Gotta go. Time to write the next chapter."

Aaron woke up on the floor of his room, and at least a dozen places on his skin were begging for a scratch. He didn't remember falling asleep; it must have happened when he was typing. He had no idea what time it was or how long he'd been asleep. All he knew was he wanted to get back to his novel-in-progress.

After taking care of his and Dusty's morning physiological needs, he returned to his laptop. He decided to reread some of his previous chapters to get him back into the flow of the novel. He started at the beginning, and after reading several pages, stared at the screen in disbelief. The writing was the ravings of a basket case. He was so disturbed by what he'd written, he deleted the entire document.

What was happening to him? Where did all these tumultuous emotions come from? He'd never in his life felt so out of control. And if this was the kind of writing his life was bringing out of him, why did he even bother? His father was right. He would never make a name for himself as a writer.

Someone knocked on his door; he glanced about his room as if seeing it for the first time in a long while. It was cluttered with Red Bull cans, M&M wrappers and other debris. He was also aware that his teeth were fuzzy, and that he smelled like the inside of a laundry hamper.

He considered ignoring the knock; there was no one he wanted to see.

"Cowboy? Are you in there?"

Bernie? It couldn't be. Bernie lived in Hoboken. Aaron talked to him only a few hours ago. He must be having auditory hallucinations. But no. Dusty barked. He heard it too.

"I know you're in there. I can hear you breathing. Open up."

Aaron opened the door. Bernie was standing outside wearing a loud Hawaiian shirt and smelling like a Philly Cheesesteak.

"Nice jammies," he said. Aaron was wearing the ones Laurie gave him.

"Thank you." Aaron was still in a state of shock at the sight of his literary agent.

"Jesus. It's worse than I thought." Bernie pinched his nostrils and waved the air. "You're not the Walking Dead, you're the Walking Decomposed. Good thing I decided to check on you." He slapped at his ankle. "Damn. This place is infested." Dusty approached and jumped on his legs. "And now I see why."

"Dusty is completely flea-free. I just need to..." Aaron blinked and stared. "Is it really you?"

"Last time I checked."

"When did we last talk?"

"Two days ago."

"I've lost two days?"

"Sounds like it. I would have come even sooner, but I had to scrounge up the cash for a plane ticket. Which I will deduct from your advance when we sell your novel."

"Why did you come?"

"Because I was afraid you were about to jump off a ten-story building without a net."

"I would never do that." He patted Dusty's head. "As you can see, there's someone who relies on me. But I can't believe you came all this way because you were worried about me."

"I sure as hell didn't come for the Falcons. Have you been following their season?"

"I think..."

"Yeah?" Bernie deposited his duffle bag on the floor.

"I think..."

"Spit it out before you choke on it."

"I think this might be one of the nicest things anyone has ever done for me."

Bernie scratched his calf; he was wearing black socks with sandals. "It's not that nice. You're my most valuable client, mostly because you're my only client."

Aaron felt a tickle in the back of his throat. He'd like to say more but wasn't skilled at demonstrating his feelings. Dusty, on the other hand, had no such reservations; he was getting a bit too friendly with Bernie's leg.

Aaron pried the dog away. "I'm sorry. He's been doing that lately. I think he misses Laurie."

"Maybe, but I also notice your little guy still has his balls. Take him in for a snip-snip, and he'll quit romancing people's extremities."

Aaron nodded. "I'll call the vet in the morning."

That night Bernie slept on the futon and snored quite loudly—he sounded like a clogged DustBuster—but Aaron didn't mind. He'd never had a male buddy before. As a school boy he was always somewhat of a loner, mostly because his father discouraged him from having friends over to the house.

By the time he got to college he was in the habit of keeping to himself. In grad school he met Emma and male companionship seemed unnecessary, especially since he didn't have the typical manly interests such as football, cars, blood sports and binge drinking.

Thus his interactions with Bernie were novel, and he was enjoying the male perspective. Bernie liked sports bars, and over the next few days they visited several in the Atlanta area. In a show of solidarity, Aaron occasionally shouted at the television when Bernie's teams scored.

One night they were at a sports bar called the Arena. Earlier Aaron had tried to order a Pink Lady (he was feeling lonesome for Laurie) and Bernie said to the bartender, "He's joking! Give him something that will turn his balls to steel. A hearty stout maybe or a shot of Jagermeister."

Bernie drained the last bit of beer from his mug and signaled the bartender for another. He grabbed a fried onion from a bristling concoction called a Blooming Onion. Aaron didn't partake; his appetite had dwindled ever since the breakup.

"So the chapters you were sending me," Bernie said, chewing with his mouth open. "Obviously about R.K. Harris, right?"

Aaron nodded. "I apologize. I temporarily lost my mind. That's never happened before."

Bernie clapped him on the back. "No apology necessary. Sometimes it's healthy to go a little psycho. And who can blame you? Your girlfriend ran off with a pretty boy multimillionaire who writes love stories for a living. Doesn't get much worse than that."

"I worry that he's a womanizer. He had a number of girlfriends in graduate school."

"Guys like that are always womanizers. Hell, if I looked like him, I'd be a womanizer too. Lucky for my wife, I look like a Brillo pad with legs and a moustache."

"Not only is he a womanizer, he's a schlock writer," Aaron said.

"Then they're two of a kind, aren't they? And I don't know about Laurie, but I'm sure R.K. sees the relationship as a savvy business move. Great publicity to hook up with a fellow romance writer who, according to *Vanity Fair*, gives new meaning to the words 'Hot Type.' My guess is he's envisioning dozens of photo ops and profile pieces, which means more book sales, and I'm sure that's the only thing he cares about."

"You think he's using her?"

"Could be. Or it might be a mutual arrangement. People like Laurie and Ross are different than you and me. They don't live the examined life because they don't have to. They're like water bugs, skimming the surface of a pond, never getting too wet. Guys like us? We're living on the floor of it with the muck and the bottom dwellers. "

"Maybe Ross, but not Laurie. She's not that way."

Bernie wiped beer foam and bits of onion from his moustache. "Gorgeous girl like that? Naturally you're hoping she has depth. But most gorgeous girls are like beautifully wrapped presents. When you open them up, all you get is packing peanuts."

"I'm not sure I can take another simile," Aaron said. "At least not on an empty stomach."

"Gotcha. I should leave the writing to you. Don't sweat this disappointment too much. I guarantee you, one day you'll get over Laurie and you'll find the girl for you, just like I found my Mookie."

Aaron knew all about Mookie. Every night Bernie called his wife and talked to her for at least a half hour. Mookie's name was actually Dolores. Mookie was her nickname, but oddly it was also Bernie's nickname. Every night Bernie would say, "You're the best Mookie...No. I'm not the best Mookie, you're the best Mookie."

They had the same exchange every night about who was the best Mookie. The dilemma was never resolved.

"How did you know Mookie was the one?" Aaron said.

"What are you? Some kind of moron?"

Bernie was hollering at the TV, not Aaron. When they were in a sports bar it was a three-way conversation between Aaron, Bernie, and the big screen.

"The thing about Mookie is...Hey, dipshit! You need to get glasses...On my own I'm kind of a schlemiel, but when I'm around Mookie...Christ! Did you see that?"

"Yes?" Aaron said, waiting.

"She makes me want to be a better man. I try harder around her."

In some ways that was true with Laurie. When Aaron was

around her he felt like an enhanced HD version of himself. But perhaps he wasn't enhanced enough. Otherwise she wouldn't have banished him from her life.

That night Aaron drank more than he should, and Bernie held his elbow as he stumbled into his room. Dusty hopped up from his doggie bed and greeted Aaron at the threshold. Aaron scooped him up, and Dusty licked his face.

"That dog loves you like you're made of liverwurst," Bernie said. "Funny thing is I wouldn't have figured you as a dog person."

"I wasn't. My father never allowed me pets, and after I was old enough to live on my own, I was so devoted to writing I didn't feel like I had time for one."

"So how did this hairy guy come into your life?"

Aaron slumped on the sofa with Dusty on his lap, and told Bernie the story.

When he got to the part about seeing Dusty all alone by the dumpster and trembling in the storm, he said, "I looked at that frightened little puppy, and I saw myself."

"Don't tell me you were abandoned in a dumpster."

"No." He told Bernie the story of his mother's death and when he was done, Bernie let out a low whistle.

"I'm sorry, cowboy. That is one of the hell of a sad story."

"There's one part I left out." Aaron could hear the slur in his voice. "A part I've never told anyone. Not even Laurie."

"Are you sure you want to tell me?"

"I do." Aaron paused for a moment. "I was responsible for my mother's death."

"What? How you figure that?"

"I'd taken the batteries from the radio and put them in my dump truck. If I hadn't done that, we wouldn't have gone upstairs early and she'd still be alive."

Bernie shook his head. "I can understand why you might think like that, but you're wrong. This world's mysterious. It's hard to understand why people come in and out of it."

Aaron sighed heavily. "I realize I didn't mean to cause her

death, but after that, I always felt tainted. Like I didn't deserve anything good in my life. Whenever I'm happy I know it's never going to last, and it never does."

"Sounds like a self-fulfilling prophecy to me. Maybe it's time to start changing your expectations."

"Maybe," Aaron said.

But he had no idea how to begin. For so many years he'd always expected the worse.

Aaron took Bernie to the Hartsfield-Jackson International Airport in the morning and when they reached the Delta terminal, Bernie said, "Thanks for the ride. It saved me scheckles on a cab."

"You're welcome."

"Take care, cowboy, and keep on writing." He mimed a pencil traveling across paper. "Daddy needs to buy himself a new pair of Docksiders."

"One more thing before you leave." A car horn blared, and Aaron raised his voice. "Why do you always call me cowboy?"

"Do you know a lot about cowboys?"

"Not really."

"Cowboys inspire me. They're out there on the range, day after day, isolated, singing their cowboy songs. They're almost an anachronism but they don't care. They have a way of life to defend, kind of the way you defend Craft. It's a noble pursuit."

"Thank you," Aaron said, although he couldn't say he deserved the compliment. During his first year in the MFA program he may have been more like a cowboy, singing the praises of Craft for the sheer joy of it. But that feeling of jubilation eventually faded, and he'd become increasingly jaded and judgmental. Laurie might not be the best writer in the world, but she had the jubilation part down pat. Aaron hoped he hadn't taken that away from her.

He and Bernie stood awkwardly facing each other, not speaking. Doors slammed; travelers passed by trailing wheeled bags that squeaked over the pavement. Exhaust curled from the backs of cars, and the heat from the sidewalk penetrated the thin soles of Aaron's shoes. It occurred to him that maybe a hug was in order, but he was afraid of offending Bernie's masculine sensibilities so instead he extended his hand.

Bernie ignored it and gave him an embrace that felt like a mauling. He said, "Aaron, deep down I think you're one of the good guys. I get you, and I also understand what you're defending. That girlfriend of yours didn't. You were over her head, cowboy."

He trod to the terminal, duffle bag slung over his shoulder. Aaron was sorry to see him leave as he had enjoyed their interactions. He also felt badly that he wasn't completely honest with his friend. Bernie wouldn't be getting new Docksiders anytime soon—at least not from the sale of Aaron's future novels. He'd decided to give up writing for a while. It was just one more thing in his life that had soured on him. It was time to get practical and focus on a back-up career. He was going to follow his father's wishes and put all his energy into a PhD program.

Eighteen

Aaron couldn't stand his own company for one more second. Earlier in the day, at Bernie's advice, he took Dusty to the vet to get him fixed. After the procedure, the vet wanted to keep him overnight because of a complication. "Just a precaution," she said. "Nothing to fret about." But Aaron couldn't stop worrying. He decided to go out to a sports bar to escape his thoughts, his lonely room and Dusty's empty dog bed.

Without Bernie, he felt like an imposter entering Player's Grill. He almost expected a bouncer to pull him aside and quiz him about which team won last year's Super Bowl. There was no room at the bar, so Aaron took a seat at one of the small tables beneath a neon Harley Davidson sign. A waitress wearing a plaid shirt and an abbreviated pair of blue jean shorts approached.

Aaron ordered Bernie's beverage of choice, a Pabst Blue Ribbon. He called it a "PBR" instead of using the entire name, which made him feel more like an insider.

Once his order was placed, he glanced up at one of the many large-screen TVs affixed to the wall behind the bar. The sport *du jour* was soccer. The beer arrived, and it was watery and nearly tasteless. He pretended to watch the game—or was it a match?—but his mind was elsewhere.

"Is this a mirage or what? Aaron Mite in a sports bar? Drinking a beer?"

Emma stood by his table. Instead of wearing her usual cross

expression she was smiling. She grabbed his beer—she never had any food or drink boundaries—and sipped it.

Her nose wrinkled. "If you're going to start drinking beer, I better teach you what kind of beer to drink."

She sat across from him and snapped her fingers to get the waitress's attention. When the waitress arrived, Emma said, "Take away this swill and bring us something decent."

"I'm surprised to see you here," Aaron said.

"I'm here under duress. See that guy over there?" She waved at a balding man a few tables away sitting underneath a NASCAR poster. He waved back and smiled. "That's my date. A blind date, I might add."

"I should let you get back to him."

"He's not a quart of milk, he'll keep. What are you doing here? Drowning your sorrows?"

"Sorrows don't drown; they briefly submerge only to float to the surface with greater fierceness."

"Who said that?" Emma said.

"Aaron Mite. Or rather, a character in Aaron Mite's unpublished novel."

"I thought it sounded familiar. I suppose this sorrow is all about the loss of the bottle blonde?"

"How did you know?"

"I'm assuming since you're here alone."

Aaron reached for his beer but remembered it was no longer there, just a watery spot where it once sat sweating. "Yes. Laurie and I are no longer a couple. She's now with another writer, and I use that term loosely. R.K. Harris."

"You're kidding."

"You know of him?"

"I met him once at a booksellers convention and read one of his books. Talk about your sentimental clap trap."

The beers arrived, and they chatted about the usual things: novels they'd read, movies she'd seen, a new coffee shop that opened. He told her about the cancellation of his book contract.

Emma pouted. The expression seemed affected, as if she was attempting to be a coquette, and it was more disturbing than alluring. "That's too bad. I was hoping to add your book to my signed shelf."

In her den Emma kept a collection of signed books that took up three shelves.

"You said you hated my book."

She elbowed him in the ribs, more gently than usual. "You know I didn't mean it."

A half hour into their conversation, Emma's date, a round-faced man in a spotless white polo shirt, approached the table. "Hi, Emma...The movie we're supposed to see starts in fifteen minutes. Maybe we should get going?" He tapped his watch, a complicated device with several gears.

"You're still here?" Emma said. "I thought it was clear from my behavior that our date is over."

He nervously jangled the change in the pockets of his khakis. They looked like they'd been carefully pressed for the occasion. "Was it something I said? I thought we were getting along fine."

Aaron felt sorry him. He could tell the man was no match for Emma.

Emma waved her hand at him as if he was a housefly. "Scat...Vamoose...Don't make me sic my friend on you. He has a black belt in jiu-jitsu."

Her date hurriedly headed for the door, looking over his shoulder a couple of times as if worried Aaron would jump him. A laughable notion. Aaron had never laid a hand on anyone in his life, and the only black belt he had was the one that tied his bathrobe together.

"Now where were we?" Emma said.

Aaron yawned. "I suppose we should call it a night." He stood, preparing to leave.

"Not so fast, mister. You need to take me home. Remember I ditched my date?"

"That's right."

"Aaron Mite. Absentminded as ever!"

It was a typical Emma comment and would usually be delivered with a pinch that was a shade too hard. But no pinch came. She simply smiled and linked arms with him.

He drove Emma to her house and she said, "Are you coming in?"

He briefly considered it, but no. Emma was not what he needed right now. When he turned her down, he expected her to make a scathing remark, but instead she patted his arm and said, "Well, if you ever change your mind, you know where I live."

Aaron went to the vet to pick up Dusty, and while he waited for a staff member to bring him out, he studied a poster on the lifecycle of the heartworm. It was much more complex than he might have imagined. Luckily Dusty took a monthly pill to prevent an infestation.

Someone touched his hand, and Aaron turned around. It was the vet. She was a redhead in her late thirties and wore a smock decorated with fire hydrants. "Mr. Mite? Dusty's owner?"

"Yes." Aaron didn't care for the term "owner." Dusty was so much more than a possession. He was a beloved companion, and at the moment, he was Aaron's only companion.

"I'm afraid I have some upsetting news," she said. Her voice was solemn, her eyes large and conciliatory.

Aaron shook his head. He knew what she was about to say, but he couldn't bear to hear it.

"This kind of complication is so rare—"

"No," he said, backing out the door. If he left before she gave him the news, it wouldn't be true.

"We did everything we could. Dusty was such a sweet, dear little—"

"No."

"Again, I am so very sorry. He must have had a weak heart because—"

"No," Aaron said softly. "His heart was strong; it was biggest and strongest heart I've ever known."

The vet nodded sympathetically. "I don't know what you want to do with his remains. We can always take care of them for you, if that's what you—"

"No," Aaron said. This time it was not a "no" of denial but a statement. He took a long inhale of air and his entire body shuddered. "I'll take Dusty with me. He belongs with his Da."

Aaron drove around for over an hour not knowing where to go or what to do. Eventually he found himself in Laurie's driveway. He stared at her house for a long while and then finally got out of the car and knocked on the door.

Her friend Ramona answered, and she said Laurie wasn't working today because she was visiting a film set.

"With Ross." She was a very dour person but seemed almost gleeful giving him this upsetting news.

Aaron left and he drove around aimlessly for another half hour with his poor departed dog in a box on the passenger seat. He briefly wondered how far it was to Hoboken, and if his elderly Buick would make it, but no, Bernie had done enough for him already. He decided there was only one place else to go: Emma's house.

When he stood on her step, telling her about Dusty, he half expected her to roll her eyes—she was not a fan of animals—but she pulled him into her house and made him a stiff gin and tonic, ordering him to drink it as if it were medicine. Then she went out to the car for Dusty's remains and put the box in her freezer.

She listened without interrupting as Aaron talked about Dusty: how he always turned around a minimum of three times before he settled down on his bed, how he liked to steal socks, how deeply he hated the UPS man, how he would look at Aaron directly in the eyes when Aaron spoke to him as if he could understand every word.

"It's cliché to call him my best friend, but he was," Aaron said.

When Aaron told Emma he wanted Dusty to have a proper burial, instead of scoffing at him for his sentimentality, she searched the internet for pet cemeteries and found one called Rainbow Bridge that was only two miles from Aaron's house. She didn't say a word when Aaron agreed to pay one hundred dollars for an eco-friendly pet pod and a small monthly maintenance fee.

Dusty was buried with his beloved squeak toy, Squirrely, and a jumbo package of Wavy Treats. Emma was there, squeezing Aaron's hand when Dusty's pod was lowered into the ground and covered with dirt.

Aaron and Emma were lying side by side on her double bed underneath her squealing ceiling fan. The fan was held together by a couple of rusty bolts, and Aaron feared it would eventually fly apart and fall down on their heads.

He'd been spending every night with Emma since Dusty's death. There were too many memories of his dog in Aaron's rented room. Every time he was home he kept waiting to hear the scritch of toenails on the floor and see a small dark form, squirming with joy at his arrival.

"I always knew you and I would get back together," Emma said. "We're so much alike. When I saw you with that bottle blonde I knew the relationship wouldn't last. If she were a novel, she'd be a guilty pleasure, but you aren't the kind of person who goes in for guilty pleasures. You require gravitas, and I respect you for that. Certainly I see why you were attracted to her...She's easy on the eyes."

He reached over to pat Emma's bare shoulder. "You're easy on the eyes as well." Aaron was being truthful. Emma looked especially fetching tonight. Her cheeks were pleasantly flushed from the exertions of their earlier sexual intercourse and she'd cut her hair shorter. Now, instead of looking lank and lifeless, it curved around her chin in soft waves. Was she as pretty as Laurie? No, but few women were.

She recoiled from him. "Ugh. Don't even start."

"Start what?"

"Start trying to be something you're not. I know that I used to say you were inattentive to my needs. And you're probably trying to change that, but it's not you, Aaron, and it doesn't suit you anyway. If I'm going to be with you, I need to accept you the way you are. Gloomy, self-involved, unemotional."

"But I think might have changed. Maybe a little."

"Oh, please. People don't change. I read in *Psychology Today* that people's personalities are solidified by the time they're five. Face it. You're going to be the same for the rest of your life."

Aaron shifted positions on Emma's scratchy sheets. She bought them from a deep-discount store, and when she took them out of the package their folds were so pronounced they could cut butter. "You believe that and you still want to be with me?"

"While we were split up, I went out with this lawyer for a while. All he wanted to do was talk about how I was feeling, and was he being nurturing enough." Emma shuddered. "After we'd been dating a month he even changed his Facebook status to 'in a relationship.' That's when I knew it was over. You'd have hated him. When the waitress in the coffee shop asked for his order, he said 'expresso' instead of 'espresso,' and one of his favorite phrases was 'for all intensive purposes.'"

"That's dreadful," Aaron said dutifully. Although lately such gaffes didn't seem to bother him nearly as much. He couldn't remember the last time he corrected someone's English.

"They say familiarity breeds contempt, but I disagree," Emma said. "I think familiarity is comforting...Turn over."

"Excuse me?"

"Turn over. I'm going to scratch your back. I always scratch your back before you go to sleep."

How odd he'd forgotten that routine. Aaron dutifully turned over even though his back didn't need scratching and usually Emma scratched too hard. Sometimes she even drew blood.

Nineteen

A film set was one of the least magical places Laurie had ever seen. Equipment was everywhere: cameras, crane-like devices, snaking cords and hot powerful lights. The coffee shop where the meet-cute happened was not a real coffee shop at all but a flimsy fake set. The actors sparkled while the cameras rolled but seemed bored and indifferent in between takes. China New, the star, was actually surly and didn't act a bit like the winning characters she portrayed on film.

The entire experience reminded Laurie of hot dogs, which she adored, but once when someone tried to tell her what went into making them, she plugged her ears and started singing, "Take Me Out to the Ball Game." Certain things were better left unknown. Now that Laurie had gotten a glimpse behind the scenes, she knew she'd never want to see the film in the theaters.

She was polite and didn't tell Ross how she felt. After visiting the studio several times, she finally begged off. If it was up to Ross he'd probably have her come with him every day.

He seemed to constantly crave her company even though she insisted on no funny business whatsoever, not even a peck on the cheek. Ross was always making evening and weekend plans for them. He claimed he didn't want to simply take a bite of the Big Peach, he wanted to gobble it up. Therefore he was always inviting her out to all the latest restaurants, clubs and shows. They frequently caused a stir while they were out—Ross was something of a celebrity—and people often took their pictures. Coming from Swainboro, it was thrilling for Laurie to experience all the pleasures of a big city, and it took her mind off Aaron. But it was also exhausting. Sometimes she didn't get home until well after midnight.

One night they were having dinner at a crowded restaurant. Laurie couldn't remember the name of it but it specialized in seafood and craft cocktails. (A new concept for Laurie. When she heard the term she imagined bartenders with scissors, glue guns and glitter.) Ross was trying to convince Laurie to come to the set again.

"I have to stay home and write." This was true. She was spending so much time with Ross she'd been neglecting her work.

"You could bring your laptop to the set."

Laurie cut into her sea bass. "Too many distractions. Don't you have a book due soon? When are you going to write it?"

For a man who made his living as a writer, he seemed to do very little of it.

"I'll lock myself in my apartment for a couple of weeks before it's due and bang it out," he said.

"You're obviously a writing savant. But I'm not. My butt needs to be super-glued to a chair for hours and hours."

"Come on. It won't be fun on the set without you."

"I owe Bridget some pages." Every time she finished a chapter, she sent it off to her editor. Originally her main character Lucy was going to end up with Art, the snobby dog owner, but she was rethinking that outcome. She'd added another character, based on her late husband, Jake. It looked like he was going to be the hero, which made a lot more sense. She and Jake never fought and he thought Laurie hung the moon.

"I have clout with Bridget. I'll tell her to give you a homework pass."

"I don't need a pass. I like writing. It's fun."

Ross took a sip of his cocktail, something called a Whisky

Smash, and frowned. "More fun than hanging out with me on the set of a rom-com?"

Definitely. Watching a movie being made was quite boring.

"How about if I talk them into giving you a small part? Wouldn't that make it more tempting?"

"That's sweet, but I need to pass."

Before she'd visited the set, she would been tickled pink to be in the movie, but now, after seeing what actors went through—standing around for hours, hitting marks on the floor, doing takes over and over—she'd much rather be home creating her own world instead of acting in someone else's.

Aaron and Emma were sitting in a coffee shop called Rise and Grind. She ordered her usual complicated coffee drink (a nonfat latte with caramel drizzle) and black coffee for Aaron without even asking him. He was craving cream and sugar in his morning brew but decided not to mention it. Emma made it clear she wanted him to be the same as always and chastised him if he evidenced any behavior that deviated from his pre-Laurie persona.

They'd been back together for two months, and living together for a week. Emma had never expressed a desire to live with him before, but because he cohabitated with Laurie she felt she had to keep up with "the bottle blonde."

Likely she already regretted her decision, because for the last few minutes, she'd been complaining about his sleeping habits, saying he was far too restless. Aaron tried to listen but his mind wandered.

"In the middle of the night, I'm shivering because you've stolen all the—"

Her lips pulsate with the fluidity of a sea anemone.

"And something must be wrong with your sinuses. All the honks and clicks you make—"

She spangles his cheeks with the sputum of her ire.

"And last night you elbowed me twice in the—"

He feels his soul contracting.

She kicked him under the table. "Dammit, Aaron. Are you writing in your head again?"

"No. Of course not."

"You better not be," she whispered. "Not if you want to get lucky later."

He nodded at the familiar threat. It'd been a long time since he "got lucky" with Emma. At least two weeks.

Emma retired to the ladies' room. Aaron automatically reached into his jacket pocket to retrieve his notebook and jot down his thoughts, but halfway through the motion he remembered he wasn't writing a novel. That's because he wasn't a novelist anymore; he was a PhD candidate.

In fact, last night his father had taken him out to dinner to celebrate Aaron's new role in life. They went to Embers, a dark-paneled restaurant in Midtown Atlanta that specialized in prime rib. Horace Flowers was in a rare jovial mood and talked about all the rewards of academic life. And he reminded Aaron that he'd still be writing. Just not fiction.

His father was in such good spirits Aaron got up the nerve to ask a question that had been nagging him for months.

"Tell me," he said. "What was wrong with *Chiaroscuro?*"

His father sighed. "Is this discourse necessary?"

"Indulge me."

His father put his fork down beside his barely touched prime rib. Usually he ate with great gusto, like a caveman celebrating a fresh kill, but tonight his progress with his meal verged on the ladylike. "It was solipsistic."

Aaron didn't necessarily see that as a negative thing.

"Airless and dreary."

Agreed. He'd been aiming for that effect.

"But its worst flaw is that it's emotionally inauthentic. The author's clearly trying to mimic what he himself has not experienced."

Inauthentic. It was the worst thing his father could say. Fiction was worthless if it wasn't authentic. The rest of the night Aaron had been silent, mulling over his father's comment.

Now, his phone buzzed. He was surprised he could hear it over the coffee shop noises. It was Bernie. "Finally you answer. I've been calling you for the last couple of days."

"Sorry. Sometimes I forget to charge my phone."

"Glad I caught you. Guess what? An editor is interested in buying your novel."

Aaron's novel had already been shopped everywhere except for the smallest of presses. He imagined Bernie had connected with one of them. If Aaron signed with a tiny publisher his print run would likely be less than five hundred copies.

"Who is it?"

"Brace yourself: It's Featherstone."

It took a few seconds for Bernie's reply to permeate the neurons in Aaron's gray matter. Once it did they started firing madly. He knew he'd heard correctly, yet how could it be possible?

"Are you there?"

"Yes."

"Now don't run off and buy the Taj Mahal. They're not offering a lot of dough. Only 10K but—"

"How did you—?"

"Six degrees of Bernie. Actually it was more like sixty degrees of Bernie, but I got an editor to read it and he loved it."

Aaron felt weightless, as if he could float up to the coffee shop's pressed metal ceiling. A troubling thought occurred. "Did you exploit the connection with my father? Because if you did—"

"I swear on my Fantasy Football scorecard I didn't. You got this contract on the merit of your writing. They want you to come to New York, and they're footing the bill. Like I said, they don't pay much of an advance, but they treat their authors like—"

"Kings," Aaron said, smiling.

Aaron talked with Bernie for a few more minutes, thanking him profusely. After he hung up the phone, he whispered the word, "Featherstone."

He was afraid to say it any louder as he didn't want to disturb the Fates who always seemed to be snatching away his happiness.

"Featherstone," he whispered again. His head was swimmy with the news.

Emma returned to the table and gave Aaron a queer look. "What's wrong? You seem...I don't know...dazed, like that time I accidentally hit you on the head with my field hockey stick."

He wished he were alone; he needed more time to let the news suffuse every molecule of his being. But he couldn't ignore Emma. If he refused to reply, she'd crack him like a pistachio.

"Featherstone."

"What? Why are you whispering?"

"My agent just called. I have a contract," he said, a little louder. "With Featherstone."

"Featherstone?" The word swept her off her feet. She plunked her narrow backside into the plastic chair across from him. Emma always ordered several copies of all the books Featherstone published to sell at The Spine. In the past she'd said, "They're the only publishing company I completely trust."

She recovered from the Featherstone spell more quickly than him. "What's your advance?"

Aaron repeated the number Bernie gave him. An advance was immaterial to him. He would write for Featherstone for free.

"Pretty modest. Guess you'll have to continue with your PhD plans."

"I don't want a PhD."

"You can't live on that kind of money. How are you going to support yourself?"

Her comments were why he wished he'd been alone when he got the call. The only thought he wanted in his mind was his newly minted status as a Featherstone author. She was sullying his rarified state with mundane matters. It was like asking him to give her the TV remote control in the midst of sexual relations.

Which Emma had done.

More than once.

"I'll go back to adjuncting," he said to appease her. "And once the novel is published, I'll be more likely to get a position teaching creative writing. Featherstone authors are always in demand in the academic world."

Emma glanced at her phone. "I wish we could sit and talk about this ad infinitum, but one of my staff called in sick, and I have to go into the store. *Someone* in our household needs to make a living wage."

They left the coffee shop, and Aaron trailed behind Emma in a state of utter bliss.

"Featherstone," he whispered again. He couldn't imagine he'd ever tire of saying the word.

Two days later Aaron received a call from his disgruntled father.

"I just got off the phone with Dr. Mullins. He tells me you've decided against the PhD program. Do you know how this makes me look? I spent valuable time getting your paperwork expedited. Care to explain?"

Aaron gave him the news about his contract with Featherstone. His announcement was met with silence. His father had always reviewed every Featherstone novel, and in general, the reviews were positive. Nicholas Windust was with Featherstone for his first two novels until he switched to a publisher called One. Windust's former editor founded One, and it was called One because it only published one novelist: Windust.

"This has to do with our relationship," his father said. "You know that it must."

"My agent assures me it doesn't, and I trust him completely."

"You're a fool if you believe that. Don't forget I read your novel. The critics won't be kind. You think I'm being cruel, but I'm merely trying to protect you."

"I'll take my chances with the critics."

His father expelled a long sigh. "I suppose there's nothing I can do."

"Here's a radical thought: You could be happy for me."

Silence.

"I have another call I need to take. We'll speak later."

Aaron suspected it would be a while before he heard from his father again. When Aaron got accepted to the MFA program, his father froze him out for weeks. (Horace Flowers urged him to get an M.A. instead of an MFA so as to be better poised for a PhD.) He refused phone calls from Aaron and on the rare occasions when he deigned to speak to his son, the conversations were brief and terse.

Twenty

Arriving at Featherstone, Aaron was offered not Diet Coke but Earl Grey tea in a fragile china cup. A steel-haired woman in a no-nonsense tweed suit and sensible lace-up footwear manned the reception area. His editor's office had an old-world ambiance. Leather wing chairs with nail heads flanked a brick fireplace, and the desk was a dignified cherry wood structure. A stark contrast from the space-age Lucite workstations he'd seen at Wilner.

Edward Bulwer dressed like a proper editor, wearing a dress shirt with a stiff white collar and spectacles with small round lenses. He invited Aaron to sit by the fireplace. They discussed his book and not once did his editor use the word platform. A few minutes into their conversation, Aaron asked about social media requirements.

His editor winced. "We discourage our authors from such practices. It's not dignified to post photos of one's dinner or to regale readers with one's mental state. The work should stand on its own."

"That's a relief."

"Any other concerns?"

"You've said nothing about the main character. Some readers have suggested he's...well, rather bleak in his outlook."

"Deliciously bleak. That's what makes him fascinating. It's like watching a train derail. At Featherstone we don't believe in diluting characters to make them palatable for the average reader. It reminds me of the way the French offer a watered-down version of their coffee for Americans. Featherstone readers can stomach unlikable characters because they demand authenticity in their fiction, and the truth is, the world contains droves of unlikeable people."

Aaron nodded along. He could have spoken those very words himself.

"Please," said his editor. "Do not alter a single hair on his unwashed and disheveled head."

Adjacent to his editor's desk stood a large oak bookshelf lined with a number of handsome volumes. Aaron pointed to it, "Are those all Featherstone books?"

"They are. Would you like to take a gander?"

"May I?"

"Be my guest."

Aaron rose and stood by the bookshelf, and his editor joined him. He scanned the titles, all of which he recognized. It was an impressive collection: Nobel Prize winners, Pulitzer Prize winners, and National Book Award recipients. There were also two Nicholas Windust novels.

The temptation to run his fingers across their spines was almost overwhelming. He'd like to open the volumes, take in the eloquent typeface and inhale the smell of ink and binding. As a precaution, he kept his hands behind his back like a schoolboy in an art museum, lest they develop a mind of their own.

"Distinguished company, isn't it?" his editor said.

"Yes, sir."

"One day *Chiaroscuro* will be on that shelf."

"Hard to fathom."

"It's exactly where your excellent novel belongs."

Aaron wished his father were present to see these books, and to hear his editor speak those words. When it came to evaluating literature, Horace Flowers rarely made missteps, but it appeared as if this time he might have lost his sense of objectivity.

Twenty One

Dear Laurie Lee,

Thanks for entering the Pink Heart Contest. We had hundreds of worthy entries, and it was difficult to choose our winners. We're sorry to say you did not place in our contest. We do hope you try us again next year.

Sincerely,

Shirley Nelson, contest coordinator

To: Laurie Lee
From: Bridget Carter
Subject: Excited!
Hi Laurie,

Thank you for the chapters you've been sending. When I read them I find myself smiling throughout. What a charming novel.

One small heads-up: Your publishing team had a recent pow-wow, and we've decided to bring in another writer to polish up your prose. Her name will be on the cover but in tiny print. In fact, you'll need a magnifying glass to read it, whereas your name will be as big as the first line on an eye chart.

We at W&W are thrilled about being the midwives for this book and getting it out into the world. You're a big star around here.

All best,

Bridget

To: Bridget Carter
From: Laurie Lee
Subject: ??
I'm confused. As my editor I thought you'd be the one doing the polishing.
Laurie

To: Laurie Lee
From: Bridget Carter
Subject: Fear not
Of course I'll be giving feedback. But your book is so special we want it to be the best that it can be. Your cowriter is AMAZING and understands she must retain the spirit of your story. BTW, big-wig authors do this all the time. James Patterson, Janet Evanovich, Clive Cussler. You're in glittering company.
All best,
Bridget

For three full days Laurie holed up in her house with the drapes closed, speaking to no one. She emailed Ramona telling her not to come to work because she was sick. She texted Ross and told him she didn't want to see him anymore because he'd lied to her. Aaron was right; he *was* the false love interest— no more genuine than the set of that rom-com she visited.

Laurie didn't go near her computer. In fact, the thought of sitting at her desk and composing a single sentence made her feel itchy all over. She almost wished she could give back the advance money and cancel the entire deal. How could she have been so foolish and deluded?

On her fourth day of isolation, someone knocked on the front door. She ignored it, but the knocking continued. A shout came through the door. It was Ross. "Are you in there? If you don't answer I'm going to assume the worst and call the police."

"Go away!"

"Bridget sent me. She said you haven't answered her emails for several days. Please open this door."

Ross saying Bridget's name was the equivalent of saying, "Open sesame." Laurie reluctantly let him in. She was unprepared for the sunlight surging through the open door. It spotlighted her unwashed hair, faded bathrobe and pale face.

"What is this about me lying to you?" Ross's hair was mussed attractively, his shirt unbuttoned to reveal a peek at the landscape of his golden chest. He looked like an advertisement for a luxury product: a Tag Heuer watch or a single-malt scotch.

"You know exactly what I'm talking about. You blurbed my book even though you knew it was no good."

"Actually I have no idea if it was good or not. I didn't read it. I had my secretary read it and she came up with the blurb."

"But you lied to me and told me you read it."

"Only because I wanted to make you feel better after Aaron skewered your work. And who cares if it's not the most polished manuscript in the world? The cowriter will fix it. There's no shame in that."

Three days of not eating was catching up with Laurie. She was unsteady on her feet and dropped into a chair. She hugged a throw pillow to her chest, and was tempted to burrow under the cushions like a chipmunk.

"But then it won't be my book."

"Yes, it will," he said. "You were the one who came up with an intriguing concept. Not everyone can do that. Writing ability isn't always the most important factor when it comes to selling books."

"It should be."

Ross moved a stack of newspapers to sit on her sofa. "Think of publishing as being like a restaurant. You have the food preparers in the back, and then you have the front-of-the house people. Both are needed to serve up a tasty meal."

"But you do your own writing."

"Yes, but I have an MFA."

"And you write so fast."

"That comes with experience."

"In all the time we've been spent together lately, I've never once seen you sit down at the computer and...Oh...my...goodness."

"What?" Ross said.

"It just occurred to me. You don't write your own books, do you?"

"Don't be ridiculous. Of course I do." The golden skin of his face flushed red.

"Ross."

"I come up with the concept. I make an outline. I—"

"Do you or don't you write your own novels? And if you lie to me, I'll never speak to you again."

He shifted position on the couch. "Listen, Laurie...You can't tell anyone. It's a well-guarded industry secret."

She narrowed her eyes at him. "You just told me there was no shame in having a cowriter."

"It's different with me. My personality's too tied up with my writing. A handsome man writing love stories reaffirms women's fantasies about romantic heroes as soulful and tender creatures."

"Did you write *any* of your books?"

"The first one. All the rest have been ghostwritten."

"I loved the first one!"

"*Love's Prophet* was a gift from the gods. It's never going to happen again."

"You don't know that."

"Sorry, but I do. Besides, I've found my niche. I'm a much better media personality than writer. It's not a bad life, being the face and personality that sells the book, and you, Laurie Lee, have what it takes. Once you're a bestseller, it's amazing how readers will continue purchasing your books no matter who writes them. In a market like that it's silly to write your own novels."

"Surely you're exaggerating."

"Not really. V.C. Andrews still makes the bestselling list, and she's been dead since 1986."

"Well, I'm not like you. I want to be more than a face and a personality. Aaron tried to tell me that W&W didn't want me for my writing, but I wouldn't listen. I'd convinced myself that he was trying to sabotage me. But I was wrong."

"Sounds to me like you miss the guy."

"I do," Laurie said softly. She'd been considering getting in touch with Aaron, at the very least to apologize. She'd even gone as far as calling the university and hoping to leave a message for him, but they said he no longer worked there.

"Aaron will never respect or understand your writing, not in a million years. Is that what you want?"

Laurie tightened the sash on her robe and got up from the chair. "I don't know, but at least he tells me the truth, unlike you."

"That's a shame. I could really help your career. In fact, I think we could help each other's careers. Everybody loves a golden couple. You may want to rethink your decision."

"My decision's firm. And I don't want your blurb either. It's not genuine."

Ross laughed. "You're as much of an innocent about publishing as Aaron. Blurbs are rarely genuine. They're just one author doing a favor for another. But luckily readers don't know that."

"I don't care what everyone else is doing. I only want a genuine blurb. Guess what else? I'm going to rewrite my novel and finish it myself. And I'm going to give it everything I have. Maybe it won't work out, but at least I tried."

Ross stood. "You're making a huge mistake."

No, she wasn't. Her mistake was letting Aaron go. But she had no idea where to find him. The only person who might know would be Emma.

Laurie entered The Spine, and no one was behind the register. It was quiet inside—almost as if the building was empty—and so dimly lit it was as if she was squinting through smog. She wandered through the labyrinth of towering stacks, looking for signs of life. In the True Crime aisle, she sensed a presence behind her. She pivoted on her heels and came face to face with Emma, who was holding a price gun. It was aimed at Laurie's heart.

"Help you?" Emma said with an unnerving smile.

"I was, uh...I hate to trouble you but...I need to speak to Aaron about something important. Do you know where I might find him?"

Emma's face was in the shadows. "Yes. I do."

"Really? That's great."

Silence.

"Will you tell me?"

Emma glanced at her watch. "Let me see. Right about now he's probably in my bed, waiting for me to get home so we can have torrid sex."

"I, uh...don't understand."

"You're not very bright, are you? Torrid means extremely hot, both in the literal and figurative sense."

"I meant...Are you and Aaron—?"

"Back together? Yes, indeed, we are. We're living under the same roof and loving every single minute." She swiped her tongue over her lips in a suggestive manner. "You're welcome to visit, of course, but if our house is rocking, which it almost always is, don't come knocking. Any more questions?"

"No. Thank you."

"Can I give him a message?"

"No. That's not necessary."

Laurie fled the store. Emma's words rang in her ears and images of the two of them together flooded her mind. It wasn't until she got in her car that she allowed herself to scream.

Twenty Two

"I need a book on novel writing." Laurie said. "The best book on novel writing there is. One that covers every aspect, because I don't have a lot of time. Suggestions?"

"One moment, please," the reference librarian said. Laurie wasn't at her temping library because she didn't want to run into former coworkers. The man's fingers danced over the keyboard. He paused and said, "Well, there's a *Dummy's Guide...*"

"Sounds like the one for me."

"Wait. It's checked out...Let's see...This is interesting. There's a book on novel writing called *Craft*, and it just so happens the author lives right here in Atlanta. He teaches at Metro Atlanta University."

He wrote down the call number for her, and Laurie took it, saying, "Much obliged."

Before going into the stacks she paused. If the author lived in town, why didn't she simply pay him a visit and see if he'd be willing to help her with her writing one on one? Surely she could learn more from a person than a book.

Horace Flowers' office was located in a looming brick building called Monroe Hall. His door was ajar, and the tinkle of classical music drifted into the hall.

"Knock, knock," she said before entering.

No response; maybe he couldn't hear her over the music.

She poked her head in the door. "Hi there. May I come in and speak to you for a moment?"

A man sat in his chair with his eyes closed as if sneaking a catnap. His resting face was disgruntled, but that didn't necessarily mean he was an unpleasant person. Some people simply looked that way when caught unawares.

Laurie lowered her voice to a whisper. "I'll come back another time when you're not—"

"I don't take student appointments. I'm a professor emeritus."

His eyes remained closed as he spoke, and his voice matched his grumpy expression.

"I'm sorry to disturb you, Professor Emeritus. I must have the wrong office."

Laurie was relieved this prickly person was not Professor Flowers.

His eyes flew open, and he stared at her. "Was that your attempt at a joke?"

She didn't recall saying anything funny. "I'm looking for Professor Flowers. Could you tell me where he is?"

He put on a pair of half-moon glasses and studied Laurie. "Are you a student here?"

"No, sir."

"And what do you want with Dr. Flowers?"

"I want him to help me improve my novel-writing skills."

He yawned and didn't even bother to cover his mouth. "That won't be possible."

"Well, maybe you should let Dr. Flowers answer that question himself. If you'd just tell me where he—"

"I'm Dr. Flowers."

"But you just said you were—"

"Professor emeritus is an honorary title. And I no longer teach classes."

Laurie blushed. She had never gone to college and didn't know all the various academic ranks. "I don't want to take a class. I want one-on-one lessons."

"I don't do that either."

"I'll pay, of course. Very well. Because it needs to be an intensive course. I've got a novel under contract, and my deadline's looming. I'd probably need to see you every day for a month."

"You have a book contract?"

She nodded.

"Who's the publisher?"

"W&W."

"A solid operation but decidedly lacking in prestige." He scratched behind his ear.

"Will you do it?"

He didn't answer immediately. Instead he unwound the wrapping from a spearmint Lifesaver and popped it into his mouth. He savored it for a few seconds before speaking.

"My advice would be expensive. I'd require five thousand dollars."

"Okay."

"And you'd have to keep our business relationship secret. I have a reputation to maintain. In other words, I don't want my name to appear in your acknowledgements."

"Sounds fair."

"And you must to do everything I say and not question it."

"Okey doke."

He glanced at her over the tops of his glasses. "And you must never say okey doke again in my presence. When would you like to start?"

"As soon as possible. As I said, I'm on a deadline."

Dr. Flowers opened a desk drawer and handed her a card with his contact information. "Very well. Send me what you have via email. I'll look it over, and we'll develop a plan of action."

Six hours later

From: Professor Flowers
To: Laurie Lee

Subject: Payment

Dear Ms. Lee:

I finished reading your work. My price has gone up. I'll need eight thousand dollars. If you agree to my terms, I'll see you in my office at ten a.m. sharp. Also, and this is crucial, even though you are quite obviously a woman, you'll need to take my criticism like a man. That means no crying or histrionics. I'll be requiring a thousand dollars in advance.

Laurie sat in Professor Flowers' office, pen poised over her brand-new daisy-patterned spiral notebook. The office was overly warm, and she kept tugging at the collar of her blouse.

Dr. Flowers stared up at the ceiling as if deciding how to begin the session. Eventually his gaze settled on her face. It was laser-like in its intensity.

"Let me begin by saying that on the sentence level, you're one of the most unskilled writers I've ever encountered. It's a miracle you've secured a publishing contract. I had no idea W&W standards had gotten so low."

Laurie's bottom lip trembled. She bit down on it almost hard enough to draw blood. *No crying.*

"Are you...Are you saying there's no hope?"

"I am not. You possess a natural sense of story mechanics, and a somewhat engaging voice. But you have a tremendous amount of work ahead of you. Your first homework assignment is to read *Strunk and White*, cover to cover."

"Skunk and who?" She looked up from her notes.

"*Strunk* and White. As I was saying, you've developed a number of bad habits that need to be addressed before we can even begin. Once you're finished reading *Strunk and White*, I'll give you a list of authors with distinctive styles. You're to read their books and try your hand at emulating them."

"That sounds like a lot of work. As you know, the clock is ticking and—"

"Young lady. You don't yet have the skills to write a decent novel. You have to develop those first and the only way to do that is through reading those who have mastered their Craft. If you work diligently, you'll make your deadline. I've devised a schedule for you. Here's the list." He handed her a typed piece of paper.

Laurie recognized many of the novels but she hadn't read a single one. She wrinkled her nose at *Pride and Prejudice*. She'd paged through it once. The writing was creaky and old-fashioned.

"Since you're a genre writer, I've selected authors who have some commercial sensibilities. Read the novels and then write several pages employing that author's style. If we want to keep to your schedule, you should allow only a week for this task."

Laurie didn't know how she would possibly finish all the books in a week—when she was bored she tended to read sentences over and over—but she'd try her best. Her career and self-respect depended on it.

Twenty Three

Exercise One (*Catcher in the Rye*)

If you really want to hear about it, I think old man Emeritus is a crummy teacher. All he does is sit behind his desk like some decrepit phony, yammering about art and aesthetics and lousy stuff like that. Don't even get me started on how goddamn bossy he is...Anyway, we're in his office, which is hot as the devil's sauna, and I ask him, "What the hell is wrong with adverbs? If they crap up your writing so badly, why do teachers shove them down your throat in elementary school?"

Teachers kill me, they really do...Old man Emeritus especially. He's so touchy about every little goddamn thing. He acts like you killed someone if you use the word "very" a few times. I said to him, look at page 102 in *Catcher in the Rye*, there's a bunch of "verys", two in a row even. He gets all high and mighty and says that's a stylistic choice...like I even know what that means. He's crazy, I'm telling you. Emeritus will be the death of me. I'm not kidding.

Exercise Two (*Pride and Prejudice*)

It is a truth universally acknowledged that a woman who is forced to read prose in an archaic style will eventually resent the man who has foisted this exercise upon her.

"My dear Professor Flowers," the pupil said earnestly. "I'm baffled as to how these exercises are assisting me. This novel's language is unfamiliar to my ear. It will take me at least a fortnight to read it, and as you're quite aware, the days until my deadline are swiftly dwindling."

"Young woman. I am highly disturbed by your impertinence," he replied coldly. "When we entered into this agreement, I daresay you made a solemn vow that you would accept my council without question. Do you wish to alter the terms of this agreement? I must say, your near-constant complaining is becoming tiresome. And what have I told you about attaching adverbs to dialogue. Are my directives unclear? Dialogue should be written so the reader will immediately discern the emotions of the character in question without need for attribution."

"Forgive me for contradicting you, Dr. Flowers, but Jane Austen is liberal in her use of adverbs with dialogue tags."

"You, madam, are no Jane Austen," Dr. Flowers replied. "Use 'said' and 'said' alone or risk my extreme displeasure."

Exercise Three (*Lolita*)

Emeritus, thorn in my side, burr in my shoe. My tormentor, my foe. Em-er-it-us, the taste of your name on my tongue is terr-i-ble.

He is Em, every day, a toad in a suit coat. He is a Flower that wilts and pricks at my fingers. He is a critic at large. He is Horace, a writer of books. But in my life he will always be a horse's patoot.

Exercise Four (*The Old Man and the Sea*)

She was a young woman who needed to write a book and she had gone a week now without writing a word of it. During that time the old man had been directing her.

The young woman thought the old man was loco which is the worst kind of crazy and the young woman thought about quitting him, but then she would lose eight thousand dollars.

It also made the young woman sad to read a book like *The Old Man and the Sea*, which was about a fish and she didn't care about fish. Not even as a dinner entrée. Not even in fish stick form. Not even those little Goldfish crackers.

*   *   *

"Are you mad at me?" Laurie said to Dr. Flowers. They were sitting in his office, preparing to discuss the work she turned in. Unexpectedly, she had fun with the writing exercises, but she knew they weren't particularly flattering to her teacher, and she hoped he hadn't taken offense. "And incidentally, I don't really think you're a horse's patoot."

Dr. Flowers nibbled a shortbread cookie. A trail of crumbs dusted his shirt and he swatted them away. (He had a whole tin of cookies but had never once offered her one.) "I've been called worse."

"I'm sorry. I probably shouldn't have—"

"To be frank, I admire your playfulness."

"You do?" Laurie was suspicious. Everything they'd done so far was serious.

"And you know what makes these exercises work?"

"Because they're fun?"

"No. Because they're truthful. I think this is exactly how you feel about me, and what I'm teaching you."

"Well, not *exactly*—"

"I won't concern myself with your opinions about me. But I do hope you consider dropping some of your resistance to what I have to say. Your exercises, irreverent as they are, indicate much promise about your potential as a writer."

"Thank you."

"But you still have a long journey ahead of you. Tell me what you thought of the books."

Laurie consulted the notes in her composition book. "I liked *Pride and Prejudice*, but I wished the language wasn't so archaic. The rest of the books I didn't care for at all."

"And why is that?"

"Not my type of reading material. Initially I thought *Catcher in the Rye* was going to be fun, but then it turns out Holden's in a mental hospital, and he gets estranged from his whole family, and then there's his bizarre obsession with that silly hat. It was all so sad. *Lolita*, on the other hand, was more creepy than sad. I wanted to take a shower and scrub my skin with a loofah after I read it. And *The Old Man in the Sea* was plain depressing; he dies in the end! I don't want to read a book where the main character doesn't survive. I like HEAs."

"Excuse me?"

"Happily Ever Afters. If you write romance, you always have an HEA."

He rolled his eyes, and she thought of how much he hated eye rolling in fiction. Smiling was another one of his bugaboos. "And God forbid you should have anyone ever grin on the page," he said during yesterday's lesson. Laurie didn't understand the problem. In real life people rolled their eyes and grinned all the time.

"The trouble with romance is there's no suspense," Dr. Flowers said. "You already know how the book is going to come out. That's one of my many complaints about genre fiction. Why bother reading it?"

"Because it's not necessarily the destination. It's the journey." She lifted her chin, feeling as if she'd made an important point.

"Yes, but you keep taking the same journey over and over; it's like cruising on a Carnival ship to the Bahamas several times a year. The passengers and menus change but essentially it's the same voyage."

"I'd love to go to the Bahamas on a cruise ship, and I bet I would never get tired of it. They have movie theaters, midnight pizza buffets, snorkeling and—"

Dr. Flowers tossed her pages across his desk. "In order to grow as artists we must leave our comfort zones and read fiction that is sometimes contrary to our world view. Then, maybe one day, you can transcend your genre."

Laurie was sleepy from the oppressive heat in Dr. Flowers' office. Today she'd worn a lightweight sundress to their meeting, but she was still perspiring and it was sticking to the back of her legs.

"How will I transcend my genre if I don't ever get to write my own work?"

"Fine. Tonight's your night. Incorporate what you've learned thus far and write a scene for me to read tomorrow."

"One more thing."

"Yes?"

"May I have a cookie? I'm starving."

He appeared to be struggling to suppress a smile. "If you want a cookie, you're going to have to earn it. Let's see how your scene goes."

Laurie wasn't sure she approved of Dr. Flowers' methods, but whenever she wanted to question him, she kept thinking about the Karate Kid waxing all those cars. *Strunk and White* was also helpful. She had no idea adverbs were so frowned upon, and had always assumed they made her writing more descriptive. Now that she'd removed most of them, she could see the way they were junking up her work.

She was hesitant to start writing on her own novel again. For the first full hour she stared at the screen, but then she had an idea, and another one followed like pennies spilling out of a jar. She'd forgotten how much she'd missed her characters.

Dr. Flowers was staring up at the ceiling, having just read her chapter. He was silent for so long she felt like biting her fingernails down to nubs. She'd spent hours on her chapter, working it and reworking it, until she couldn't bear to look at it anymore.

"Well?" she said.

He made an adjustment to his tie and took a sip from his tea cup. She was certain he enjoyed torturing her with his delaying tactics. He reached into the tin of cookies, withdrew one and snapped off a piece and handed it to her.

"It's slightly better."

Laurie stared at the cookie piece in her hand which was hardly larger than a crumb. But since she didn't have breakfast she pushed it into her mouth.

"On the sentence level. You're a quick study. The prose is much cleaner and easier to read. You've eliminated some of the hokey corn pone, and I saw fewer clichés."

Laurie knew there was more to come. Comments that would probably make her want to throw herself in a well.

"It's still extremely facile. The characterization's skimpy, and the relentless cheeriness grates. Not to mention, I don't believe a word of it."

"You're not supposed to believe it." She spoke slowly, as if dealing with someone who was slightly touched in the head. "It's fiction."

"Surely you've heard the quote, 'fiction is the lie that tells the truth'?"

She hadn't, but she nodded her head as if she had.

"A novel must have a sense of authenticity for it to be taken seriously."

Laurie flung her hands in the air. "How many times do I have to tell you this? I'm not writing serious fiction. I'm writing a lighthearted romance."

"That doesn't exempt you from being authentic. While it's true that genre fiction will rarely be intellectually authentic, it must, at the very least, be emotionally authentic. That's what's missing here."

Laurie squared her shoulders, prepared for battle. "I don't know what you're talking about. My chapter's brimming with emotion. On the second page the heroine's bawling like a shorn lamb."

Dr. Flowers gave her a cold look, and Laurie shivered even though the room was much too warm. "Yet I feel nothing for her."

"I think you're being unkind. Plain and simple."

"What's more, it's clear you don't either. As Robert Frost said, 'No tears in the writer, no tears in the reader.'"

"I have no idea what you're talking about." She placed a hand over her heart. "I feel for Lucy."

"I don't think you do. It's obvious to me she's the toy doll you're maneuvering around in service of your plot. You clearly have little knowledge of who Lucy is."

"Now I know you're crazy. Because guess what? Lucy's mostly me. What do you think of them tomatoes?"

He smiled, the rarest of events, but it was not a warm smile. Rather, it was the smug smile of someone who's just said, "Checkmate."

"I suspected as much. It's common for beginning writers to borrow heavily from real life. It's usually a mistake because, ironically, the one person we tend to know the least is ourselves."

"I know myself very well."

He ignored her comment and said, "What is Lucy's idea of perfect love?"

"Hmm. Let me give it some thought."

"You should be able to answer me immediately. You're writing a romance, which in a sense is a book-long argument between two lovers about whose version of love is superior. Also, what event in her past is haunting her? What's her wound?"

"Is that important?"

"For someone who writes romance, you seem to know very little about it. Lovers are usually attracted to each other because, on a subconscious level, they're hoping to find healing of their deepest wounds through the union."

"I never really thought about it that way."

"That's quite obvious. Tonight, write about your main character's wounds."

"Okay," Laurie said tentatively. Nothing immediately came to her. "How many pages?"

He closed his eyes, which meant he was preparing to dismiss her. "For as many pages as it takes for you to understand her pain."

*   *   *

"She's claustrophobic?" Dr. Flowers said. He sat behind his desk, his chin resting on his folded hands. The sun was bright behind him and his face looked ghostly. Laurie muffled a yawn; she was up late trying to complete her writing assignment.

"Yes, sir."

"Are you claustrophobic?"

"Sometimes."

He leaned forward, his watery eyes never straying from her face. But she'd gotten used to his penetrating gaze, and barely flinched. "What's the underlying reason for your claustrophobia?"

"I have no idea. I've experienced it on and off all my life."

"That's worth exploring. You might want to give it some thought."

"Is this therapy or writing lessons?"

Dr. Flowers dunked his tea bag into a cup of water. How could he drink tea when his office was so hot? Laurie had taken to bringing Polar Pops of Diet Coke to their sessions.

"That's the thing about writing. It tends to reveal what we're obsessed with and also what we're avoiding, and sometimes the things we avoid are exactly the things we should be writing about."

"I'm not avoiding anything."

He was quiet for a moment, but she could sense the machinery in his mind whirring as he plotted his next move.

"Let's try another tactic. Instead of writing about your character's wounds, write about mine."

"But I don't know anything about you."

"You write fiction. Make it up. Give me a backstory."

Exercise Five

Dr. Flowers is a somewhat disagreeable man with a permanently anguished expression, but he wasn't always that way. Once he was an aspiring novelist; words sang in his heart and he happily put them on the page. He also had a lovely young wife who read his work and told him it was brilliant. Her love and support gave him courage, and he submitted his work to a prestigious press. It happened to land on the desk of an editor who'd been continually passed over for promotion and was extremely bitter about it.

The manuscript had immense promise; even the editor recognized that. The author simply needed to spend a year or two perfecting his craft. Ten years ago, the editor might have taken on the author, nurtured him so that he could grow into the kind of novelist people would remember for a long time.

But the days of guiding a young novelist were over for the editor. He was nearing the end of his career. Publishing had changed so much since he started, and he'd lost much of his idealism. The manuscript on his desk stunk of hope and youth, and all of the things the editor had lost.

So, instead of writing a kind yet supportive rejection note to the greenhorn author, the editor typed out a scathing letter several pages long, exposing every single flaw and not mentioning a single one of the manuscript's many strengths.

In the meantime, the young Flowers had gotten into the habit of impatiently waiting for the mail and running out to the street as soon as it came. It was such a letdown when the mailbox contained only bills and ad circulars.

He also had long pillow talks with his young wife, and they'd spin tales about how their lives would change when he got published. But the longer he waited for a response, the more superstitious he became, and he told his wife not to talk about it anymore because it might jinx him. She assured him nothing could jinx him because he was brilliant. The next Fitzgerald or Hemingway.

Finally a letter from the press arrived. His heart practically flew out of his chest when he saw the return address. The envelope was thick. He knew rejection letters were usually one-page long or sometimes no more than a slip of paper. Was it possible the letter contained a contract for the novel?

He couldn't bear to read it. He asked his wife to open it for him, which she did, her hands trembling all the while, but her face beamed. She felt sure it was going to contain good news. But then she began to read, and her expression got more and more serious as she went along.

"What is it? Tell me." He could barely stand it.

She tucked the letter back into the envelope. "There are other publishers. This one isn't for you."

"Let me see it."

"Please, honey, I don't think you should read this."

But the young Flowers had a stubborn streak, so he insisted. As he read, it felt as if the bottom had fallen out of his stomach. His wife tried to comfort him, but he shirked away from her.

Over the next few days he read the letter dozens of times. He read it so many times he could quote from it verbatim. The editor's poisonous voice was the only one he heard in his head, and it drowned out the voice of his young wife who kept telling him he was talented and that he should try another press and not let this single rejection get to him. He also could no longer write; every time he sat down at the typewriter, he imagined the editor standing over his shoulder in judgment.

In time the corners of his mouth froze into a permanent frown, and he started to view the whole world through the critical eyes of the editor. Suddenly he saw his young wife not as nurturing and loving, but as simple and Pollyannaish. He was often short with her and discounted almost everything she said. Eventually he became cruel and unfeeling toward her, which caused her to pack her bags and leave. He was left alone with his defeated spirit and judgmental eye.

Dr. Flowers finished reading Laurie's work. He rearranged a few items on his desktop and didn't say anything for a long time, as was his custom. Finally he said, "'Words singing in his heart?' 'Stunk of hope?' Could you be more mundane? People beaming? Beaming's a word that should be struck from the dictionary. 'Happily on the page?' What do Strunk and White say about adverbs?"

"There's only one adverb, and I thought that one was—"

He held up a hand. "That's not the worst of it. Can't you see it's all so predictable? Couldn't you have come up with something more original?"

"I'm sorry. It was the first idea that came to mind and—"

"Never, ever follow your first thought." His voice sounded hoarse, and he lowered it to a loud whisper. "Write until you surprise yourself."

"Do you want me to do it over?"

"No." He closed his eyes and leaned back in his chair as if preparing for a nap. "Just continue writing on your novel and bring me more pages tomorrow."

The next morning Laurie knocked on Dr. Flowers' office door, and when she got no response, she jiggled the handle, thinking he might be napping, but the door was locked. She visited the English suite office and spoke to a receptionist who told her that Dr. Flowers was feeling extremely ill yesterday afternoon and was taken to the hospital by ambulance.

Distressed, she immediately drove to the hospital to check on him, stopping by the gift store first, but all the offerings seemed far too cheery for a man like Dr. Flowers: a plush teddy bear hugging a vase of carnations, Mylar balloons decorated with bees that say, "Bee well."

She was tempted to ask the clerk, "Don't you have anything for people with a gloomy outlook?" In the end, she selected a fruit basket, but removed the oversized ladybug-patterned bow after she left the store.

When she arrived in Dr. Flowers' room, he was sleeping. There were no flowers or family members. She sat by his bedside for a few minutes, debating whether she should stay. Her purse fell from her lap and cosmetics rained on the tile floor, making a terrific clatter.

Dr. Flowers' eyes flew open; he looked startled, as if he wasn't sure where he was.

Laurie was on her hands and knees, retrieving a silver lipstick tube of Pinky Nude that had rolled under the bed.

"I'm sorry. I didn't mean to wake you. I was—"

"What are you doing here?" His voice sounded parched and weak.

"I was worried silly about you."

He closed his eyes again. "There's no need for concern. I had a bout with severe heartburn. They kept me overnight for observation, but I'll be going home soon."

A broad-chested male orderly came in and told Dr. Flowers he could start getting dressed because his doctor has given him the okay to be discharged. The orderly glanced at Laurie and gave her an appreciative look. "Is this pretty lady your daughter? Will she be taking you home?"

Dr. Flowers said, "No. She's not my daughter, and I'll catch a cab home, thank you very much."

"A cab?" Laurie said. "I won't hear of it. I'll drive you."

He refused, and they argued back and forth until he finally relented. The orderly told her to go ahead and get the car and meet them underneath the portico in front of the building.

On the way home, Dr. Flowers was uncharacteristically quiet, and instead of wearing his usual crabby expression, he simply looked like he'd been beaten with a broom handle. When they arrived at his house, a small condo near the university, she insisted on seeing him in.

The air inside smelled stale, like the house has been closed up for a while. The walls of his front room were painted a forest green and looked almost black in the dim light. Dusty damask drapes covered every window, and dark wood bookshelves lined an entire wall. Nearly every surface was awash with newspapers, magazines and books, some yellowed with age.

Laurie got Dr. Flowers settled on an easy chair.

"Are you sure I can't do something for you? Make you a cup of chicken noodle soup or maybe some red Jell-O with those little marshmallows? That always perks me up."

"I'm fine."

She shrugged her purse over her shoulder but continued to linger, reluctant to leave him alone. His eyes were closed, and he seemed as if he might be drifting off to a nap. She was about to ask if she could fetch him a blanket when he said, "You got most of it right."

"What's that?"

"The writing exercise. Most of it was chillingly accurate, believe it or not. The bitter editor, although I received more than one rejection. Also the young wife. You didn't mention children. We had a son. My wife left me when he was still a toddler."

Slowly Laurie lowered herself into a chair, listening intently.

"She remarried, the boy took his name and five years later, she was killed in a freak accident. The boy came to live with me. I didn't do well with him. I was too married to my work. We barely speak."

"I'm sorry...I honestly never imagined..."

"I asked you to write it, didn't I?"

That was the most confessional thing he'd ever said to her. She squeezed his hand. The texture of his skin felt dry and papery, as if he was dehydrated. "I'm sure that's not all true. You're just being hard on yourself."

"Sadly, I'm not. Anyway, last night I started writing something about you. I didn't finish it. The heartburn got in the way. Why don't you take a look?"

He leaned down and withdrew a piece of paper from a battered leather satchel. He handed it to her.

She smiled, flattered. "I can't imagine what you might have come up with."

Her clothes, so colorful I long for an eyeshade. Her voice is a brook, happy, gurgling; her smile as bright as the sun. Her hands move like two hummingbirds; so fast you can barely see.

She's a walking inspiration poster. Hang in there! Don't worry, be happy! When life gives you lemons, squeeze it into your sweet tea.

And yet, amongst all the light, the party balloons, the sparklers, rare flashes of something slightly darker...What is she hiding?

Laurie looked up from the paper, startled.

"I have no idea what you're getting at...I mean, well. I did recently lose my husband but—"

"How long ago?" His voice was incredulous.

"It's been over a year. But if I'd told you, you'd want me to probably write about it and frankly I'd rather not. For months afterward I was so depressed. If I write about it I might stir things up again."

Dr. Flowers met her eyes. Usually his gaze was meant to be intimidating, but today it held only softness.

"No light without dark."

"Excuse me?"

"No joy without pain." His voice sounded weak initially but got stronger with every syllable. "Don't deny your demons. Come to terms with them, and they'll make you a more compassionate writer. The reader reads your work and wonders why you're hiding from him. More importantly he wonders what you're hiding from yourself."

"I don't feel as if I'm hiding a thing," she said.

"So you say, but I think you need to dig deeper. Why don't you try writing about the day of his death?"

"I can't. And not because it was too painful, it's because I was so doped up on sedatives, I can barely remember it."

"Or maybe there's something you'd rather not remember."

Dr. Flowers closed his eyes again as if their conversation had spent him. The room was silent.

Laurie got up from her chair. The condo was so cluttered she was starting to feel boxed in. "Well, I should go and let you get some rest." She paused by the door, gathering her thoughts. "I hope you feel better soon. And thanks for all you've done for me. I'm a much better writer because of you."

He opened his eyes. The whites were mapped with blood vessels. "Is it my imagination or are you saying goodbye to me?"

"I think I'm done for the time being. Yes."

"According to our schedule you have two more days left."

"I'll skip them. I honestly think I've gone as far as I can."

A resigned expression crossed his face. "As you wish."

Laurie exited the living room and opened up the front door, relieved to depart from his company and to be out in the sunshine once again.

Twenty Four

Twelve hours a day every day Laurie worked on her novel. Her output thus far was impressive, but she had no idea about the quality of her work, and whether or not her sessions with Dr. Flowers had helped. Finishing the book was what mattered most now. After she was done writing her pages, Ramona proofed them for her.

Two weeks later, Laurie was at the seventy-thousand-word mark, which meant it was time to wrap up plot points and slide into a climax. She started the day typing and the words flew, but around eleven a.m. they stopped abruptly. She made a few false starts but nothing happened. It was as if her muse has knocked off for the day and was now stretched out on a La-Z-Boy eating Cheese Nips and binge-watching Netflix.

Ramona approached her desk. She'd drawn a single black tear coming out of her right eye. "Where are the pages?"

"I don't have any."

"What do you mean you don't have any? I've been waiting for them."

The cursor blinked on a screen that seemed excessively blank and white. "I'm feeling off today."

Ramona's eyes were unblinking. "I need those pages."

"Can't you find something else to keep you busy?"

She vigorously shook her head. Her hair was stiff with black dye and barely moved. "You don't understand. I want to know what happens."

"But...you don't like real-life romance. You like heroes with scales or fur." Laurie glanced at her assistant's t-shirt. It said, "Some Day My Succubus Will Come."

"I like *this* romance."

"You think it's good?"

"Remember? When we started this arrangement, you asked me to only correct mistakes, not to comment on your work."

"Only if you *don't* like it. Are you saying you're enjoying the book?"

"It doesn't make me want to shove lit matches under my nails..."

"You sweet-talker, you."

"I'll leave you now so you can write." She looked over her shoulder. "Type fast."

Ramona's backhanded compliment encouraged Laurie, but it didn't help with the block. She kept rereading and rereading the last few paragraphs she'd written, hoping they'd juice the ones to come, but nothing happened. She'd start a sentence, and it went nowhere.

Maybe some light household chores would unclog her brain. She folded laundry warm from the dryer and ran a vacuum over the carpet even though it didn't need it. Still feeling blocked, she baked a batch of Tollhouse cookies and devoured six of them, getting a sugar rush. Jittery with energy, she returned to her desk, but when she sat down to write...

Nothing.

The next morning the clock radio blared a commercial for a monster truck rally, and Laurie muffled it with her pillow. She didn't want to get out of bed because she knew nothing had changed. She could still sense the block in her mind. Overnight it seemed to have solidified into a permanent structure, like an iceberg or a kidney stone. A few minutes later there was a knock at the front door. It was Ramona.

"Did you oversleep?"

No doubt Ramona was noting the baby doll gown, the wild hair, the crusty eyes.

"No."

"I'll go in the office and wait for you to get ready."

"I'm not working today." Laurie swallowed, hoping to chase away the sour taste in her mouth.

Ramona frowned. "But there's only a week until your deadline. You can't afford to miss a day."

"I know that. And I'm not being lazy. I just can't get past the block. It's like trying to muscle through a bricked-up door with ten snarling German Shepherds guarding it."

"You're giving up?"

"I don't know what else to do." Tears pricked her eyes. Things had been easy until now. She was so close, only fifteen or twenty thousand words more. If she wasn't blocked she could easily write that many words in a week.

"Sit at your desk," Ramona said. "Something will happen. I'll keep the Red Bull coming."

"You don't get it. This is a serious block. The story's completely stalled. I'm just going to send off what I have to my editor. Let the cowriter figure out the rest."

"But if the cowriter writes it, it won't be your story anymore."

Laurie ran her hands through hair tangled by a restless night. "I'm too emotionally exhausted to argue with you about this. Here's what I need you to do: Proofread and then send it off to my editor."

Ramona left, grumbling. As soon as she'd gone, Laurie climbed back into bed and pulled the covers over her head. Fatigue settled over her, heavy as her goose-down duvet. Maybe she'd spend the rest of the day there. With no book to write, there didn't seem like much point in getting up.

Aaron was finishing up the dregs of his morning coffee when someone banged on his front door. Ramona, Laurie's assistant, was outside. She was huffing and puffing like she was out of breath. What could she possibly want?

"May I help you?"

Ramona peered over Aaron's shoulder, as if looking for someone. "Are you alone?"

"Yes."

Emma left for the bookstore several minutes ago.

"Good. I need to talk to you."

"What does this concern?"

Her expression was stony. She kept looking over her shoulder as if she was being watched. "A matter of grave importance."

"Perhaps you could be more specific?"

Ramona ignored the question and pushed past him to enter the house. She bumped into a coffee table.

"It's dark in here," she said.

Emma kept the drapes closed and favored forty-watt bulbs. Aaron had adapted to the dim lighting and barely noticed it anymore. He reached for the lamp switch and Ramona touched his shoulder and said, "I like the dark."

Aaron ignored her and turned on the lamp. Ramona was not the sort of person he wanted to be alone with in the gloom of Emma's den.

"How did you find me?" Aaron said.

"It doesn't take a detective. I went to The Spine website, and it listed an Emma Grimes as the manager, and then I looked up her address. I took a chance and, sure enough, here you are."

She sat on the sofa without being invited. The springs groaned and the smell of camphor rose up. It was an unyielding piece of furniture passed down to Emma from a spinster aunt.

"Did someone die on this sofa?"

"I have no idea."

"I sense a presence."

Enough of that. The girl was making him anxious. "Exactly what is this important matter you need to discuss?"

Ramona didn't answer. She rose from the chair and stood in

front of the bookshelf where Emma kept her autographed books and scanned the titles. She examined the back cover of one volume, frowned and stuck it back in upside down.

Aaron immediately righted the book to its correct position. Emma was extremely particular about those books. She didn't like anyone touching them. Not even Aaron.

"Would you please tell me the nature of your—"

She poked his chest with a stubby finger. "Do you still care about Laurie?"

Her question was disarming, and it took him a moment to answer. "Of course. Just because we've parted doesn't mean—"

"I suspected as much. And that's why you have to write the ending of her book."

"I don't understand. Why doesn't she—?"

"She's blocked. And it's your fault."

"Well, I—"

"You roughed up her muse, and the effects are still lingering. You owe her." The threat hung in the air.

"Are you saying Laurie sent you over here to—"

"No. She'd lock me up in an Iron Maiden if she knew what I was up to."

Ramona was so close to him Aaron could smell the licorice on her breath and count the blackheads on her nose. She seemed to have no regard for the conventions of personal space.

"What about Ross? He's a novelist, and I've been told he's proficient at writing love stories. Couldn't he possibly—"

"I haven't see him around lately. I think he's back in New York."

Interesting, Aaron thought. Still, he didn't know how he could help Laurie. "I don't know anything about writing a romance novel. It has all sorts of tropes and conventions I'm not familiar with."

"You've never read a romance?" She managed to press in even closer. He was practically flattened against the wall.

"Only one of Laurie's."

Which he now regretted deeply. Although he had watched

more than a dozen romantic comedies. Perhaps the tropes were similar?

"It's not that hard. Laurie's already done most of the work."

"You don't understand. Novels are such personal affairs. I can't imagine trying to finish someone else's story."

She grabbed his sleeve and gave it a vigorous shake. "But it's your story too. In the book your name is Art."

"Really?" Aaron said. The news intrigued him. "How do you know it's me?"

"Messy hair, broken glasses, pessimistic, snotty...Who else could it be?"

The description of his character didn't sound particularly positive. Laurie's book might be a painful manuscript for him to read.

"Is this Art character by chance the villain?"

"No," Ramona said. She expelled a droplet of spit, and it hit the lens in Aaron's glasses. "He's part of the love triangle. Like in *Twilight* when Bella has to choose between a vampire and a wolf."

Aaron raised an eyebrow. Neither choice sounded remotely appealing for this poor Bella person.

"Or in *The Hunger Games* when Katniss has to choose between—"

Aaron tried to shrink farther into the wall but there was nowhere to go. "Is Art human at least?"

"This isn't a paranormal. And if you write it, you can choose who Lucy gets to be with, Art or Drake. But there's really only one choice to be made."

"Drake? Is he modeled after—"

"Jake. Bingo. And Jake is much more suited to Lucy. Art's a dud."

Aaron frowned. "If the female protagonist chooses Jake or rather, Drake, maybe that will make the novel too predictable."

Ramona shook her head so hard Aaron wondered if she was in danger of straining her neck. "She needs to choose the one readers will root for. That's Drake, not Art."

"Perhaps you should write it yourself then?"

"Do I look like a professional writer to you? You need to write it." She clamped her hands on his shoulders. "It's the least you can do."

"How long do I have?"

"A week."

"A week? Impossible. Sometimes it takes me a week just to write one paragraph. I couldn't—"

"You can and you will." Ramona didn't name specific consequences, but she didn't have to. Whatever she had in mind was bound to be extremely dark and disturbing. Witchcraft perhaps. Or maybe voodoo.

She stuck a flash drive into the front pocket of his shirt and gave it a solid pat. "The novel's on here. Email it to me when you're done."

When she backed away from him Aaron felt such a sense of relief he didn't argue.

But Ramona wasn't finished with him yet. She lumbered back into his personal space, so close he could feel the heat from her face, and said, "Don't. Let. Laurie. Down."

The front door slammed, and the pictures on the wall shook.

Aaron reluctantly printed out Laurie's novel on Emma's laser printer. It was hard to imagine Laurie had improved much since their breakup, and he feared that reading her prose would be like venturing into the tangled foliage of a jungle armed only with a plastic butter knife.

He began to read, and to his immense surprise, he was immediately engrossed in the story. The work was still genre, but it was much improved. In fact, it was hard to believe Laurie wrote it, and yet he knew she did, because her distinctive warmth shined through.

Aaron recognized himself in Art, the owner of a purebred poodle that Lucy's mutt impregnated, and he was touched by

Laurie's portrayal of him. It was clear that the heroine loved him. But Art's character was slow to redeem himself, and his condescending behavior and distain for Lucy's dog drove her into the arms of Drake, a dog trainer who'd been hired to get Lucy's mutt in line.

Lucy was torn between the two men, and this is where Laurie had left off. Aaron felt a sense of loss. He'd known, of course, that Laurie's novel lacked an ending, but he'd become invested in the characters and felt let down that their complications weren't resolved.

Aaron had no idea how to complete Laurie's novel. Were it a literary novel the conclusion could be left ambiguous, allowing room for the readers to make their own decisions, but Aaron knew that romance readers expected all the conflicts to be tied up in big pink bow.

Twenty Five

Laurie's baby doll nightie was growing funkier each day. For the better part of a week she did little more than watch TV or loll on her couch eating Honey Nut Cheerios straight out of the box. She hadn't heard a word from her editor, but Ramona assured her the manuscript had been sent off. Likely it was already in the hands of the cowriter.

One afternoon she got so disgusted with her lapsed grooming she forced herself to take a bath. While toweling off, her home phone rang. She decided to ignore it and the answering machine picked up. It was Dr. Flowers. "Could you please come see me? It's urgent. I'll be home all day long."

A half hour later she was on the front stoop of Dr. Flowers' condo, ringing the bell. Three newspapers were piled up outside, and a wasp was busily constructing a small wicked-looking nest under the eaves. A woman wearing a medical smock answered the door. She had orange-red hair tied back into a professional knot.

"You must be Laurie. I'm Lola, Dr. Flowers' nurse. He's expecting you. The bedroom's down the hall, second door on the left."

Dr. Flowers' bedroom had the stale, sour odor of a body fretful with infection. Her former teacher was a motionless white mound in his queen-sized bed. Only his face was visible, and he looked drawn, as if he had shed a few pounds since she last saw him. She thought he must be sleeping but then his eyes opened partway.

"You came." His voice was a raspy whisper.

"As soon as I got your message. What's going on?"

It was a silly question. Sickness was obviously going on. Laurie was a natural nurturer and had the urge to smooth his sheets or feel the temperature of his forehead, but Dr. Flowers would likely shoo her away.

"My condition has gotten worse, I fear."

"How long have you been laid up like this?" She took a seat on a high-back chair beside his bed.

"A little less than a week. But I didn't bring you here to discuss my illness. I wanted to give you something." An arm emerged from the blanket and reached for an envelope on the night table. He wagged it in her direction. "This is for you."

She took it and opened it. It was a check addressed to her for eight thousand dollars.

"I don't understand. This is yours. You earned it."

"I'm not certain about that, and I charged you far too much. At the time I felt I might need the money, but it turns out I was wrong."

"I'm sure everyone can use an extra eight grand."

"Yes, everyone who's planning to be alive in the next few years, but that won't be me."

Laurie widened her eyes. "What do you mean?"

"That nurse you met...She's with hospice."

"But...I don't understand...I thought you had heartburn."

"The heartburn's a symptom of esophageal cancer. I've had it for several months now, and it's inoperable. I knew it would one day debilitate me and that's why I insisted on such a large fee for my services. I have a solid nest egg, but it doesn't take long for private nursing care to eat away at it. I didn't want to spend my last days in a hospital. But now it appears as if I'll be leaving this earth much quicker than I'd planned."

Laurie inhaled sharply. Normally she'd try to minimize the impact of his news by saying something cheerful like, "You'll beat this thing!" or "Lift that chin off the floor!" But even she knew those were empty words. She glanced down at her hands, which looked pale and useless. "I don't know what to say."

"Neither do I. Someone should write a book called *Small Talk in the Face of Death* or *What to Say When You're On the Way Out.*"

She laughed and quickly cupped a hand over her mouth in horror. "Oh my God. I'm sorry."

"It's fine. Anything to lighten the moment."

Laurie noticed there were no flowers or cards on display. What was wrong with his family?

"Have you had many visitors? You mentioned a son once."

"I did, but we're not close. My fault entirely."

"But you've told him about your illness?"

"No."

"You have to. He'll want to say goodbye."

Dr. Flowers seemed to shrink into his bedclothes.

"Not after what I've done to him. I was never a good father when he was growing up. I was so involved in my career, I was barely there for him. But that's not the worst of I In fact, I hesitate telling you this."

"I'll try not to judge."

"My son wrote two novels, and I told him both were an embarrassment." Dr. Flowers' body shuddered as if he was shaking off a fever.

"It's not the nicest thing to say, but if the novels were awful than you were probably doing him a favor...Believe me. I know better than anyone else how hard it is to have your work ripped to shreds and thrown to the hyenas but—"

"I didn't read either of the novels."

"I don't understand."

"I've been a literary critic for most of my life, and each year I become more discerning. Perhaps too discerning. I can barely enjoy novels anymore. I also believe only a few select writers were destined for greatness, and it was impossible for me to imagine my son would be one of them."

"Are you sure there wasn't another reason you didn't read his novels?"

"What are you getting at?"

She refilled his water glass with a pitcher on the nightstand. "You know what you're always saying to me: Dig deeper."

Dr. Flowers closed his eyes and remained silent for a moment.

"I suppose I might been afraid he was extremely talented. Then I would have to confront my own failures." He sighed. "I'm not a very good man."

Laurie sat and moved her chair closer to his bed. "Sorry, I didn't mean to make you feel bad about yourself...it's just that you're always stressing the importance of honesty. But you shouldn't rough yourself up too much. If your son quit writing because of what you said...well, he wasn't really committed anyway. Real writers stick with it."

"He didn't quit. It's the only time in his life that he's ever defied me. His second novel will be coming out from Featherstone next year. That's always been his dream publisher."

"Featherstone?" Laurie's stomach fluttered. "What's your son's name?"

"Aaron...Aaron Mite. He was adopted by my late wife's second husband. That's why we have different last names. When my ex-wife died, her husband was so distraught he started drinking heavily. So Aaron came to live with me."

"Aaron," she whispered.

"Do you know him?"

She nodded. "He's Art. He's one of the heroes in my novel."

Dr. Flowers' eyes flew open. "Aaron and you—?"

"Yes. We met at a writers' colony."

"An incredible coincidence." Dr. Flowers' face contorted in pain.

"Should I get the—?"

"No." His features relaxed slightly. "His mother died when he was seven. I suppose he told you."

"He did." Laurie was silent, remembering the night of Aaron's bad dream and how close she'd felt to him then.

"Listen...Would you call Aaron for me?"

She shook her head. "It has to come from you. It'll be much more meaningful that way. I haven't spoken to him in a long time...Our ending was on the messy side."

"And yet..."

"Yet, what?"

"At one time you loved him. I read part of your work, remember?"

I still love him, she thought. "He's living with another woman. She manages a bookstore."

"Emma. Yes. They've been together since Aaron was in grad school. I always felt as if that relationship was more of a habit than true love."

"But they have a lot in common."

"True. But sometimes I wonder if that's a positive thing. How can a person grow if they are constantly having their opinions validated?" Dr. Flowers reached for a glass of water on his night table, and winced when he swallowed. "I'll bet you were good for Aaron. Have you finished your novel?"

"Not yet." Laurie didn't want to admit that she couldn't finish it.

"Something about the Drake character bothers me. Is he based on someone real as well?"

Laurie nodded. "My late husband."

"I see. I can't quite put my finger on it but I'll let you know if it comes to me. By the way, I'm going to call my son."

"Great idea."

"But I have to ask you a favor first. I need you to go to the university and get Aaron's manuscripts. I've stored both of them in a locked file cabinet under M for Mite. I want to read them before I see him. It's the least I can do. The keys to my office and the file cabinet are on my dresser."

"I'd be delighted."

"And one more thing. It's about your writing. There's

something there. In fact, it's the same quality that always attracted me to Nick Windust's work."

"And what quality is that?"

"An exuberant spirit. It's clear you're enjoying yourself. By the way, there's a tin of shortbread cookies on my desk. Feel free to help yourself to as many as you'd like."

It was the nicest thing he'd ever said to her. Too bad she didn't deserve any cookies.

Laurie returned to Dr. Flowers' house with a single manuscript. She looked through the "Ms" in the file cabinet but couldn't find more than one. The nurse let her in and said, "I just gave him morphine. He's probably asleep."

"I'm going to leave something on his bedside table," Laurie said. She entered the bedroom and heard gentle snoring. Dr. Flowers looked like a different man in his morphine-induced sleep. It was as if someone had taken an iron to his face and gently smoothed out all the frown lines. She kissed his forehead and placed Aaron's manuscript on his nightstand before she left.

When she got home there was an email from Bridget: "Call me ASAP."

Laurie couldn't imagine her editor had anything good to say. She probably wanted to chuck the whole thing and let the co-writer take over. After all, what good was a romance novel without an ending?

Her editor answered the phone and skipped the social niceties. "I just finished reading your manuscript."

"I'm sorry...I'm sure you curse the day our paths crossed. I had such a hard time—"

"What are you talking about? I loved it. It's so much improved."

"But the ending?"

"Very sweet and satisfying. I wasn't sure who Lucy would end up with. I think you made the right decision. Needless to say, we won't be requiring the services of that cowriter. I'm sending this straight to copyediting. Congratulations. We'll be talking more soon."

Laurie ended the call, completely mystified. As far as she knew, there was no such thing as a manuscript fairy. How in the world did the novel finish itself?

Ramona.

It must have been her, but that seemed odd. Because if Ramon finished it, you'd think one of the heroes would have shape-shifted into a zombie or a werewolf. But who else could it be? She was the only person who had access to Laurie's work.

The next morning Laurie drove to Dr. Flowers' house. She needed to properly thank him for all he'd done for her. Also she was curious about how far along he'd gotten on Aaron's manuscript and what he thought.

Laurie knocked on the front door. She was expecting the hospice nurse to appear, but instead it was Aaron.

He looked just as she remembered. His longish hair curled around his chin, his glasses was taped at the bridge, and he was wearing that shabby corduroy jacket he refused to give up.

"I'm sorry. To interrupt, I mean...I can come back another time..."

"I'm confused. Why are you here?"

"To see your father."

"You know him?"

"Your father and I are friends...Well, not friends exactly, but...He gave me some private writing lessons. I had no idea he was your father when I started. Listen, I don't want to disturb your visit with him. How is he, by the way?"

Aaron paused a couple of beats before he answered. "He's..." He plunged his hands into the pocket of his jacket. "He's not with us anymore. He died a couple of hours ago."

"No!"

"I'm afraid so."

What happened next was almost involuntary. Aaron was obviously hurting, and it was Laurie's inclination to make things better for him. She flung her arms around him and he returned her embrace. It felt like the most natural thing; their bodies always meshed well together, and she inhaled the familiar smell of moth balls and a roasted nut aroma that was part of his natural body chemistry.

"What's going on here?" Emma appeared in the doorway. Laurie and Aaron guiltily pulled away from each other.

Emma jabbed a finger in Laurie's direction. "You! What are you doing here?"

Laurie stammered out an explanation and ended by saying, "I had no idea Dr. Flowers was Aaron's father. I just found out last night."

Emma's brows were low on her forehead. "I find that highly implausible."

Laurie ignored her and said to Aaron, "I'm sorry about your dad. I got to know him well over the last few weeks. I saw him almost every day. We talked last night, and he said he was going to call you. I hope he was able to reach you before—"

Aaron's head was down, and he was addressing his comments to his scuffed pair of loafers.

"He was dead before I got here. The hospice nurse called me. Apparently in his last few moments, he was able to give her my phone number."

"Oh no. That means he didn't have the opportunity to say anything about your novel."

Aaron glanced up. "What about my novel?"

"He was going to read it last night."

"You must have misunderstood. He's read my work. Long ago."

"No, he hasn't. He only said he did."

Aaron shook his head as if to process this new information. "Are you saying he lied?"

"I'm afraid so. It was difficult for him. There was a time when he desperately wanted to be a novelist, and your aspirations reminded him of that abandoned dream."

"My father wanted to be a novelist?"

She nodded.

"And you don't know if he read my work?"

"He didn't have a lot of time. I brought the manuscript to him yesterday from his office, and he was asleep. Maybe he woke up and read some last night or this morning. You should ask the hospice nurse. She could tell you what he was doing in his last hours."

"She's already gone. I didn't get her name. I suppose I could call and—"

Emma tsked loudly. "What does it matter, Aaron? You don't require your father's approval. Featherstone's publishing your work, for God's sake. That's all the validation you need."

How could she be so clueless? Of course Aaron wanted his dad's approval. What son didn't? If Dr. Flowers had read his son's work, it was a shame he didn't leave a note or something. But maybe he'd been too weak.

"Again, Aaron, I'm so sorry about—"

"Why are you still here?" Emma said. "This is a private family matter. We don't have time to stand around inanely chatting with you."

Aaron said nothing. His head was bowed again, revealing the stark white of his scalp in the part of his hair. He looked vulnerable and sad, and Laurie wished she could gently guide him through his grief. Emma, no doubt, would yank him through it.

"I'll leave then," Laurie said. "Again, I'm sorry. If there's going to be a memorial service—"

"It'll be family only," Emma said. "Professor Flowers was a public figure. We don't want a circus."

Laurie descended the three steps that lead to the walk outside the condo and glanced over her shoulder to take one last look at Aaron. All she saw was his corduroy-covered arm; Emma was pulling him inside, and Aaron offered no resistance. That image of him being passively tugged along stayed in her mind for a long time.

Twenty Six

It was hard for Aaron to imagine that a few rogue cells could destroy someone as formidable as his father. Over the next few days, he was grateful for Emma's help in dealing with the endless details that accompanied a person's death. She was the one who found his father's will in his top desk drawer. His assets were left to Aaron, and his father requested cremation and no service. The condo was a long-term lease. His father was never interested in the responsibilities of home ownership.

Emma also helped him choose a funeral home to deal with the remains. Aaron knew the word "remains" was a euphemism, but it bothered him still. He preferred the word corpse; then maybe his father's death would seem more real to him. Euphemisms like "palliative care," "the remains," and "the departed" distanced a person from reality.

He did see his father's motionless form before it was taken away, and he could immediately sense he was no longer contained within his diseased shell of a body. Aaron didn't understand how people used to be buried alive. Dead people didn't resemble sleeping or unconscious people any more than a mannequin resembled a real person.

He was given his father's ashes in a box. They were heavier than expected, and again, his mind couldn't associate a large cardboard box with his father's permanent departure from this earth. Nor did he know what to do with the ashes. His father didn't make any special requests regarding ash scattering. He wasn't a nature lover, so it would be disingenuous to scatter them in the usual popular sites like oceans, mountains or canyons.

The mortician noted his hesitation and said Aaron didn't have to take the ashes; he would dispose of them. Aaron knew the ashes were not his father—in fact they are a probably a medley of various dead people—but he still felt protective over them and did not want to surrender them to a stranger. He stored them in Emma's attic until he could decide what to do with them.

Aaron occasionally thought about Laurie, but she wasn't a subject he could deal with for more than a few minutes at a time. His father's death took up too much of his gray matter. Perhaps it'd be wise to put her out of his mind for good. Likely they'd never be together again. He was with Emma now, and he couldn't help but feel he would never measure up to Jake.

Still, every once in a while, he was freshly startled that Laurie took writing lessons with his father and how quickly she improved, which meant she was clearly talented. How odd that Horace Flowers—a person with incredibly high standards when it came to literary aesthetics—managed to coax this gift out of her. And how strange that she became close to his father in a way that had always eluded Aaron.

Did Laurie know he'd finished writing her novel? He'd dithered back and forth about how to end it, but it eventually became clear that there was only one choice to make.

Aaron was also still absorbing the news that his father never read his novels. Laurie said she gave his father a manuscript—he assumed it was *Chiaroscuro*—but he couldn't locate it in the condo. The day after Horace Flowers' death, he received a phone call from the hospice nurse and was able to ask about his father's last few hours.

"I'm sorry. I'm not sure what he was doing. I wasn't in his room. But he was sleeping most likely."

"You didn't check on him at all?" Aaron said.

"No. He asked me to only come in when he summoned me. I'd

set a monitor in his room so I could hear him if he needed me, but he didn't interact with me that night. He did, however, call me in the morning."

"And?"

"He asked for a paper and a pen. He wanted to write some letters. I fulfilled his request and later he asked me to mail two letters and a package. I stuck them in the mailbox."

"Who were the letters to?"

"I'm sorry. I have no idea. I didn't glance at them."

Aaron suspected at least one of the letters was for him, and the package the nurse mailed was his manuscript. At some point he expected it would arrive at Emma's house like a missive from the grave.

Twenty Seven

"What's with the mauling?" Ramona said.

Laurie continued to hug her assistant even though she smelled like a musty attic. "I know what you did, and I'm so grateful I'd give you one of my kidneys if you needed it. My editor loves the book. And, of course, I insist your name be on the cover along with mine."

"She likes it, huh?"

"Bridget's beside herself."

Ramona extricated herself from Laurie's embrace and said, "Well, I wish I could say I wrote the ending, but that would be a lie."

"Then who?"

"What's-his-face. Your ex."

"Aaron?" Laurie's mouth hung open.

"You got it."

"And he agreed?"

"It took some not-so-veiled threats on my part, but yes. What did you think of the ending?"

"I haven't read it yet. I just found out about it. Wait. Who did Lucy end up with?"

"The person she's supposed to be with, of course: Drake."

"I see."

"That was the only possible outcome. Readers would have hunted you down with torches and pitchforks if she ended up with Art."

But that wasn't the point. The point was Aaron was given a perfect opportunity to express his true feelings for her, and he didn't take advantage of it, in the vein of a true grand romantic gesture. The second Ramona mentioned he'd written the ending, Laurie had a small hopeful thought: "Will Aaron reveal he still loves me?" Obviously she now had her answer.

"He did a satisfactory job of tying things up. If you want to read what he wrote, it's in Dropbox."

"I will."

Not yet though. She wasn't ready to face the ending. Sometimes she wondered if she would ever be.

Laurie called her editor and revealed that her novel now had a collaborator, who happened to be her ex-boyfriend.

"I should have told you but I—"

"Who cares how the ending came about? Only that it did. Everyone here is thrilled. What's his name? We'll need to give him cover credit."

"He won't want his name on the cover."

"Have you asked?"

"No. But I do know he isn't a fan of genre fiction. He's a literary novelist. He has a book coming out with Featherstone next year."

"Is that so? What an interesting twist."

Laurie knew the gears in her editor's head were spinning and not in a good way.

"Bridget. I know what you're thinking but—"

"Publicity would have a field day."

"Please put it out of your mind."

"And it just so happens that the senior editor at Featherstone lives in my building. Easy on the eyes if you like the stodgy sort. Now I'll have an excuse to talk to him."

"Forget it. Aaron takes his status as a literary writer very seriously. He'd never want his name on a romance novel."

"Laurie. Laurie. Laurie. I think you underestimate your allure. I'll bet you could easily talk him into it."

"It's not happening. Discussion over."

"You need to ask him just in case," she said, sounding huffy. "We can't have him demanding credit after the book is on the shelves."

Twenty Eight

Aaron made his daily trek to the mailbox, wading through ground cover and pushing beyond vines and other foliage that scratched the skin on his arms. Emma said she liked a natural-looking yard, and that overgrowth discouraged trick-or-treaters and magazine subscription salespeople. Most likely she was just too cheap to hire a yard person.

He needed a Weed Wacker just to leave the house and twice he'd gotten poison ivy. Also, the possibility of snakes slithering in the underbrush unnerved him.

The mailbox contained the usual junk—pizza ads, Bed Bath and Beyond coupons—but also a bright pink envelope that smelled faintly of peaches. Aaron took a long deep whiff and rushed back to the house as the fast as the overgrowth and his limp would allow. Carefully he opened the envelope, taking care not to tear it. His hands quivered as he pulled out a piece of stationary.

It read:

Dear Aaron,

Thank you for finishing my novel in my time of need. I couldn't have done a better job myself. Normally your name would appear on the cover with mine. I can't speak for you, of course, but I told my editor you'd rather be skewered on a fondue stick and boiled in peanut oil. If you feel otherwise, please let her know as soon as possible. Also I'll be happy to share a portion of the royalties with you. Thanks again. You created the perfect ending.

Sincerely,
Laurie
P.S. I'm so sorry about your father's death. I was very fond of him.

Aaron read the note several times and each time his gaze lingered on "the perfect ending." Naturally he'd wanted Lucy to end up with Art. In fact, he'd made a few false starts in that direction, but it was wrong for the novel. The material preceding it demanded that Lucy choose Drake, and thus, Aaron had to put his preferences aside and do the right thing. Aaron could no more cheat on a novel than he could use the word "party" as a verb.

There was a time when Aaron hoped Laurie's struggles with the ending were due to her conflicted feelings about him. But judging by her letter, it sounded as if she was perfectly satisfied with the novel's ending and their real-life ending as well.

Aaron received a call from Edward, his editor, and he sounded irate.

"I ran into a commercial editor from W&W, a woman named Bridget Carter. She lives in my building. I thought, why is this flamboyant woman engaging me in conversation? But then your name came up. Is it true you've collaborated on a bodice ripper?"

Aaron was sitting at his desk. He closed the document he'd been working on. "Collaborated is not the correct description. What I did was—"

"Forgive me if I say I'm not interested in the details. Nor do I care what you do in your spare time, but please understand your name cannot appear on the cover of this novel. The woman intimated that it might be good for publicity. Preposterous! Featherstone doesn't want one of their authors to be associated with a genre novel; we have a reputation to protect."

"Of course not. Although it is an accomplished genre novel. I was surprised to find it engaging, and I—"

"Let me repeat myself. Under no circumstances can your name appear on the cover of a penny dreadful. Understood?"

"Yes."

"Then this conversation has come to an end. Good day."

Not long afterward Aaron received a package in the mail from his publisher. He took it into Emma's den and found an advance copy of his debut novel.

It had the distinguished look of an important book. His name and the title were printed in gray on a black background. He ran his fingers over the raised lettering on the dust jacket and examined the binding. Then he cracked open the spine and noted the fine typography, marveling at this physical representation of a lifelong dream. He had no one to share it with. Emma was attending her bi-annual bookseller convention.

The phone rang. It was Bernie.

"Hey, cowboy. You get the book in the mail yet?"

"It just now arrived."

"What do you think? Pretty fancy package, wouldn't you say? Featherstone's one publishing company that still cares about a book's appearance. They make their advance reader copies look like the real deal."

Aaron didn't say anything.

"Is there a problem? Maybe you don't like the color? Or maybe it's the font; now's the time to chirp up if there's something that bugs you. Not that they'll necessarily fix it, but—"

"It's a handsome cover. I just..."

"What?"

"I wish my father was here to see it. Even if he wouldn't have approved." Every afternoon Aaron made the treacherous safari to the mailbox, hoping to receive a package from his departed father, but it never came.

"I'm sorry about your old man. I know that's rough. Lost mine five years ago."

"And I would also have liked to share it with...Well...never mind."

"Still mourning Laurie, huh? I thought since you and Emma were together—"

Aaron glanced at his screensaver, which was a huge photo of Emma's face, blown up large so he could count every pore. Emma installed it a few weeks ago. Her eyes, large and vaguely accusatory, seemed to be following him, waiting for his answer.

"I'm satisfied with Emma's company..." He turned his back on the screen and lowered his voice even though she wasn't in the house. "But I must admit, now and then, I do get nostalgic for Laurie."

"Does she know you still miss her?"

"I imagine she does."

"How?"

"Well, I never told you this because it was embarrassing, but shortly after we broke up, I tried to get her back. I employed a romantic gesture."

"Not sure what you mean."

"Have you ever watched a rom-com?"

"What's that?"

"A romantic comedy."

"Never. I like my movies with explosions and a high body count."

"One weekend, I watched more than a dozen rom-coms. And in every single one, the hero makes a romantic gesture. I tried giving Laurie a jar of Jif peanut butter, but it failed miserably."

"You tried to woo a girl with a jar of peanut butter?"

"I know. Far too subtle. A romantic gesture has to be something grand like chasing the girl through an airport or breaking up a wedding."

"I don't know. Sounds kind of phony and flashy to me. I know grand gestures didn't work with my Mookie."

"You extended one?"

"Once. When we split."

"I didn't know the two of you had ever parted."

"That's because I don't like to talk about it. After she dumped me I took every cent I had and hired a skywriter to write 'Sorry, Moo' and fly over her house. That's as many letters as I could afford. Bottom line? She was unimpressed, and I had to eat Ramen noodles for weeks because the skywriter took all my savings."

"Then how did you get her back?"

"Just started acting like a better guy. Quit drinking so much. Stopped hanging out with my buddies all the time. Started taking my life more seriously. It took a year and I'd long given up on her coming back, but she eventually did, and the rest is Mookie history."

"That would never work in a rom-com."

"Yeah, well, life isn't a rom-com, is it?"

The conversation ended, and Aaron paged through his novel, thinking it might cheer him up. It'd been a long time since he'd read his work and now that it was a real book with a different typeface it almost seemed like the work of a stranger.

Aaron spent the entire day engrossed in the novel, breaking only to use the bathroom. By the time he closed the book, twilight was darkening into evening and his stomach protested its hollow state.

Once he finished, he sat in a chair, trembling and blinking. Aaron felt as if he'd undergone a minor trauma. He shoved *Chiaroscuro* under the chair and went into every room of the house, turning on all the lights with their weak forty-watt bulbs. He also opened all the windows, letting in fresh air. Last, he entered the bathroom and splashed cold water on his face. It was as if he was trying to exorcise himself and the house from the aftereffects of his novel.

It wasn't that he was disappointed in the quality of his work. Oh no. In fact, more than ever, he was able to see why Featherstone acquired it. It was an extremely accomplished character study.

Sadly, the character who was being studied was a sorry excuse of a human being. Eric always expected the worst and let life buffet him around like a badminton birdie. Aaron remembered those traits in him, of course, but to be repeatedly exposed to them over a period of hours was sobering.

He dried his wet face with a bathroom towel. It was thin and rough, like something you might find in a prison. Emma always bought the cheapest ones. As usual, he avoided his reflection in the mirror. Matters of vanity had never interested him, but then a voice in his head said, "Look at yourself."

The glass revealed long hair, overdue for a wash, which flopped into his eyes. His glasses were broken again, this time at the bridge. Emma stepped on them a few weeks ago. She claimed it was an accident, but the breakage occurred after a squabble, and how his glasses got in the way of her size-ten foot was anyone's guess. Aaron was showering at the time.

The glasses were held together with the usual electric tape. But the worst thing was his eyes behind the lenses; they were flat, with no light in them.

He averted his gaze, because he knew he was seeing Eric in the mirror. Aaron was the living embodiment of a character so pathetic that even he, his creator, could barely stand to be in his company for the several hours it took to read the novel.

He heard the sound of a key turning in the lock. The front door creaked open and Emma called out, "Why are all the lights on? This place is lit up like a football field on game night."

Aaron was grateful she was home; he welcomed the distraction from his troubling thoughts. He left the bathroom to greet her, and she dropped her travel bag at his feet.

"What a flight. Delayed for two hours and then turbulence almost the entire time. I need a gin martini stat. Make me one while I jump in the shower. I bought a bottle in the airport duty-free shop. Use that."

"Of course." He was happy to have a chore to distract him from his upsetting thoughts.

Emma headed for the bathroom, snapping off lights as she went, and Aaron sorted through her bag, looking for the gin. During his search he came across an advance reader copy of the new Frank Zenn book. He must have been one of the authors appearing at the booksellers' conference Emma attended. Aaron was anxious to read it; he hoped it was better than his last effort.

He flipped through the pages, eager to read the first line, as he always believed that first lines of novels should be representative of the entire work. The novel was personalized on the title page. The message said, "Emma. See page 212. That's what's going to happen between us tonight. All best, Frank." He turned to the page and found himself reading a graphic sex scene.

Footsteps. Aaron shoved the book under the cushion. Emma came into the room wearing a terrycloth robe. She glared at Aaron.

"What are you doing? Where's my drink?"

"I thought you were taking a shower."

"I decided I wanted my drink first."

"I was just—"

"Jesus, Aaron, I ask you one simple thing." She came toward him, and he knew he was about to get pinched. He braced himself for the sting and decided he wouldn't mention the book because he hated confrontation.

Emma swooped in with her pinchy fingers. Time seemed to slow for a moment, and her fingers grazed his skin. The two of them could be acting out a scene from *Chiaroscuro*. How many times did Louise torment Eric? More than he could count. Aaron held up his hand.

"Wait."

Emma's brow lowered. She was not used to having her pinches aborted. "I don't want to wait. I want my damn drink."

"It'll keep." He withdrew the book from beneath the cushion. "What would you like to say about this?"

She stared at the Zenn novel like she'd never seen it before. "What about it?"

"I read the inscription inside."

"I don't know what you're talking about." Her voice was screechy and false sounding. She'd always been a terrible liar.

"Allow me to read it then." Aaron opened the book, and Emma snatched it from him.

"That's my book! Why are you pawing through my things?"

"You asked me to get your—"

"But I didn't ask you to snoop around in the rest of my stuff."

She stared at him wide-eyed, like a mouse cornered with a broom.

"Emma, listen."

"It was just a one-nighter. It meant nothing. They never do."

"What do you mean *they*?"

Emma froze, realizing her mistake. "I meant to say he! Zenn meant nothing to me."

Aaron stared at her flushed face. Then he glanced up at the shelves where she kept all her signed books. For the first time he noticed one of them was R.K. Harris's. Slowly he withdrew a book as Emma anxiously looked on. He was about to open it to the title page when Emma screamed, "Don't do that! Don't touch my books."

"Okay."

He gently replaced the book.

"It's a...hobby. Some people collect stamps or coins, I collect...well...As I said, it doesn't mean a thing."

Aaron nodded but said nothing.

"It's only sex. You've never been the jealous type. I'm surprised you even care."

"You're right," he said softly. "If this had happened yesterday...I would have just..."

He'd have done nothing. That was his habit. To let the waves of life wash over him, like a dead jellyfish on the beach.

Silence fell between. They'd reached an impasse.

"I deserve better than this."

"What?"

"This is not the life I want anymore."

"Like I said, it was—"

"You've cheated on me the entire time we've been dating,

Emma." He glanced at the case. "There must be at least thirty books on those shelves."

"But—"

"No buts. You also break up with me a couple of times a year. And you pinch me and throw things at me. Your lawn's a jungle and your house is lit like a cave. You're extremely cheap, except when it comes to coffee and booze."

"Now wait a minute—"

"And I've never said a word about it."

"So why start now?"

He sighed. "I'm very grateful for your help with my father's arrangements, but I can't be in this relationship anymore. I'll do us both a favor and leave."

Her eyebrows flew into her thatch of bangs. "You can't leave me. I won't let you. I'm the one who decides this stuff."

"I'm sorry."

She grabbed his arm and twisted it, giving him an Indian burn.

"Emma, let go of me."

"No. I say when you leave."

Aaron wrenched free of her, and she stumbled backwards, hitting a corner of the lamp table.

"Owww!" Emma shouted. She covered her eyes with her hands. "You're a brute. I can't believe you're doing this to me."

"I'm sorry. Are you okay?" He took a tentative step in her direction. "Emma? Don't cry." He touched her shoulder.

She lunged at him, knocking him to the ground, and kneed him in his crotch. Sharp pain shot from his groin and radiated throughout his body.

"By the time I get dressed you'd better be gone." She kicked him in the shin with a bare foot and stomped away.

Twenty Nine

A freckle-faced girl who looked to be about eight was standing on Laurie's step. She'd just rung the bell.

"Is it Girl Scout cookie time again? I certainly hope so."

"No. My mom asked me to bring this letter to you. It was delivered to our house by mistake. She says sorry for not bringing it over earlier but Garrett stole it."

"Garrett?"

"He's my three-year-old baby brother. We found it in his toy chest. Oh. And she's also sorry about the strained spinach stains."

Laurie took the letter. "Thank you very much for bringing this to me."

The little girl skipped away, and Laurie glanced down at the envelope. She gasped at the return address: Dr. Horace Flowers. Her hands shook as she tore open the envelope. What could he have sent her?

Dear Laurie,

Thank you for bringing my son's manuscript to me. I intend to read it tonight. One last lesson from me: I insist you read "The Story of an Hour" by Kate Chopin. It's a short story in the public domain so you should be able to find it online. Incidentally, I just wanted to say that it was a pleasure teaching someone with so much enthusiasm for writing. I do hope you keep at it.

Sincerely,

Horace Flowers

He must have written the note right after she'd dropped off Aaron's manuscript. Laurie hugged the note to her chest. She missed her sessions with Dr. Flowers and the man himself. She was also very curious as to why he wanted her to read "The Story of an Hour." She'd never heard of the story or the author.

Laurie went inside and found the story on her computer. It was very short, and wouldn't take more than a few minutes to read. It was about a woman named Mrs. Mallard who'd just received a telegram that her husband died in a railroad accident. A widow story. Well, that made sense.

She kept reading. It turned out the woman wasn't a widow at all. Her husband was alive, but the news of his survival was so startling, she had a heart attack and died. The doctors said she died "of the joy that kills." Laurie read the story two more times and when she was finished she sat stunned for several minutes. While she read, memories of the day of Jake's death came rushing back to her. There was one particular retrieved memory that made her gasp out loud.

"How did he know?"

She remembered Dr. Flowers once saying she was hiding something from herself. He'd been right. Now she finally knew what it was.

Laurie called Delilah. "I need to see you. Are you free this afternoon? Could you slip away for an hour or so?"

"Good timing. Bart's taking the kids to a movie at two. Where do you want to meet?"

"How about the cemetery? Jake's grave."

"A little bit morbid but okay. Are you going to give me a hint about what this about?"

"No. I need to tell you in person."

Two hours later, Laurie and Delilah were sitting on the bench a few feet away from Jake's headstone. Marvel and Brick had to pay extra for the proximity to the bench. Jake's grave was decorated with miniature American flags, a small toy football and a violet plant. Laurie knew that Marvel tended to it regularly.

"Ask me the question again," Laurie said softly. "About who I loved more. Aaron or Jake."

Delilah got out the flask she always carried in her oversized purse in case of emotional emergencies. She took a swig and handed it to Laurie.

"I don't usually ask questions when I already know the answer."

Laurie winced at the taste of the whiskey but she swallowed it anyway.

"That's why you're my best friend. You know me better than myself. And so did my writing teacher, Dr. Flowers. He sent me this before he died."

She reached into her purse and pulled up "The Story of an Hour" on her phone.

"It's a story about a woman who's just been told her husband died. First she weeps with 'wild abandon.'"

"Like you."

Laurie nodded. "And then she goes into a room alone to contemplate his death. May I read it to you? It's what happens a few minutes after she gets the news."

"Fire away."

Laurie cleared her throat and started to read:

"There was something coming to her and she was waiting for it, fearfully. What was it? She did not know; it was too subtle and elusive to name. But she felt it, creeping out of the sky, reaching toward her through the sounds, the scents, the color that filled the air."

She took a deep breath, and Delilah gave her a nod to go on.

"Now her bosom rose and fell tumultuously. She was beginning to recognize this thing that was approaching to possess her, and she was striving to beat it back with her will—as powerless as her two white slender hands would have been. When she abandoned herself a little whispered word escaped her slightly parted lips. She said it over and over under her breath: 'free, free, free!'"

Laurie put down her phone. "There's a lot more, but I think you get the gist."

Delilah sighed but didn't say a word. She was likely waiting for Laurie to speak. Laurie glanced up at the sky; it was empty of clouds and such a deep blue it was hard to look at it long. Two squirrels chased each other up an oak tree, their tails scraping against the bark.

"On the day Jake died, the family was in the hospital waiting room. The doctor came and said they'd lost him. I immediately fell to my knees and got so hysterical, he gave me a sedative. A few hours later, the sedative was wearing off. We were all at Brick and Marvel's house, and I stumbled outside. It had just finished raining and the trees were dripping and everything was so green and in the distance was the most beautiful rainbow I'd ever seen." She paused, recalling the moment with great clarity. How could she have forgotten it? "And that's when it came at me, just like in the story: this delicious, heady sense of relief. I couldn't help myself. I kicked off my shoes and danced right there in the wet grass. Jake was dead, but I felt more alive than I had in a long time."

Laurie stole a glance at Delilah, expecting a look of shock. But all she saw was a look of concentration on her friend's face, as if she were listening intently.

"But then I sensed someone watching me. There was movement at the kitchen window. I'm sure it was Jake's sister. I immediately ran inside in shame, swallowed another sedative and took to bed. From that time on I convinced myself it was the drugs or the shock that brought on my relief. I'd convinced myself those weren't my real feelings..." Her voice halted and she swiped at a tear in the corner of her eye. "But they were. I loved Jake. Truly I did, but I didn't love being married to him. It didn't feel right. I'm a terrible person, aren't I?"

Delilah took her hand and squeezed it. "You are not terrible. Jake was a great guy, he just wasn't a great guy for you. He wanted this conventional lifestyle, and although I think you convinced yourself you wanted that lifestyle too, it stifled you."

Laurie sniffed. "How long did you know? The whole time Jake and I were together?"

"Pretty much. But you were so convinced. And everyone in town seemed to think you belonged together, and of course, you'd recently lost your grandmother. Naturally you craved a family. Who was I to make waves? But I think I really knew it on your wedding day, when you got claustrophobic in the church dressing room. The room was small, but not that small."

"It didn't matter. Nothing you could have said would have stopped me from marrying him. I really thought Jake was who I wanted."

"Still, I was tempted to say something."

"It's not like I ever wished him dead." Laurie guiltily glanced at his grave. "That thought never ever occurred to me."

"Of course not."

"But when he died, I couldn't own the part of myself that felt freed up. And I think that's why I plunged myself in a long funk. I was punishing myself. But somehow Dr. Flowers suspected."

Delilah and Laurie finished the flask. Meanwhile, it started to sprinkle so they got up to leave. Laurie went to Jake's grave and gently laid an envelope on it. Inside was a card with two words written on it: "I'm sorry."

Thirty

Three months later

Laurie decided not to return to Swainsboro. Every time she entered the city limits she felt a tightness in her chest and wanted to turn her car around. Marvel was disappointed, but she was preoccupied planning a wedding. Kate had recently gotten engaged and she was crazy about her future son-in-law, who used to play football with Jake.

Laurie applied and was accepted to Metro Atlanta University. She wanted to continue growing as a writer and planned to major in creative writing. "The Story of the Hour" broadened her reading choices. She read all of Kate Chopin's books, and after she exhausted Chopin, she asked the librarian for more recommendations. She suggested Joan Didion, Virginia Woolf and, believe it or not, Laura T. Leer.

Laurie reread *Torpor in the Suburbs*, this time a little bit more thoughtfully. She wished she could discuss the novel again with Aaron. Now, at least she knew what fabulism meant. It was a form of magic realism in which fantastical elements are placed into an everyday setting. Like when the main character turned into a couch.

One Friday afternoon she was working on a new novel, and the doorbell chimed the song, "Please Mr. Postman," interrupting her. Laurie went to answer the door and discovered a large box on her porch. She took it into the kitchen and split it open with a pair of scissors. Underneath a nest of bubble wrap were several copies of *Canine Cupid*. The cover was a drawing of a dog who left heart-shaped paw prints all over the jacket. Her own name was printed prominently in red cursive, to match the paw prints, and below it...

No.

She gasped. Aaron's name was on the cover.

Her editor made a terrible mistake, one that couldn't be fixed, as her books had already started shipping to stores. How could Bridget let a blunder like that get by? It didn't seem possible...Unless, of course, it wasn't a mistake at all, and her editor had done it on purpose. Laurie remembered how disappointed Bridget seemed when she refused to involve Aaron in the book's promotion. Perhaps her editor decided to go over Laurie's head.

She picked up the phone to call Bridget but remembered it was after two p.m. on Friday. The office would be deserted. She'd have to wait until Monday.

Meanwhile, she needed to explain herself to Aaron. At the very least, she didn't want him to think she had anything to do with this calamity. Laurie looked up Emma's address on the internet. She decided to drive over to her house, hoping to see Aaron's car. Emma would likely be at work.

When she arrived at Emma's address, the driveway was empty of cars and the yard was so completely overgrown she couldn't imagine anyone living there. A "For Sale" sign was barely visible with a sticker that said, "Under Contract."

Laurie drove in a drizzling rain, trying to figure out her next move. She remembered Dr. Flowers' condo. Maybe Aaron and Emma had moved in there.

By the time she reached the condo it was raining hard, and the sky was an ominous blue-gray. Laurie opened her umbrella against the deluge and dodged a couple of puddles on the way to Dr. Flowers' former front door.

The heavy curtains were gone from the bay window and the lights were on inside. Aaron stood in the living room, doling out treats to three little black dogs. His hair was neatly trimmed and it looked as if he was wearing new glasses with fashionable frames.

The condo looked completely different from the last time she saw it. Clutter was cleared away, and the front room was painted a cheerful daffodil color. Several bright throw pillows dotted a salmon-colored sofa, and a vase of daisies graced a glass coffee table.

Her gaze swept the room. In a corner, Emma was talking animatedly. A cozy domestic tableau unfolded behind the window glass. Emma smiled at Aaron and ruffled the hair on one of the dog's heads. A ring glinted from the appropriate finger. Laurie's stomach dropped. *Aaron? Married?*

But that was only the beginning. The pair chatted for several seconds, and Emma patted her slightly rounded midsection and glanced down at it with a dreamy look on her face. It was clear she was in the early stages of pregnancy. Laurie startled and dropped her purse. Several items rolled out but she scarcely noticed.

Thunder muttered in the distance, and Aaron's glance drifted in direction of the window. Laurie ducked out of sight. She scrambled to pick up her purse and then ran to the car, accidentally stepping into a puddle that filled her shoes with cold water.

She drove away. Rain walloped the roof of her VW bug. It seemed almost angry, and the wipers couldn't keep up with the downpour. Inside the car, Laurie sat almost motionless, watching the water sluice down the windshield until tears blurred her vision.

Thirty One

The rain had stopped, and Aaron was walking Emma out to her car. He happily splashed through one of the puddles.

"What are you doing?" Emma said.

"Just having a little fun."

"Oh brother."

Aaron paused, noticing something swollen and water-logged lying on his doorstep. He leaned down to pick it up and discovered a book of daisy-patterned checks belonging to Laurie Lee.

How strange.

"What is it?" Emma asked.

"It's Laurie's checkbook."

Emma glanced at it. "Daisies. Just the kind of checkbook I would expect her to choose." Her tone wasn't unkind. Marriage and pregnancy seemed to have softened her.

Emma's old house had been sold and while she was clearing it out, she came over to give Aaron some things he'd left there, including his father's ashes. She didn't seem the least bit angry with him anymore, but then again, Aaron was ancient history to her. She was now expecting Frank Zenn's baby, and they recently got married. And yes, according to Emma, Zenn was still bitter about the papyrus comment.

"I wonder how this got here," Aaron said, referring to the checkbook.

"It doesn't take a *CSI* detective. Your bottle blonde obviously paid a visit." That sounded more like the Emma he knew.

"But I've been home all day. I wonder why she didn't knock."

"Maybe she saw me through your picture window and it scared her away. Who could blame her? I almost killed her with a price gun once."

"What?"

"She came to the shop looking for you months ago. We were still together."

"And you didn't tell me?"

She snorted. "Does that sound like something I would do? Jesus, Aaron, all these years and you still don't know me very well."

He rifled through the checkbook. Most of the checks were so wet they were useless but a couple weren't soaked through and could be salvaged.

"I hope you're planning on returning it. It's obvious you still have feelings for her. And you're looking pretty sharp these days. Maybe she'll take your sorry self back."

"Maybe," he said softly.

"Gotta run." Emma clapped him on the back, a little harder than necessary. "Have a nice life, Aaron Mite."

No matter what happened, that was his new intention.

Aaron's heart twinged when he arrived at Laurie's familiar rose-vine-covered cottage, and the site of countless pleasant memories. Her car was not in the drive; instead Ramona's hearse was parked out front.

He walked up the flagstone path and knocked on the door. It opened, and Ramona appeared. Her face was Kabuki white and she was garbed in a black Morticia-like long dress—a specter of gloom and doom on an otherwise cheerful sunny day.

"Help you?"

"I was looking for Laurie. She left her checkbook on my step and—"

She snatched the book from his hand. "I'll see that she gets it..." Ramona rifled through it and narrowed her eyes. "Did you use any of these?"

"Of course not...I don't suppose Laurie's here? I didn't see her car."

"She was here earlier and seemed depressed, which is not like her. Did you upset her?"

"Not that I know of. I don't suppose you know where she went."

Ramona shrugged. "She said she was feeling blocked and needed some inspiration. Any more questions?"

"No. Will you please—"

Too late. Ramona had already shut the door.

Aaron stood on Laurie's porch, feeling an urgency to see her as soon as possible. But where would she have gone? For several moments his mind was blank and then an idea occurred to him. *Of course.* She had to be there. Where else could she be?

He jumped into his car and got on I-285. After driving for over ten miles he took the exit to Hartsfield International. Jets were flying so low they seemed to be almost on top of his car. He drove to the international terminal and parked in short-term parking. Once inside the terminal, he strolled for several minutes among the crowds, glancing about, wondering if his trip was a waste. Then, several yards away, he spotted someone garbed in hot pink, sitting on a bench. It was her. A book was by her side: *The Peculiar Sadness of Lemon Cake.*

"Laurie."

She was so startled she nearly fell off the bench. Her eyes were swollen and the rims flared red. Frankly, she'd never looked worse, and yet, in some ways, she'd never seemed lovelier.

"Aaron! What are you...? How did you...?"

He sat beside her.

"I was looking for you, and Ramona said you went off to seek inspiration, and I had this wild idea you might be at the airport. And I'll be damned if you aren't."

"You were looking for me?"

"I found your checkbook on my step."

"And you came all the way out here to give it to me? That wasn't necessary."

"I left the checkbook with Ramona. I came here to see you. Have you been crying?"

"No! I mean...maybe a little. Airports always make me sentimental. I still don't understand why you came here to see me."

"Why wouldn't I?"

She jutted her chin. "I can think of two very good reasons. Your wife and your baby."

Aaron struggled not to smile. How ironic that he and Laurie were presently engaged in the most common of rom-com tropes, the silly misunderstanding. He didn't imagine such situations happened in real life.

"I'm not married."

Laurie gasped. "Is this a *Knocked Up* situation? Aaron Mite, shame on you. You need to do the right thing by Emma. I thought I saw a ring on her finger."

"Emma is not carrying my child. She and I aren't together anymore."

"But I saw her at your house."

"Emma's moving and she stopped by to give me some things I'd left behind. She's happily married to another writer."

"But if Emma's not your wife then..." She looked him up and down. "Who's been taking care of you?"

"No one."

"You've been taking care of yourself?" Her voice was tinged with disbelief.

"Correct."

"And now you have three dogs?"

"Yes. Sadly, Dusty died."

"Oh no!" She grimaced. "That's awful. I loved Dusty."

"Me too. I missed him so much I decided I needed three dogs to take his place. I was jogging, and I saw a sign that said, 'Free puppies'—"

"Back up a second. *You* were jogging? As in doing exercise? As in sweating?"

He nodded.

"I've taken it up recently out of necessity. I was gaining so much weight from all the cooking I've been doing. I've learned to make a somewhat palatable version of your chicken and dumpling dish, but I prepare it far too often."

Laurie stared at him like she didn't recognize him.

"Enough about me. Why did you come by and see me today?"

Her forehead bunched. "Something awful happened. You're going to hate me."

"I doubt that very much. What is it?"

"Your name's on the cover of my book. I swear on a stack of Harlequin Blazes, I had nothing to do with it."

Aaron smiled. "I know."

"You do?" She honked into a tissue. "How so?'

"Because I was the one who requested my name on the cover."

"You did *what*?"

"You seem upset. Would you rather not have my name on your book?"

"Of course not. But it's a crippling career move. Did you discuss it with your editor?"

He nodded.

"And he was okay with it?"

Aaron paused before answering, "No. He wasn't."

"I'm confused. Surely you care what your editor thinks?"

"Not anymore. Featherstone canceled my contract. They won't be publishing my novel after all."

"No!"

"It wasn't unexpected. My editor warned me it would happen."

"And you asked to have your name on my cover anyway? I'm confused. Why would you do such a crazy thing?"

"I suppose it was my way of saying I admire all the improvements you've made in the Craft."

"But you sacrificed your book contract. That's all you ever wanted."

Aaron shrugged. "Hopefully there will be other book contacts. This seemed more important. I was very proud of you."

"Proud?" Laurie said.

Aaron nodded. "You're an accomplished writer."

"That's very sweet of you to say but I have to confess something: I changed your ending."

"You did? Why?"

"I got a letter from your father. He sent it before he died, and after that, I called my editor and said I needed to change the ending."

"What did the letter say?"

"He asked me to read 'The Story of An Hour.' Are you familiar with it?"

"I am. I teach it in my composition classes. It's about a woman who thinks her husband...." Understanding suddenly dawned on Aaron. "Oh," he said softly.

"Your ending was great, but Lucy ended up with the wrong guy. Drake, sweet as he is, would have kept Lucy in the same place, physically, spiritually and intellectually, for the rest of her life. There was a time Lucy thought that's what she wanted, but she was wrong. She needs someone like Art who will inspire her to grow."

"But Art can be such a snob."

"Sometimes. But underneath the snobbery is a fine, decent human being who Lucy loves dearly."

"Really?"

Laurie nodded.

"That's a relief to know, because Art is so crazy about Lucy he can't think straight."

"He is?"

"Perhaps Art needs to show Lucy just how crazy about her he is."

Aaron was about to zoom in to kiss Laurie, when he noticed a little girl with saucer-sized eyes watching them.

"We might need to find a more private place for the Art and Lucy reunion," Aaron said. "Shall we go to my house?"

Laurie squeezed his knee. "I don't think I can wait that long."

Aaron glanced in the direction of the gate. "We could always join the mile-high club."

"Aaron, how very rom-com of you."

He shrugged. "I'm trying. But you might get claustrophobic."

"I'm never claustrophobic with you, and that's a fact. But I think Art and Lucy need a little more room. You know another great thing about airports?"

"What?"

"They're always located very close to hotels." She grabbed his hand. "Come on."

He picked up her book, *The Peculiar Sadness of Lemon Cake*, and opened it to see what romance novel she was hiding underneath the dust jacket. But to his surprise, it ended up being the actual novel.

"You're reading this?"

"I finished it just before you walked up to me."

"I read it too, a couple of years ago. What did you think?"

"It was peculiarly sad."

He laughed.

"But I loved the fabulist elements."

Aaron raised an eyebrow. "Do tell. I'm impressed."

"Yes, I ended up rereading *Torpor in the Suburbs* and liked it so much I wanted another fabulist novel. Also, I adore lemon cake."

"Me too. With a nice sugary glaze on top."

"Glaze? It has to be at least an inch layer of butter cream frosting."

"But glaze is so much more subtle and nuanced."

"Who wants nuance when you're eating cake?"

The two of them walked hand-in-hand, happily squabbling as they headed toward the exit.

Epilogue

Aaron was impatiently prowling the house, pent up with nervous energy. He had a special surprise planned for Laurie tonight. Only a few more minutes, and she'd be home from her classes at Metro Atlanta University.

Dusty II, III and IV barked; someone was ringing the doorbell. Aaron answered it, and outside stood a plump woman with cottony white hair, wire-rim spectacles and eyes that...Dare he say it? *Twinkled*. In fact, if she weren't wearing a mustard yellow pantsuit she could be mistaken for Mrs. Claus.

"Down, Windusts," Aaron said to his dogs. He used their more formal names when he was being stern with them. All three dogs liked to greet strangers by jumping on them and licking their faces. The dogs ignored him and clawed at the woman's pantsuit as if trying to climb her. Aaron gently pulled them down by their collars.

"Windust?" the woman said.

"My favorite author."

"You must be Aaron."

"I am. And you are...?"

"Sorry for dropping in. I tried calling but the phone rang and rang."

"Oh, yes. I forgot to plug it back in. I was writing earlier and I—"

"No need to explain," she said with a smile. "There's an important matter I need to discuss with you. Are you alone?"

"I am," Aaron said. It was an odd question from a complete stranger, and perhaps he should be wary, but frankly this woman looked as harmless as a teddy bear.

"This won't take long."

"I'm sorry. I still didn't catch your name..."

"Windust," she said.

At the sound of their names, the dogs nudged the woman's hand, angling for head pats.

She smiled. "I'm Windust. Nicholas Windust, to be precise. You can call me Nicole."

Aaron opened his mouth but nothing came out. The language portion of his brain seemed to be temporarily disabled. "I'm sorry. Did you say—?"

"Could I come in? I promise to be brief."

"Yes. Please do."

Aaron ushered her inside. He'd never been around such a famous person before. When he imagined such encounters he was as unflappable as a Buckingham Palace guard. Not so with Nicole Windust. Aaron fluttered about, offering her drinks, mixed nuts and the most comfortable seat in his condo. She refused everything except the chair. When she sat, it squeaked. She glanced behind her and picked up a bunny rabbit.

Aaron took it from her and tossed it to one of the dogs. "Forgive me. We have toys everywhere."

"I have two dogs of my own." She sat again and said, "I was sorry to hear about your father, Aaron. We never met, you know."

That much was clear. Aaron was one hundred percent certain his father did not know Nick Windust was female.

"I did, however, have a high regard for him."

"Thank you. And he thought of you as the most talented author in the world...but you probably already knew that."

"I do. I don't generally read my own press, but I made an exception for your father. I read every word he ever wrote about me. He had such a keen understanding of a novelist's mind. I was surprised he wasn't a novelist himself."

"He was...for a time...It didn't suit him."

"It's not for everyone." She touched her cheek. "Is there something on my face?"

"I'm sorry I was staring. I'm so surprised—"

"I understand. Only a handful of trusted confidantes know that Nick Windust is female. I hope you'll keep my secret?"

"Of course. But my curiosity has gotten the better of me. Why did you—?"

"In the fifties I wrote two novels under Nicole Winston, my real name. They were summarily dismissed. My first novel under the name Nick Windust was widely reviewed...I understand you're a novelist, Aaron."

"I am. Not yet published, but...Well, I'm working on that. How did you know?"

"Your father told me. In fact, he sent me a copy of your manuscript through my publisher."

So that's what happened to it. Aaron had always wondered what had become of the package his father sent off before his death. He assumed it'd been lost in the mail.

"I've been on deadline and couldn't read it until recently."

"I'm confused. Why did he want you to read my novel?"

"Because he was impressed with it. In fact, he compared it to my earlier works."

"You can't be serious."

Nicole smiled. "Of course, he *was* biased."

Aaron nodded solemnly. "He was dying, and his mind may have been clouded with painkillers."

Or maybe, in his last hours, he got sentimental about Aaron's work. To compare Aaron with a young Nick Windust, the world's most accomplished author, was frankly ludicrous.

"Maybe you should read what he wrote."

She retrieved the manuscript from her briefcase and handed it to Aaron. A note on Metro Atlanta University letterhead was clipped to the top page.

Dear Mr. Windust:

My name is Dr. Horace Flowers. We've never met but I daresay that the only person who knows your writings better than you is me. Over the years your fiction has given me much to chew on, e. g. your narrative instincts, command of language and keen sense of characterization. But as admirable as those qualities are, they aren't why I became a Nicholas Windust authority.

I could never express this in a scholarly paper, but I've always wanted to say this about your work: Your stories appeal to aspects of myself that literary aesthetics can't touch. While immersed in the pages of a Nicholas Windust novel, I briefly forget I'm a critic. Instead I'm merely a reader, hopelessly engrossed in the world of your characters. Your novels help me to connect with my own humanity.

Recently I stumbled across the work of another novelist who, in my opinion, possesses this same quality. Full disclosure: He's my son, Aaron Mite. How he could write with such clarity, wisdom and exuberance after having me as his father is a mystery. But he's done it. Admittedly, there's some rawness in his work, but it strongly reminds me of your earlier novels. Forgive me for being presumptuous, but I feel the only publishing company that can do Aaron's work justice is One.

Regards,

Horace Flowers

Aaron looked up from the letter, speechless.

"Quite the compliment, isn't it?" she said.

He glanced back at the letter and then closed his eyes. It was the best gift his father had ever given him. "Thank you for this. I can't tell you what it means to me. It was very kind of you to share it with me."

"Actually, my motive for visiting involves more than kindness."

"Excuse me?"

"I'm here because I'd like to talk to you about being published by One."

"I don't understand...Only you're published by One."

"True, but that's because my editor and I haven't found any authors whom we both agreed on. At my urging, he read your novel last week, and he was as excited about your talent as I am."

"But...you just said my father was biased about my work."

"He was, meaning he didn't give you sufficient praise. Your novel shows far more promise than my earliest efforts."

Aaron blinked uncontrollably, having trouble absorbing her message. "You want to publish *Chiaroscuro*?"

"I'm sorry. I don't know anything about *Chiaroscuro*. Your father sent me a novel called *Klieg*."

"*Klieg*? That's my first novel. I wrote it during my MFA program."

"It doesn't read like a debut."

"I barely remember finishing it. I was caught up in a crazy state of euphoria over the love of writing. It scarcely felt like work at all."

"The best way to write a book."

"I agree. Recently I've been back in touch with that feeling again." Thanks to Laurie, he thought.

"I'm delighted to hear it. So, Aaron, can my editor contact your agent with an offer?"

Dusty II jumped on Aaron's lap and bathed his face, almost as if he understood Nicole's question. Aaron gently tried to control him. "I'm so honored. I can't wait to tell Bernie, my agent. And my fiancée."

"You're engaged?"

"Not officially. I recently purchased the ring, and I'm asking her tonight. I'm not one to make assumptions, but I do believe she might say yes."

"Congratulations. I hope your assumptions are correct." Nicole Windust picked up her purse. "I don't want to take any more of your time, particularly on such a special night of your life."

"Can't you stay for a while longer? I'd like you to meet Laurie."

The front door opened, and a voice rang out: "Who's ready for happy hour?"

The three Dustys greeted their mistress, tails spinning wildly. If Aaron had a tail it would be spinning as well.

"Can I offer you a cocktail?" Aaron asked Nicole.

"I don't want to put you out."

"I make a superb Pink Lady."

"A Pink Lady? Why, I haven't had one of those in years."

Laurie entered the living room, all white teeth, ivory skin and golden hair. The light bulbs seemed to have upped their wattage. One day Aaron expected her to blow a fuse or two.

"Great class. My mind's buzzing like ten beehives." She noticed Nicole and blushed. "Oh. I'm sorry. I didn't know we had company."

"Laurie. This is Nicole, an old friend of the family. I invited her to have a drink. Will you entertain her while I make the Pink Ladies?"

"I'd love to. Why don't we go out on the patio? It's gorgeous this evening."

Laurie guided Nicole outside, chatting her up as if she'd known her for years, her voice musical and lively. Aaron retired to the kitchen and assembled the gin, grenadine, egg whites and, of course, the paper umbrellas. He could scarcely concentrate on his task, he was so exhilarated. Aaron had heard the expression "dizzy with happiness" before, and until now, he assumed people weren't being literal. Why would happiness make a person dizzy?

Yet here he was feeling woozy, as if joy had settled into his body cavity and made his muscles and bones so light he could float away. It was ironic. He'd never been one to believe in HEAs, and yet fate appeared to have handed him one.

He thought about Laura T. Leer's novel *Torpor in the Suburbs*, and how, in the end, the main character turned into a decrepit old couch. Which made Aaron wonder: If he were a character in a novel, what would he turn into?

Not furniture. Far too static, and devoid of life. No. It would have to be something light-filled and spacious, a place where butterflies fluttered, insects thrummed and the landscape was vast and open. Maybe a meadow. Yes, that would suit him nicely.

Karin Gillespie

Karin Gillespie is national bestselling author of five novels and a humor columnist for *Augusta* Magazine. Her nonfiction writing had been in the *New York Times, The Writer* and *Romantic Times*. She maintains a website and blog at Karingillespie.net. Sign up for her newsletter on her website, follow her on Twitter or connect with her on Facebook.

Books by Karin Gillespie

GIRL MEETS CLASS
LOVE LITERARY STYLE

The Bottom Dollar Series

BET YOUR BOTTOM DOLLAR (#1)
A DOLLAR SHORT (#2)
DOLLAR DAZE (#3)

Henery Press Books

And finally, before you go...
Here are a few other books
you might enjoy:

GIRL MEETS CLASS

Karin Gillespie

(from the Henery Press Chick Lit Collection)

The unspooling of Toni Lee Wells' Tiffany and Wild Turkey lifestyle begins with a trip to the Luckett County Jail drunk tank. An earlier wrist injury sidelined her pro tennis career, and now she's trading her tennis whites for wild nights roaming the streets of Rose Hill, Georgia.

Her wealthy family finally gets fed up with her shenanigans. They cut off her monthly allowance but also make her a sweetheart deal: Get a job, keep it for a year, and you'll receive an early inheritance. Act the fool or get fired, and you'll lose it for good.

Toni Lee signs up for a fast-track Teacher Corps program. She hopes for an easy teaching gig, but ends up assigned to Harriet Hall, a high school that churns out more thugs than scholars.

What's a spoiled Southern belle to do when confronted with a bunch of street smart students who are determined to make her life as difficult as possible? Luckily, Carl, a handsome colleague, is willing to help her negotiate the rough teaching waters and keep her bed warm at night. But when Toni Lee gets involved with some dark dealings in the school system, she fears she might lose her new beau as well as her inheritance.

Available at booksellers nationwide and online

Visit www.henerypress.com for details

BET YOUR BOTTOM DOLLAR

Karin Gillespie

The Bottom Dollar Series (#1)

(From the Henery Press Chick Lit Collection)

Welcome to the Bottom Dollar Emporium in Cayboo Creek, South Carolina, where everything from coconut mallow cookies to Clabber Girl Baking Powder costs a dollar but the coffee and gossip are free. For the Bottom Dollar gals, work time is sisterhood time.

When news gets out that a corporate dollar store is coming to town, the women are thrown into a tizzy, hoping to save their beloved store as well their friendships. Meanwhile the manager is canoodling with the town's wealthiest bachelor and their romance unearths some startling family secrets.

The first in a series, *Bet Your Bottom Dollar* serves up a heaping portion of small town Southern life and introduces readers to a cast of eccentric characters. Pull up a wicker chair, set out a tall glass of Cheer Wine, and immerse yourself in the adventures of a group of women whom the *Atlanta Journal Constitution* calls, "... the kind of steel magnolias who would make Scarlett O'Hara envious."

Available at booksellers nationwide and online

Visit www.henerypress.com for details

BLOGGER GIRL

Meredith Schorr

(From the Henery Press Chick Lit Collection)

What happens when your high school nemesis becomes the shining star in a universe you pretty much saved? Book blogger Kimberly Long is about to find out.

A chick lit enthusiast since the first time she read *Bridget Jones's Diary*, Kim, with her blog, *Pastel is the New Black*, has worked tirelessly by night to keep the genre alive, and help squash the claim that "chick lit is dead" once and for all. Not bad for a woman who by day ekes out a meager living as a pretty, and pretty-much-nameless, legal secretary in a Manhattan law firm. While Kim's day job holds no passion for her, the handsome (and shaving challenged) associate down the hall is another story. Yet another story is that Hannah Marshak, one of her most hated high school classmates, has now popped onto the chick lit scene with a hot new book that's turning heads—and pages—across the land. It's also popped into Kim's inbox—for review.

With their ten-year reunion drawing near, Kim's coming close to combustion over the hype about Hannah's book. And as everyone around her seems to be moving on and up, she begins to question whether being a "blogger girl" makes the grade in her offline life.

Available at booksellers nationwide and online

Visit www.henerypress.com for details

A STATE OF JANE

Meredith Schorr

(From the Henery Press Chick Lit Collection)

It's more about finding yourself than finding a man.

Jane Frank is ready to fall in love. It's been a year since her first and only relationship ended and far too long since the last time she was kissed. With the LSAT coming up, she needs to find a boyfriend (or husband) before acing law school and becoming a partner at her father's firm. There's just one problem: all the guys in New York City are flakes. Interested one day and gone the next, they seemingly drop off the face of the earth with no warning and no explanation.

In her misguided belief that life doesn't really start until you get married and have kids, Jane jumps from one extreme to the next trying to force a happily ever after until she breaks. Will she ever find her path, and can she do it without alienating her friends and family and risking her career in the process?

A State of Jane is a hilarious, heartwarming, and honest coming-of-age story of what happens when a good girl discovers there is more to finding love than following the rules.

Available at booksellers nationwide and online

Visit www.henerypress.com for details

Made in the USA
Middletown, DE
21 October 2016